the ENGINE of RECALL

KARL SCHROEDER

Introduction by Stephen Baxter

Robert J.
SAWYER
BOOKS

ROBERT J. SAWYER BOOKS ARE PUBLISHED BY
Red Deer Press
Trailer C
2500 University Drive N.W.
Calgary Alberta Canada T2N 1N4
www.reddeerpress.com

CREDITS
Edited for the Press by Robert J. Sawyer
Cover and text design by Erin Woodward
Cover image courtesy Fotosearch
Printed and bound in Canada by Friesens for Red Deer Press

ACKNOWLEDGMENTS
Financial support provided by the Canada Council, the Government of Canada
through the Book Publishing Industry Development Program (BPIDP), the Alberta
Foundation for the Arts, a beneficiary of the Lottery Fund of the Government of
Alberta, and the University of Calgary.

COMMITTED TO THE DEVELOPMENT OF CULTURE AND THE ARTS

THE CANADA COUNCIL | LE CONSEIL DES ARTS
FOR THE ARTS | DU CANADA
SINCE 1957 | DEPUIS 1957

NATIONAL LIBRARY OF CANADA CATALOGUING IN PUBLICATION
Schroeder, Karl, 1962–
The engine of recall / Karl Schroeder ; editor: Robert J. Sawyer.
ISBN 0-88995-323-6
1. Science fiction, Canadian (English) I. Sawyer, Robert J.
II. Title.
PS8587.C515E53   2005   C813'.6   C2005-900418-5

✶ ✶ C O N T E N T S ✶ ✶

✴ ✴ I N T R O D U C T I O N ✴ ✴

by Stephen Baxter

Of the ten science fiction stories in this very welcome collection, it is perhaps "Solitaire" which, for me, best epitomizes the work of Karl Schroeder.

The "Solitaire" of the title is an unusual sort of intelligent alien. It is an interstellar traveller that is technological but not social, and so lacks anything of our sort of consciousness, of self or others. Schroeder's invention is to be marvelled at: here is a truly *alien* alien, with utterly inhuman motivations, drawn with the clarity of Larry Niven.

But this is a human story: when Theresa, the protagonist, sails away with the Solitaire, the alien becomes a mirror for her own humanity. In the form of the Solitaire a human's inventiveness and sociality are unpicked; Theresa sees that by contrast, for a human even the act of becoming a hermit is a social statement. And yet even so she longs for escape into the Solitaire's isolation.

This comparatively brief story explores themes that are developed repeatedly in Schroeder's works. At the heart of the story is a debate about the nature of our intelligence, its interaction with technology, and the environment which they create. Another of the pieces here, "The Pools of Air," is set in another marvellous science-fictional setting, the clouds of Jupiter, but at its center is a human story about how imaging technology creates a barrier between us and reality.

And Schroeder's stories are often driven by an impulse to escape, as in "Solitaire." "The Dragon of Pripyat" is a jaunt into the heart of Chernobyl—a place, as one character remarks, that has been effectively deleted from the human world for thousands of years. What better place to escape to, even if only by telepresence?

If you are familiar with Schroeder through the reputation he is establishing with his novels, you will not be surprised to discover here several inventive and memorable tales that may be described as hard SF, or space opera. In addition to "Solitaire" and "Pools of Air," "The Engine of Recall" is a classic tale of interstellar derring-do, with an ancient alien artifact, a memorable voyage past a pulsar—and a very neat twist. "Halo" is a story of a colony orbiting a brown dwarf, a body intermediate between a planet and a star. In "The Cold Convergence" we are taken to a bleak Titan, moon of Saturn. The guy knows how to put together the essential prose of a science fiction story; in "Pools of Air" Schroeder delivers in a few sentences evocations of titanic Jovian cloudscapes that we lesser mortals spend whole pages trying to capture.

I suspect, though, that Schroeder may be uncomfortable with either or both of the labels "hard SF" or "space opera," as I often am. As the genre has matured such labels have become so broad as to be of little use critically—and perhaps too simplistic.

Schroeder's gift is an ability to generate genuinely new ideas, and to use them to derive effective stories. For example the brown-dwarf setting of "Halo" (which Schroeder revisits in his novel *Permanence*) sketches a whole new model for our future colonization of space, for brown dwarfs may be far more numerous, and closely spaced, than stars. Schroeder's stories develop ideas new to human discourse, and so expand the range of our imagining: this is ideative fiction, regardless of the labelling.

But if you do think of Schroeder as a hard SF writer, you may be pleasantly surprised by some of the pieces here.

"The Dragon of Pripyat," set in the near future, has the feel of a technothriller, as does its sequel "Alexander's Road." "Allegiances" is a dark tale set against the background of the modern-day Balkan conflict. "Making Ghosts" describes experiments to download human consciousness into machines—not in some arbitrarily advanced future but in the present day, or near to it, and the limitations of modern technology are used to lay bare the philosophical quandaries of the replication of minds.

Perhaps the most unexpected tale here is "Hopscotch," the story of a woman who discerns patterns behind *National Enquirer* oddities like the "raining fish" of the story's very first sentence. This is genuine SF, a story of strangeness behind our consensual reality—but it is also an effective character study which explores why we want to believe in such oddities.

I believe this collection is a good introduction to Schroeder and his wider oeuvre. He has published three science fiction novels to date: *Ventus* (2000), *Permanence* (2002) and *Lady of Mazes* (2005). Again in these novels the themes hinted at in "Solitaire" and other stories recur. In *Permanence* intelligence proves to be not the culmination of life but a transitory feature, to be evolved and then discarded; it is like the flight of birds which, once it has enabled the species to reach some island free of predators, is quickly abandoned. Meanwhile *Lady of Mazes* is an echo of Arthur C. Clarke's *The City and the Stars,* perhaps, in which far-future humans are trapped in a stale technological utopia. But while Clarke's Alvin discovers a history of transcendence beyond the walls, Schroeder's protagonists find an extraordinary ecology of intelligences, post-human and artificial, in which humanity is only one player. (It is a measure of the quality of Schroeder's ideas that his exploration of the evolutionary purpose of consciousness in *Permanence* has inspired at least one academic paper in response, "*Permanence:* An Adaptationist Solution to Fermi's Paradox?" by Milan Cirkovic, published in the *Journal of the British Interplanetary Society,* 2004.)

And just as in "Solitaire," in both these novels the protagonists are driven to escape from prisons psychological and physical; and as in some of the stories here, the novels' structures deliver conceptual breakthrough via the device of the characters' successful escapes.

Of the stories in this collection "The Dragon of Pripyat" may be most familiar to North American and British readers through its deserved reprinting in a Gardner Dozois best-of-its-year anthology. But Schroeder is not a "new" writer: most of these stories, the earliest dating to 1991, were first published in Canadian markets, and Schroeder has become a significant figure in the Canadian SF writing community. In this collection, Schroeder's first, it is possible to trace the development of his ideas and his talent, and to glimpse a potential now being realised fully in his novels.

If I may say so I believe the best of Karl Schroeder is yet to come. In the meantime, enjoy these stories, and immerse yourself in the vision of a powerful and important talent.

When I was a kid I read everything I could get my hands on about UFOs. One of the most interesting books was The Mothman Prophecies *by John Keel; what struck me was Keel's contention that UFOs tend to appear in the same areas where Bigfoot and ghosts are sighted. But instead of imagining that this was due to some creepy government conspiracy (as* The X-Files *did after this story came out), I wondered: what if there were some previously unrecognized force at work here? A law of nature that manifests by breaking all the other laws . . .*

"Hopscotch" was nominated for the 1993 Aurora Award; ironically, another story of mine, "The Toy Mill," written with David Nickle, won the award instead.

Originally published in On Spec *magazine (Summer 1992), "Hopscotch" was reprinted in* On Spec: The First Five Years, *Tesseract Books, 1995.*

✳ ✳ H O P S C O T C H ✳ ✳

It was raining fish.

Linda gave a whoop of triumph which made him jump. Alan clutched the dashboard and stared. An absurd thought came to him: *lucky we're parked.*

The vista of marshlands outside was drawn in thatches of yellow grass under a perfectly blue sky. Yet, out of the clarity a steady downpour of fish was falling. They were no more than six to eight inches long, silvery and seemingly alive. Three were already flopping on the gold hood of the Honda.

"I don't know my fish," mumbled Alan.

"What?" Linda, bouncing in her seat, turned to him. "Get the camera. It's in the glove compartment under the maps."

". . . what kind they are," he half-finished. He was reaching for the glove compartment when she opened her door.

Alan dragged her back and Linda fell across the stickshift. "Ow! What are you doing?"

"Don't go out there! It's crazy."

"The camera! The camera!" She fought past (knocking him in the chin with her bony shoulder) to get it. He made sure he had a good grip on her arm.

"You're not going out there."

"Let go of me." She hastily rolled down the window, and began snapping shots.

"Lens-cap!"

"Yeah-yeah." She popped it off and kept shooting

Thud. Some little mackerel or minnow or other left a smear of ocean on the windshield. He watched it slide down over the wiper. "Jesus, this is weird, you know? I mean, *really* weird."

"I told you I expected it. What did you think, I was crazy?" He shrugged and she, not seeing it, looked back. "You like that in women?"

He gave her a shit-eating grin. Then he sprawled against the door with one arm along the seat-back. "You told me. People tell me a lot of stuff I don't believe."

"Good for you." She poked her head out. "It's slackening off." Before he could react she had the door open and hopped out. He followed with a curse.

Man killed by falling fish. "Christ, Linda. Get in the car. You'll be brained or something."

"Wow! Look at this!" She craned back to take a photo straight up. He banged the roof in frustration.

Then he did look around, and the reality of it finally hit him: the marsh flats, surprised birds huddling in the grass, and everywhere fish, flapping, bloody or dead, lying like the sticks of some fortune-telling operation thrown but never read.

He reached out to touch one of the fish which lay on the roof. It was very cold, with the slick feel of decay. He snatched his hand back. For a moment he was very afraid of Linda, as if she'd just *done* this or something, to impress him.

"We're on the trail of it, you know Alan? The big *it*, the nameless dread everybody blames when something really *off* happens. We got its scent."

"Yeah." He tried to smile. "Like a fish market."

Later when they were driving back to town, his right leg started to hurt badly, mostly in the calf and knee. It took a bit of thought before he realized that, for a few moments when it all started, he had been pushing at the floor of the car with that foot, like he was trying to put on the brakes.

* * * * *

He lay with his face buried in her hair. Linda was asleep. He was on the comfortable side of awake, most likely to join her. He couldn't stop thinking, though.

About fish, for one thing. About the blank spaces on his bank statement where there should be numbers. About the way summer liked to fall into autumn suddenly, just when he was getting used to things. And about Linda, whom he might never get used to.

Linda was always zipping off in ten different directions at once. Always talking, always thinking even during sex. He tended to be passive except when inspired, so together they evened out, he calming her down, she revving him up.

She was terrified of conforming. "If I got a normal job, Al, settled down, had kids . . . I'd disappear. Gone. Faded into the background. There's four billion people in the world, and maybe a couple hundred stick out." So she was on a constant hunt for the outré. She'd pore over the headlines of some lurid tabloid and crow when she found a particularly strange title. "Rhinoceros delivers woman's baby in zoo!" or "Apparition of Elvis appears on bingo cards."

She'd get all excited: "What if it were *true*, Al! Say the universe is more twisted than we thought? No one's ever scientifically studied the really weird. Maybe it's real—like it's the natural equivalent of the Big Lie. Think about it!"

Well, he tried. They had met because they shared a love of practical jokes. He'd concluded lately that his jokes were just been an attention-getting device. Her nonconformism went deeper than he could follow. Ultimately he still dreamed of a big house, a fast car and a gorgeous wife. Linda wanted to pop out of what she called the "programmed world" like a bubble, unique. He figured it was because her parents had started out as hippies and ended up as right-wing stock-brokers. That would confuse anybody.

Everything she experienced, she tried to re-experience in a new way, as different from the ordinary. They'd seen some kids playing hopscotch once. "That game is three thousand years old," she said as they walked past. "Each square represents a stage on your way to Egyptian heaven or hell. When you play it you're practicing for the afterlife." Simple as that, then she was pointing out the way the windows of the Faculty Club caught the evening light in rose squares, while he gawked back over his shoulder and the kids posed like storks.

But he was broke now and it was august. Linda had her grants and bursaries; whatever she did she was really good at it. Alan hadn't yet told her he didn't have the money to go back to school. The fact was, he was sponging off her, had been all summer. And he no longer wanted to be an engineer.

Linda had this grant and was doing her Ph.D. on statistical studies of irreproducible phenomena. He'd known in a vague sort of way that it had to do with UFOs but he didn't believe in them and couldn't believe she would. When she said why didn't he come along for a couple of weeks while she went into the field, he'd jumped at it.

She went to strange places. Never holiday spots. But the fields in Ohio in July were surreal, faced by soft mists with the faint factory smell of distant cities, and they'd made love there to the buzz of insects and sigh of big trees. The Atlantic, in Maine, was unimpressive, slate gray, somehow unbelievable but he was paying more attention to her than it and even it got pretty romantic.

Alan was prepared to admit he was in love, but love was one of those things Linda didn't believe in—it was another "program"—so he didn't know what to say to her. Yes, she cared for him, but she thought it was some kind of betrayal to express love in the normal fashion. While she believed they were freer this way, her attitude was coming between them; and his lack of money was also, and then this afternoon the thing with the fish, was like a wedge to pry her away from him.

He didn't know where that had come from. Really. What was she up to? He didn't know and if he didn't know the really basic things about her, why she was here, how she could be looking for miracles and finding them, while he drowsed and whittled wood on the hood of the car . . . then, they weren't making it.

∗   ∗   ∗   ∗   ∗

"You have to tell me how you're doing this."

In the car again. Hell. And it was dark this time. Linda draped herself over the wheel, staring across a cabbage field at a black line of trees. They had the windows open and a cooler of beer in the back but it didn't help. He was hot.

"Statistics."

"You say we're gonna see a UFO tonight."

She brightened. "If I'm right."

"Like we've graduated from falling fish?"

"Not exactly."

"So explain."

Annoyed, she turned to him, resting her cheek on the wheel. "You never asked before."

"Well I'm asking now. Getting whacked by a mackerel from space got my attention, okay?"

She chuckled. "Sure. Anyway, I didn't want to talk about it because it was so off the wall and probably wrong.

"The thing is UFOs and things like that've been around since Moses. They're all part of one big stew—UFOs, apparitions of the Virgin Mary,

Bigfoot, poltergeists, even visitations by Liberace. You see, all these things appear in the same places, sometimes at the same time. And, say in 1880, they saw dirigibles, not flying saucers. When *we* build flying saucers, we'll be seeing something different, something new."

"How?"

She squinted at him. "Most people ask *why*, you know. They get obsessed with the details. When a UFO lands and gives somebody a starmap, it sets them off for years. But the guy from the UFO is just as likely to give you a plate of pancakes." He laughed, but she sat up and shook her head. "It happens. Scouts honor. The point is, these things are like TV. All form, no content. All picture with no message to it. Try and figure out the *meaning* as a way of getting at origins, and you're fucked. So I'm doing it differently."

"Shit. You really are chasing the things, aren't you?"

"You saw. Alan, you *saw* the fish." Uneasy, he was silent. She had that look in her eye again. "It's a matter of correlating the data on when and where, and ignoring the details of the individual events," she went on. "So I've been doing that. And I found an equation that matched up the incidences of things. I found a *pattern*."

"Like you know where they're from? Venus, or something?"

"No, that's not what I'm looking for, if it was I wouldn't have got this far. It's the raw pattern I was after. When fish fall in Virginia, something else is going to happen along a sort of line, a space-time line, a measurable distance away. You do the statistics, follow that line through space and time, and, in this case, it winds up here."

"Here. How do you know it's gonna be a UFO?"

"I checked the literature. They've never had fish falls here, but they do see flying saucers every now and then."

"Simple as that? No reasons, no clue why?"

"Who cares?" She beamed at him. "That's the beauty of it. Like quantum mechanics, it lets you describe the workings of something without having to deal with the plain impossibility of what you're describing. It's crazy, but it works. A way of getting a handle on all of this without having to believe in the divinity of Liberace. See?"

Fireflies were coming off the fields. He stared at them. "Huh. An equation to catch Elvis? Flying tortillas and little-girl poltergeists? Ha!" He sat back, seeing nothing but the humor in it. He started to laugh.

"Alan!" Oh there she went, pissed off again. But Linda grabbed his arm and pointed, and there, rising behind the black line of trees across the field, was the mother of all fireflies.

* * * * *

And *bang*, she was out of the car again. Him still sitting with his jaw down.

But there, that vision of her as a silhouette, too thin, with this green light like an umbrella over the forest all seen past the rearview, the fly-specked glass and the hood; it froze him up. So she was twenty feet away before he could cut his hand finding the door handle and run after.

Cabbages everywhere. "Get back to the car! Get back to the car, God-damn it! Now!" but she ran away. Had the camera again. Alan went after but wanted to run the other way; he couldn't look at that big light or he'd stop dead. She was trying to take pictures and run at the same time so she tripped over a cabbage. Great. He did a dog-pile fall on her.

"Get off! Get off!" she shrieked.

Alan found the adrenaline rush astonishing. He was terrified and he'd never been before. She elbowed him in the stomach but he didn't even feel it. "You're not going in those trees," he shouted. "Get back!"

They rolled over and over and then she was up and on her way again. He caught snatches of words: "—see it, right up close—got to get close, catch it—"

It was all the places she was going where he couldn't follow. It was the University, and the corners of her mind where he couldn't fit, all in this green thing so maybe he was just as pissed off as scared now. He was jealous of it.

Wild idea. Funny what you thought when terrified.

He caught her again near the woods and they went down. This time they were both silent but he had her good. Now he was aware of a kind of hiss, more silent like the memory of a sound, but definitely there. They both looked up, her head under his. *We must look pretty stupid,* he thought, floundering in cabbage.

The light went out like it was blown out by a wind; it flickered away over the trees in shreds. For a long time they lay in the dirt, not speaking or even moving. Then she said, "You're heavy."

*　*　*　*　*

At a diner under a huge neon Stetson, she fidgeted over a sundae and he glared at the camera. "Think you got it?" he asked at last.

"I don't know." She was pissed off but trying not to be. She looked at him, resigned. "You didn't have to knock me down."

"Just trying to keep you from getting killed."

"They're not dangerous."

"How the hell do you know? It's like the nineteen fifties: 'a little radiation never hurt nobody!' None of the people who said that are around anymore, are they?"

"Get this straight," she said tightly. "I know what I'm doing. I'm a scientist, and I'm trying to learn objectively about a phenomenon of nature."

"Nature, hell! We were in gunsights back there!"

She shook her head quickly. "No gunsights. No little green men. Oh, yeah, maybe there would have been some. But they're not *real* aliens. They're real like the virgin Mary and Liberace. You honestly think Elvis lives in a UFO? Come on." She tapped her spoon on the table. "Christ, I need a cigarette."

"Then what was it, if it wasn't aliens?"

"I . . ." She stopped. "Don't know. Don't want to know. That's the point, isn't it? We can't lose our objectivity. Can't go flying off the handle like you did. Like you were Rambo versus the space gooks."

"Come on." But he bit back on the rest of his retort because he remembered so clearly the wild look in her eye when he had her down. Reason gone.

"You ran after it," he accused. "Like it *was* something."

Linda acted casual. "I wanted to get as close as I could. Doesn't that make sense? Have to study it."

"You wanted—" he stopped again. He didn't want to argue; this was where she drew the line, he knew. She would never admit to what she really wanted, and he couldn't think how to stop her wanting it.

But he was sure she'd wanted to be taken up in that flying saucer, if only so she could argue with the aliens.

*   *   *   *   *

The old man droned on over the tape recorder. Linda couldn't still be listening and Alan hadn't started out interested anyway. He was too busy thinking about the big two-letter word *us*. There were all these contradictory impulses he wanted to follow, most of them stupid and what she wouldn't laugh at she'd be insulted by.

Hell. He poked at the plastic over the window of this seething hot trailer, and glanced back at the old man, who was telling some incoherent story about hurricanes and walking radio towers. Linda had her eyes on the old guy so Allan's gaze drifted to her and stayed, locked.

A lot of men stayed away from her because she was "too intense." At moments like this she sure looked it, with all her attention going to something he'd given up on already. It was this *focus* that was scary.

It was great when you were the one focused on, and he'd thought that, fundamentally, it was him. But right now she had her eyes fixed like searchlights on the old man, or rather on what the old man was telling her, and Alan was somewhere in the penumbra of shadow around her.

Originally he'd been able to get her attention back, with tricks and humor. Not any more. In fact, it would feel kind of like cheating to have to be dragging her back with neon signs, instead of letting her go where ever her quick blade of intellect cut.

Later at the car, while Linda unlocked the doors, Alan picked at the weather-stripping on the window then said, "I'm tired."

"Yeah, we're done. Let's go back to the hotel."

"No, I mean tired of all this. This . . . weirdness. What are you trying to do, anyway?"

She paused, continued unlocking and got in. He half-expected her not to unlock his side but she did. She watched him get in.

"You're scared."

"Bullshit."

"That bit with the UFO scared you. Admit it. It's okay to be scared."

"I'm *not* scared." He hopped a bit in the seat, waving his hands to start talking, getting nowhere. "It's—just—" Brainlock set in. He slumped back. "Just . . . not what I signed up for."

She stared out stonily, started the engine. "I think you're doing exactly what you keep telling me not to. You're acting out a script of some kind you've made up. 'Daring researcher makes blinding breakthrough,' You're thinking in headlines. Admit it."

"What?" She was getting heated up. "I *know* what I'm doing. I'm the first person to have a handle on this stuff! I've found the answer, this could be as big as discovering electricity, bigger than going to the moon!"

"Sure." He held up his hands. "Sure. You . . . got the figures. But I think you're turning it into a crusade. I saw you running after the UFO. You've fallen for the mythology, you're not just doing statistics now. You want to *get* the thing behind all this. I mean you believe there is something behind it now, don't you? And you want it."

Linda drove silently for a bit. Then she said, "What do *you* want?"

"I'm just an ordinary guy. I don't want to know what I want. It gets too complicated that way."

Despite herself, she smiled, glanced at him and jigged her eyebrow. "Everytime you say something like that, you guarantee you'll never be 'ordinary,' " She turned her eyes back to the road, pensive.

"What are you going to do next?"

"I know where the next anomaly will appear," she said. "Michigan. Are you coming?"

He thought it over. "No. It's not what I came for."

"Fine. I'll draw you a map, in case you change your mind." Her voice had gotten cold. "You want me to drop you off somewhere?"

"Don't chase it, Linda. That's what everybody else does, you said so yourself."

"You want me to drop you off somewhere?"

∗ ∗ ∗ ∗ ∗

He wanted to kill something. Killing off a few beer was no substitute. Alan kicked about his friend Murray's apartment for a couple of days. The map she'd drawn, with her calculated date for the next appearance, lay on the kitchen counter. Murray was not happy about having guests, especially non-paying ones. Alan had two hundred in the bank and no idea where more might come from.

Of course, after a couple of days he decided it had been a stupid idea to run off the way he'd done. She needed him now more than ever. Now that things were happening. But she was such a pig-headed, insensitive bitch sometimes, when she got notions in her head . . . And this latest stuff was way out of his league. He'd drag her away from it if he just knew how. But it was too strange, he couldn't get a handle on it.

She pretended to be so objective. Ha. He'd held her when she cried over the stupidity of life, when they'd talked about what it would be like to win a lottery, just *make it* some day. She always came down on him for being too unimaginative, for plotting out his life and his relationships according to simple models he got from TV and movies. Linda went too far the other way; she thought she could keep it all up in the air, and some treasure would rain down on her someday. Like the fish . . .

Drunk and watching something safe—*Dallas*—he was worrying again about what might be waiting for her in Michigan, feeling futile about being unable to even *know* that, when he remembered something she'd told him. He got up to pace.

She'd said she knew the Ohio thing was going to be a UFO because UFOs had been seen in that area before. Bet she knew the fish would be fish for the same reason. He knew where she did her newspaper-morgue research, had seen her at it. That must be how she knew.

If he just knew what it was going to be, he'd feel better. He kicked the TV off and headed for the door, just as Murray came in.

"Christ, can't you do the dishes for a change?" said Murray.

"When I get back."

"Oh, you're coming back?"

He took the bus down to the newspaper. He hated buses, but they were it from now on. At least till he had a job. He didn't want to get onto that train of thought, better think about something more fun . . . like the fields at night, and the blanket she kept in the back of the Honda.

Shit. It hurt to remember.

They let him into the morgue and he sat down, feeling useless, at a microfiche of headlines. Thousands of them, fading away in a kind of miniature landscape he cruised over. After an hour or two of blue-gray figure and ground, he was getting nowhere, but somehow felt like he was doing something and so kept at it. It was late afternoon, they were going to kick him out soon, but maybe he'd be back tomorrow. Nothing else to do.

Then the headline popped out at him. The place was right. He stared. MAN VANISHES BEFORE WITNESSES.

*   *   *   *   *

The Honda sat in the middle of a broken, tilted concrete lot. Some ex-gas station, he figured as he drove up. This was the middle of nowhere. He couldn't see her at first and felt a pulse of anxiety. He got out of his rented car.

Linda had been checking her tires. She stood up from behind the Honda, surprised. For a moment neither of them spoke.

Then she sort of smiled, and tried to frown at the same time. "I was hoping you'd come, you know. And I was afraid you'd show up right now, just when things should start happening."

He went over. They embraced okay, just like before, and he started to relax. "You're crazy to go for this one," he said, and felt her tense. "Sorry. I was just remembering you're crazy all the time, so why should I object."

"Thanks. I'm glad you're here." She broke from the embrace and went to rifle the car for something. She came up with a battered notebook. "The numbers say a disappearance should happen. So I'm going to keep an eye on *you*."

"It's scary. That's all. I'd feel safer if you gave this one a miss."

"Can't. I won't know if I'm on the wrong track unless I verify this one." She scribbled something in the notebook.

Alan thought about it. "I don't buy that. If somebody vanishes, first off it probably won't be noticeable for days, and second it'll eventually make the papers. So you don't have to be here."

"Sure I do. This is science in action, Al."

"Now that is bullshit. You're hunting again, that's all. You want to actually be there when it happens. You want to catch the gremlins in the act."

She frowned at the notebook, squinted up at him, and shrugged. "So?"

"Aha! You admit it! You've fallen for the whole paranormal schtick after all."

"That's not it at all," she said hotly. "It's something else. It's something bigger than just 'psychic.' So okay, I admit I want to find out what. Why not? I've taken the first step. I've proven it exists. And this is something I have to do for *me*. Because I know you, and I know you don't believe in any of it. Despite what you've seen. When you left I was thinking all kinds of things, things to say or do to make you stay. But I kept coming back to: *he doesn't believe me. Even after what he's seen.* So I let you go." She put a hand to her forehead quickly like a soap queen, and looked at him under it. "You see what I'm saying?"

Alan opened the driver's door and sat down on the edge. Heat wafted off the concrete. He smelled hot vinyl. She went around and opened the hatch of the Honda, and rooted around in the back of the car. He stared into the hazy distance.

"It's not you I don't believe in," he said slowly. "It's the idea that you're unlocking the secrets of the universe."

"Maybe that's what I'm doing," she said, her voice muffled. "You wouldn't believe it even if it were true. You have to play the role of the 'rational man,' So you're blind to the things I'm seeing. You don't really see me. Maybe I can't see your way either. We're different, Al. I guess we'll never see eye to eye."

Alan stared at his hands, depressed. "Playing roles," he said. "Like by falling in love. And worrying. And things like that?" He shook his head. "We all do that. We can't not do it. You do it too, you're doing it now with your obsession with these stupid incidents. There's only a few ways to live. I have to follow the way my life is laid out. Even if it's been done a million times before. I'm conventional and I think conventionally, I feel conventionally. You have to see that."

The sounds from the back had stopped. He looked over again but didn't see her. "You can't just break out and look down at yourself," he said more loudly, "to see what's really you and what isn't.—That's what you really want to do. Isn't it?"

But she didn't answer, and he stood up and walked around the car, and found she was really gone. Stepped through some door while he'd been looking the other way.

He walked the big square slabs of concrete calling her name, until it started to get dark. And then he sat down on the hood of her Honda and cried.

How do you live where it's impossible to live? For me, space travel isn't about finding replacement Earths; it's about accommodating ourselves to places strange and hostile to life, but wondrous and worthy on their own terms. When I first heard about brown dwarfs, those strange celestial orphans that wander the galaxy in their billions, I thought: here's a setting worthy of an entire series of stories, short and long. "Halo" was the first short work set in this milieu; my novel Permanence *is also set here.*

"Halo" first appeared in the Tesseracts 5 *anthology (Tesseract Books, 1996), and was reprinted in* The Hard SF Renaissance, *edited by David G. Hartwell and Kathryn Cramer (Tor Books, 2002).*

* * H A L O * *

Elise Cantrell was awakened by the sound of her children trying to manage their own breakfast. Bright daylight streamed in through the windows. She threw on a robe and ran for the kitchen. "No, no, let me!"

Judy appeared about to microwave something, and the oven was set on high.

"Aw, mom, did you forget?" Alex, who was a cherub but had the loudest scream in the universe, pouted at her from the table. Looked like he'd gotten his breakfast together just fine. Suspicious, that, but she refused to inspect his work.

"Yeah, I forgot the time change. My prospectors are still on the twenty-four hour clock, you know."

"Why?" Alex flapped his spoon in the cereal bowl.

"They're on another world, remember? Only Dew has a thirty-hour day, and only since they put the sun up. You remember before the sun, don't you?" Alex stared at her as though she were insane. It had only been a year and a half.

Elise sighed. Just then the door announced a visitor. "Daddy!" shrieked Judy as she ran out of the room. Elise found her in the foyer clinging to the leg of her father. Nasim Clearwater grinned at her over their daughter's fly-away hair.

"You're a mess," he said by way of greeting.

"Thanks. Look, they're not ready. Give me a few minutes."

"No problem. Left a bit early, thought you might forget the time change."

She glared at him and stalked back to the kitchen.

As she cleaned up and Nasim dressed the kids, Elise looked out over the landscape of Dew. It was daylight, yes, a pale drawn glow dropping through cloud veils to sketch hills and plains of ice. Two years ago this window had shown no view, just the occasional star. Elise had grown up in that velvet darkness, and it was so strange now to have awakening signaled by such a vivid and total change. Her children would grow up to the rhythm of true day and night, the first such generation here on Dew. They would think differently. Already, this morning, they did.

"Hello," Nasim said in her ear. Startled, Elise said, "What?" a bit too loudly.

"We're off." The kids stood behind him, dubiously inspecting the snaps of their survival suits. Today was a breach drill; Nasim would ensure they took it seriously. Elise gave him a peck on the cheek.

"You want them back late, right? Got a date?"

"No," she said, "of course not." Nasim wanted to hear that she was being independent, but she wouldn't give him the satisfaction.

Nasim half-smiled. "Well, maybe I'll see you after, then."

"Sure."

He nodded but said nothing further. As the kids screamed their goodbyes at full volume she tried to puzzle out what he'd meant. See her? To chat, to talk, maybe more?

Not more. She had to accept that. As the door closed she plunked herself angrily down on the couch, and drew her headset over her eyes.

VR was cheap for her. She didn't need full immersion, just vision and sound, and sometimes the use of her hands. Her prospectors were too specialized to have human traits, and they operated in weightlessness so she didn't need to walk. The headset was expensive enough without such additions. And the simplicity of the set-up allowed her to work from home.

The fifteen robot prospectors Elise controlled ranged throughout the halo worlds of Crucible. Crucible itself was fifty times the mass of Jupiter, a "brown dwarf" star—too small to be a sun but radiating in the high infrared and trailing a retinue of planets. Crucible sailed alone through the spaces between the true stars. Elise had been born and raised here on Dew, Crucible's frozen fifth planet. From the camera on the first of her prospectors, she could see the new kilometers-long metal cylinder that her children had learned to call the *sun*. Its electric light shone only on Dew, leaving Crucible and the other planets in darkness. The artificial light made Dew gleam like a solitary blue-white jewel on the perfect black of space.

She turned her helmeted head and out in space her prospector turned its camera. Faint Dew-light reflected from a round spot on Crucible. She hadn't seen that before. She recorded the sight; the kids would like it, even if they didn't quite understand it.

This first prospector craft perched astride a chunk of ice about five kilometers long. The little ice-flinder orbited Crucible with about a billion others. Her machine oversaw some dumb mining equipment which was chewing stolidly through the thing in search of metal.

There were no problems here. She flipped her view to the next machine, whose headlamps obligingly lit to show her a wall of stone. Hmm. She'd been right the night before when she ordered it to check an ice ravine on Castle, the fourth planet. There was real stone down here, which meant metals. She wondered what it would feel like, and reached out. After a delay the metal hands of her prospector touched the stone. She didn't feel anything; the prospector was not equipped to transmit the sensation back. Sometimes she longed to be able to fully experience the places her machines visited.

She sent a call to the Mining Registrar to follow up on her find, and went on to the next prospector. This one orbited farthest out, and there was a time-lag of several minutes between every command she gave, and its execution. Normally she just checked it quickly and moved on. Today, for some reason, it had a warning flag in its message queue.

Transmission intercepted.—Oh, it had overheard some dialogue between two ships or something. That was surprising, considering how far away from the normal orbits the prospector was. "Read it to me," she said, and went on to Prospector Four.

She'd forgotten about the message and was admiring a long view of Dew's horizon from the vantage of her fourth prospector, when a resonant male voice spoke in her ear:

"Mayday, mayday—anyone at Dew, please receive. My name is Hammond, and I'm speaking from the interstellar cycler *Chinook*. The date is the sixth of May, 2418. Relativistic shift is .500435—we're at half lightspeed.

"Listen:

"*Chinook* has been taken over by Naturite forces out of Leviathan. They are using the cycler as a weapon. You must know by now that the halo world Tiara, at Obsidian, has gone silent—it's our fault. *Chinook* has destroyed them. Dew is our next stop, and they fully intend to do the same thing there. They want to "purify" the halo worlds so only their people settle here.

"They're keeping communications silence. I've had to go outside to take manual control of a message laser in order to send this mayday.

"You must place mines in near-pass space ahead of the cycler, to destroy it. We have limited maneuvering ability, so we couldn't possibly avoid the mines.

"Anyone receiving this message, please relay it to your authorities immediately. *Chinook* is a genocide ship. You are in danger.

"Please do not reply to *Chinook* on normal channels. They will not negotiate. Reply to my group on this frequency, not the standard cycler wavelengths."

Elise didn't know how to react. She almost laughed—what a ridiculous message, full of bluster and emergency words. But she'd heard that Obsidian had gone mysteriously silent, and no one knew why. "Origin of this message?" she asked. As she waited, she replayed it. It was highly melodramatic, just the sort of wording somebody would use for a prank. She was sure she would be told the message had come from Dew itself—maybe even sent by Nasim or one of his friends.

The coordinates flashed before her eyes. Elise did a quick calculation to visualize the direction. Not from Dew. Not from any of Crucible's worlds. The message had come from deep space, out somewhere beyond the last of Crucible's trailing satellites.

The only things out there were stars, halo worlds—and the cyclers, Elise thought. She lifted off the headset. The beginnings of fear fluttered in her belly.

*   *   *   *   *

Elise took the message to a cousin of hers who was a policeman. He showed her into his office, smiling warmly. They didn't often get together since they'd grown up, and he wanted to talk family.

She shook her head. "I've got something strange for you Sal. One of my machines picked this up last night." And she played the message for him, expecting reassuring laughter and a good explanation.

Half an hour later they were being ushered into the suite of the police chief, who sat at a U-shaped table with her aides, frowning. When Elise entered, she heard the words of the message playing quietly from the desk speakers of two of the aides, who looked very serious.

"You will tell no one about this," said the chief. She was a thin, strong woman with blazing eyes. "We have to confirm it first." Elise hesitated, then nodded.

Cousin Sal cleared his throat. "Ma'am? You think this message could be genuine, then."

The chief frowned at him, then said, "It may be true. This may be why Tiara went off the air." The sudden silence of Tiara, a halo world half a light-year from Elise's home, had been the subject of a media frenzy a year earlier. Rumors of disaster circulated, but there were no facts to go on, other than that Tiara's message lasers, which normally broadcast news from there, had gone out. It was no longer news, and Elise had heard nothing about it for months. "We checked the coordinates you reported and they show this message *did* come from the *Chinook*. *Chinook* did its course correction around Obsidian right about the time Tiara stopped broadcasting."

Elise couldn't believe what she was hearing. "But what could they have done?"

The chief tapped at her desk with long fingers. "You're an orbital engineer, Cantrell. You probably know better than I. The *Chinook*'s traveling at half lightspeed, so anything it dropped on an intercept course with Obsidian's planets would hit like a bomb. Even the smallest item—a pen or card."

Elise nodded reluctantly. Aside from message lasers, the Interstellar Cyclers were the only means of contact with other stars and halo worlds. Cyclers came by Crucible every few months, but they steered well away from its planets. They only came close enough to use gravity to assist their course change to the next halo world. Freight and passengers were dropped off and picked up via laser sail; the cyclers themselves were huge, far too massive to stop and start at will. Their kinetic energy was incalculable, so the interstellar community monitored them as closely as possible. They spent years in transit between the stars, however, and it took weeks or months for laser messages to reach them. News about cyclers was always out of date before it even arrived.

"We have to confirm this before we do anything," the chief said. "We have the frequency and coordinates to reply. We'll take it from here."

Elise had to ask. "Why did only I intercept the message?"

"It wasn't aimed very well, maybe. He didn't know exactly where his target was. Only your prospector was within the beam. Just luck."

"When is the *Chinook* due to pass us?" Sal asked.

"A month and a half," said the tight-faced aide. "It should be about three light-weeks out; the date on this message would tend to confirm that."

"So any reply will come right about the time they pass us," Sal said. "How can we get a confirmation in time to do anything?"

They looked at one another blankly. Elise did some quick calculations in her head. "Four messages exchanged before they're a day away," she said. "If each party waits for the other's reply. Four on each side."

"But we have to act well before that," said another aide.

"How?" asked a third.

Elise didn't need to listen to the explanation. They could mine the space in front of the cycler. Turn it into energy, and hopefully any missiles too. Kill the thousand-or-so people on board it to save Dew.

"I've done my duty," she said. "Can I go now?"

The chief waved her away. A babble of arguing voices followed Elise and Sal out the door.

*   *   *   *   *

Sal offered to walk her home, but Elise declined. She took old familiar ways through the corridors of the city, ways she had grown up with. Today, though, her usual route from the core of the city was blocked by work crews. They were replacing opaque ceiling panels with glass to let in the new daylight. The bright light completely changed the character of the place, washing out familiar colors. It reminded her that there were giant forces in the sky, uncontrollable by her. She retreated from the glow, and drifted through a maze of alternate routes like a sombre ghost, not meeting the eyes of the people she passed.

The parkways were packed, mostly with children. Some were there with a single parent, others with both. Elise watched the couples enviously. Having children was supposed to have made her and Nasim closer. It hadn't worked out that way.

Lately, he had shown signs of wanting her again. Take it slow, she had told herself. Give him time.

They might not have time.

The same harsh sunlight the work crews had been admitting waited when she got home. It made the jumble of toys on the living room floor seem tiny and fragile. Elise sat under the new window for a while, trying to ignore it, but finally hunted through her closets until she found some old blankets, and covered the glass.

*   *   *   *   *

Nasim offered to stay for dinner that night. This made her feel rushed and off-balance. The kids wanted to stay up for it, but he had a late appointment. Putting them to bed was arduous. She got dinner going late, and by then all her planned small talk had evaporated. Talking about the kids was easy enough—but to do that was to take the easy way out, and she had wanted this evening to be different. Worst was that she didn't want to tell him about the message, because if he thought she was upset he might withdraw, as he had in the past.

The dinner candles stood between them like chessmen. Elise grew more and more miserable. Nasim obviously had no idea what was wrong, but she'd promised not to talk about the crisis. So she came up with a series of lame explanations, for the blanket over the window and for her mood, none of which he seemed to buy.

Things sort of petered out after that.

She had so hoped things would click with Nasim tonight. Exhausted at the end of it all, Elise tumbled into her own bed alone and dejected.

Sleep wouldn't come. This whole situation had her questioning everything, because it knotted together survival and love, and her own seeming inability to do anything about either.

As she thrashed about under the covers, she kept imagining a distant, invisible dart, the cycler, falling from infinity at her.

Finally she got up and went to her office. She would write it out. That had worked wonderfully before. She sat under the VR headset and called up the mailer. Hammond's message was still there, flagged with its vector and frequency. She gave the *reply* command.

"Dear Mr. Hammond:

"I got your message. You intended it for some important person, but I got it instead. I've got a daughter and son—I didn't want to hear that they might be killed. And what am I supposed to do about it? I told the police. So what?

"Please tell me this is a joke. I can't sleep now, all I can think about is Tiara, and what must have happened there.

"I feel . . . I told the police, but that doesn't seem like *enough*, it's as if you called *me* for help, put the weight of the whole world on my shoulders—and what am I supposed to do about it?" It became easier the more she spoke. Elise poured out the litany of small irritations and big fears that were plaguing her. When she was done, she did feel better.

Send? inquired the mailer.

Oh, God, of course not.

Something landed in her lap, knocking the wind out of her. The headset toppled off her head. "Mommy. Mommy!"

"Yes yes, sweetie, what is it?"

Judy plunked forward onto Elise's breast. "Did you forget the time again, Mommy?"

Elise relaxed. She was being silly. "Maybe a little, honey. What are you doing awake?"

"I don't know."

"Let's both go to bed. You can sleep with me, okay?" Judy nodded.

She stood up, holding Judy. The inside of the VR headset still glowed, so she picked it up to turn it off.

Remembering what she'd been doing, she put it on.

Mail sent, the mailer was flashing.

"Oh, my, *God!*"

"Ow, Mommy."

"Wait a sec, Judy. Mommy has something to do." She put Judy down and fumbled with the headset. Judy began to whine.

She picked *reply* again and said quickly, "Mr. Hammond, please disregard the last message. It wasn't intended for you. The mailer got screwed up. I'm sorry if I said anything to upset you, I know you're in a far worse position than I am and you're doing a very brave thing by getting in touch with us. I'm sure it'll all work out. I . . ." She couldn't think of anything more. "Please excuse me, Mr. Hammond."

Send? "Yes!"

She took Judy to bed. Her daughter fell asleep promptly, but Elise was now wide awake.

* * * * *

She heard nothing from the government during the next while. Because she knew they might not tell her what was happening, she commanded her outermost prospector to devote half its time to scanning for messages from *Chinook.* For weeks, there weren't any.

Elise went on with things. She dressed and fed the kids; let them cry into her shirt when they got too tired or banged their knees; walked them out to meet Nasim every now and then. She had evening coffee with her friends, and even saw a new play that had opened in a renovated reactor room in the basement of the city. Other than that, she mostly worked.

In the weeks after the message's arrival, Elise found a renewal of the comforting solitude her prospectors gave her. For hours at a time, she could be millions of kilometers away, watching ice crystals dance in her headlamps, or seeing stars she could never view from her window. Being so far away literally gave her a new perspective on home; she could see Dew in all its fragile smallness, and understood that the bustle of family and friends served to keep the loneliness of the halo worlds at bay. She appreciated people more for that, but also loved being the first to visit ice galleries and frozen cataracts on distant moons.

Now she wondered if she would be able to watch Dew's destruction from her prospectors. That made no sense—she would be dead in that case. The sense of actually *being* out in space was so strong though that she had fantasies of finding the golden thread cut, of existing bodiless and alone forever in the cameras of the prospectors, from which she would gaze down longingly on the ruins of her world.

A month after the first message, a second came. Elise's prospector intercepted it—nobody else except the police would have, because it was at Hammond's special frequency. The kids were tearing about in the next room. Their laughter formed an odd backdrop to the bitter voice that sounded in her ears.

"This is Mark Hammond on the *Chinook*. I will send you all the confirming information I can. There is a video record of the incident at Tiara, and I will try to send it along. It is very difficult. There are only a few of us from the original passengers and crew left. I have to rely on the arrogance of Leviathan's troops, if they encrypt their database I will be unable to send anything. If they catch me, I will be thrown out an airlock.

"I'll tell you what happened. I boarded at Mirjam, four years ago. I was bound for Tiara, to the music academy there. Leviathan was our next stop, and we picked up no freight, but several hundred people who turned out to be soldiers. There were about a thousand people on *Chinook* at that point. The soldiers captured the command center, and then they decided who they needed and who was expendable. They killed more than half of us. I was saved because I can sing. I'm part of the entertainment." Hammond's voice expressed loathing. He had a very nice voice, baritone and resonant. She could hear the unhappiness in it.

"It's been two and a half years now, under their heel. We're sick of it.

"A few weeks ago they started preparing to strike your world. That was when we decided. You must destroy *Chinook*. I am going to send you our exact course, and that of the missiles. You must mine space in front of us. Otherwise you'll end up like Tiara."

*   *   *   *   *

The kids had their survival class that afternoon. Normally Elise was glad to hand them over to Nasim or, lately, their instructor—but this time she took them. She felt just a little better standing with some other parents in the powdery, sand-like snow outside the city watching the space-suited figures of her children go through the drill. They joined a small group in puzzling over a Global Positioning Unit, and successfully found the way to the beacon that was their target for today. She felt immensely proud of them, and chatted freely with the other parents. It was the first time in weeks that she'd felt like she was doing something worthwhile.

Being outside in daylight was so strange—after their kids, that was the main topic of conversation among the adults. All remembered their own classes, taken under the permanent night they had grown up with. Now they excitedly pointed out the different and wonderful colors of the stones and ices, reminiscent of pictures of Earth's Antarctica.

It was strange, too, to see the city as something other than a vast dark pyramid. Elise studied it after the kids were done and they'd started back. The city looked solid, a single structure built of concrete that appeared pearly under the mauve clouds. Its flat facades were dotted with windows, and more were being installed. She and the kids tried to find theirs, but it was an unfamiliar exercise and they soon quit.

A big sign had been erected over the city airlock: HELP BUILD A SUNNY FUTURE, it said. Beside it was a thermometer-graph intended to show how close the government was to funding the next stage of Dew's terraforming.

Only a small part of this was filled in, and the paint on that looked a bit old. Nonetheless, several people made contributions at the booth inside, and she was tempted herself—being out-doors did make you think.

They were all tired when they got home, and the kids voluntarily went to nap. Feeling almost happy, Elise looked out her window for a while, then kicked her way through the debris of toys to the office.

A new message was waiting already.

"This is for the woman who heard my first message. I'm not sending it on the new frequency, but I'm aiming it the way I did the first one. This is just for you, whoever you are."

Elise sat down quickly.

Hammond laughed, maybe a little nervously. His voice was so rich, his laugh seemed to fill her whole head. "That was quite a letter you sent. I'm not sure I believe you about having a 'mailer accident.' But if it was an accident, I'm glad it happened.

"Yours is the first voice I've heard in years from outside this whole thing. You have to understand, with the way we're treated and . . . and isolation and all, we nearly don't remember what it was like before. To have a life, I mean. To have kids, and worries like that. There's no kids here anymore. They killed them with their parents.

"A lot of people have given up. They don't remember why they should care. Most of us are like that now. Even me and the others who're trying to do something . . . well we're doing it out of hate, not because we're trying to save anything.

"But you reminded me that there are things out there to save. Just hearing your voice, knowing that you and Dew are real, has helped.

"So I decided . . . I'm going to play your message—the first one, actually—to a couple of the people who've given up. Remind them there's a world out there. That they still have responsibilities.

"Thank you again. Can you tell me your name? I wish we could have met, someday." That was all.

Somehow, his request made her feel defensive. It was good he didn't know her name; it was a kind of safety. At the same time she wanted to tell him, as if he deserved it somehow. Finally, after sitting indecisively for long minutes, she threw down the headset and stalked out of the room.

*　*　*　*　*

Nasim called the next day. Elise was happy to hear from him, also a bit surprised. She had been afraid he thought she'd been acting cold lately, but he invited her for lunch in one of the city's better bistros. She foisted the kids off on her mother, and dressed up. It was worth it. They had a good time.

When she tried to set a date to get together again, he demurred. She was left chewing over his mixed messages as she walked home.

Oh, who knew, really? Life was just too complicated right now. When she got home, there was another message from Hammond, this one intended for the authorities. She reviewed it, but afterwards regretted doing so. It showed the destruction of Tiara.

On the video, pressure-suited figures unhooked some of *Chinook*'s whip-thin Lorentz force cables, and jetted them away from the cycler. The cables seemed infinitely long, and could weigh many hundreds of tonnes.

The next picture was a long-distance, blue-shifted image of Obsidian's only inhabited world, Tiara. For about a minute, Elise watched it waver, a speckled dot. Then lines of savage white light criss-crossed its face as the wires impacted.

That was all. Hammond's voice recited strings of numbers next, which she translated into velocities and trajectories. The message ended without further comment.

She was supposed to have discharged her responsibility by alerting the authorities, but after thinking about it practically all night, she had decided there was one more thing she could do.

"Mr. Hammond," she began, "This is Elise Cantrell. I'm the one who got your first message. I've seen the video you sent. I'm sure it'll be enough to convince our government to do something.

"Hitting Dew is going to be hard, and now that we know where they're coming from we should be able to stop the missiles. I'm sure if the government thanks you, they'll do so in some stodgy manner, like giving you some medal or building a statue. But I want to thank you myself. For my kids. You may not have known just who you were risking your life for. Well, it was for Judy and Alex. I'm sending you a couple of pictures of them. Show them around. Maybe they'll convince more people to help you.

"I don't want us to blow up *Chinook*. That would mean you would die, and you're much too good a person for that. You don't deserve it. Show the pictures around. I don't know—if you can convince enough people, maybe you can take control back. There must be a way. You're a very clever man, Mr. Hammond. I'm sure you'll be able to find a way. For . . . well, for me, maybe." She laughed, then cleared her throat. "Here's the pictures." She keyed in several of her favorites, Judy walking at age one, Alex standing on the dresser holding a towel up, an optimistic parachute.

She took off the headset, and lay back feeling deeply tired, but content. It wasn't rational, but she felt she had done something heroic, maybe for the first time in her life.

*   *   *   *   *

Elise was probably the only person who wasn't surprised when the sun went out. There had been rumours floating about for several days that the government was commandeering supplies and ships, but nobody knew for what. She did. She was fixing dinner when the light changed. The kids ran over to see what was happening.

"Why'd it stop?" howled Alex. "I want it back!"

"They'll bring it back in a couple of days," she told him. "They're just doing maintenance. Maybe they'll change the color or something." That got his attention. For the next while he and Judy talked about what color the new sun should be. They settled on blue.

The next morning she got a call from Sal. "We're doing it, Elise, and we need your help."

She'd seen this coming. "You want to take my prospectors."

"No no, not *take* them, just use them. You know them best. I convinced the department heads that you should be the one to pilot them. We need to blockade the missiles the *Chinook*'s sending."

"That's all?"

"What do you mean, that's all? What else would there be?"

She shook her head. "Nothing. Okay. I'll do it. Should I log on now?"

"Yeah. You'll get a direct link to your supervisor. His name's Oliver. You'll like him."

She didn't like Oliver, but could see how Sal might. He was tough and uncompromising, and curt to the point of being surly. Nice enough when he thought to be, but that was rare. He ordered Elise to take four of her inner-system prospectors off their jobs to maneuver ice for the blockade.

The next several days were the busiest she'd ever had with the prospectors. She had to call Nasim to come and look after the kids, which he did quite invisibly. All Elise's attention was needed in the orbital transfers. Her machines gathered huge blocks of orbiting ice, holding them like ambitious insects, and trawled slowly into the proper orbit. During tired pauses, she stared down at the brown cloud-tops of Crucible, thunderheads the size of planets, eddies a continent could get lost in. They wanted hundreds of ice mountains moved to intercept the missiles.

The sun was out because it was being converted into a fearsome laser lance. This would be used on the ice mountains before the missiles flew by; the expanding clouds of gas should cover enough area to intercept the missiles.

She was going to lose a prospector or two in the conflagration, but to complain about that now seemed petty.

Chinook was drawing close, and the time lag between messages became shorter. As she was starting her orbital corrections on a last chunk of ice, a new message came in from Hammond. For her, again.

In case this was going to get her all wrought up, she finished setting the vectors before she opened the message. This time it came in video format.

Mark Hammond was a lean-faced man with dark skin and an unruly shock of black hair. Two blue-green ear-rings hung from his ears. He looked old, but that was only because of the lines around his mouth, crow's-feet at his eyes. But he smiled now.

"Thanks for the pictures, Elise. You can call me Mark. I'm glad your people are able to defend themselves. The news must be going out to all the halo worlds now—nobody's going to trade with Leviathan now! Total isolation. They deserve it. Thank you. None of this could've happened if you hadn't been there."

He rubbed his jaw. "Your support's meant a lot to me in the past few days, Elise. I loved the pictures, they were like a breath of new air. Yeah, I did show them around. It worked, too; we've got a lot of people on our side. Who knows, maybe we'll be able to kick the murderers out of here, like you say. We wouldn't even have considered trying, if not for you."

He grimaced, looked down quickly. "Sounds stupid. But you say stupid things in situations like this. Your help has meant a lot to me. I hope you're evacuated to somewhere safe. And I've been wracking my brains trying to think of something I could do for you, equal to the pictures you sent.

"It's not much, but I'm sending you a bunch of my recordings. Some of these songs are mine, some are traditionals from Mirjam. But it's all my voice. I hope you like them. I'll never get the chance for the real training I needed at Tiara. This'll have to do." Looking suddenly shy, he said, "Bye."

Elise saved the songs in an accessible format and transferred them to her sound system. She stepped out of the office, walked without speaking past Nasim and the kids, and turned the sound way up. Hammond's voice poured out clear and strong, and she sat facing the wall, and just listened for the remainder of the day.

*   *   *   *   *

Oliver called her the next morning with new orders. "You're the only person who's got anything like a ship near the *Chinook*'s flight path. Prospector Six." That was the one that had picked up Hammond's first message. "We're sending some missiles we put together, but they're low-mass, so they might not penetrate the *Chinook*'s forward shields."

"You want me to destroy the *Chinook*." She was not surprised. Only very disappointed that fate had worked things this way.

"Yeah," Oliver said. "Those shits can't be allowed to get away. Your prospector masses ten thousand tonnes, more than enough to stop it dead. I've put the vectors in your database. This is top priority. Get on it." He hung up.

She was damned if she would get on it. Elise well knew her responsibility to Dew, but destroying *Chinook* wouldn't save her world. That all hinged on the missiles, which must have already been sent. But just so the police couldn't prove that she'd disobeyed orders, she entered the vectors to intercept *Chinook*, but included a tiny error which would guarantee a miss. The enormity of what she was doing—the government would call this treason—made her feel sick to her stomach. Finally she summoned her courage and called Hammond.

"They want me to kill you." Elise stood in front of her computer, allowing it to record her in video. She owed him that, at least. "I can't do it. I'm sorry, but I can't. I'm not a executioner, and you've done nothing wrong. Of all of us, you're the one who least deserves to die! It's not fair. Mark, you're going to have to take back the *Chinook*. You said you had more people on your side. I'm going to give you the time to do it. It's a couple of years to your next stop. Take back the ship, then you can get off there. You can still have your life, Mark! Come back here. You'll be a hero."

She tried to smile bravely, but it cracked into a grimace. "Please, Mark. I'm sure the government's alerted all the other halo worlds now. They'll be ready. *Chinook* won't be able to catch anybody else by surprise. So there's no reason to kill you.

"I'm giving you the chance you deserve, Mark. I hope you make the best of it."

She sent that message, only realizing afterwards that she hadn't thanked him for the gift of his music. But she was afraid to say anything more.

*   *   *   *   *

The city was evacuated the next day. It started in the early hours, as the police closed off all the levels of the city, then began sweeping, waking people from their beds and moving the bewildered crowds to trains and aircraft. Elise was packed and ready. Judy slept in her arms, and Alex clutched her belt and knuckled his eyes as they walked among shouting people. The media were now revealing the nature of the crisis, but it was far too late for organized protest. The crowds were herded methodically; the police must have been drilling for this for weeks.

She wished Sal had told her exactly when it was going to happen. It meant she hadn't been able to hook up with Nasim, whose apartment was on another level. He was probably still asleep, even while she and the kids were packed on a train, and she watched through the angle of the window as the station receded.

Sometime the next morning they stopped, and some of the passengers were off-loaded. Food was eventually brought, and then they continued on. Elise was asleep leaning against the wall when they finally unloaded her car.

All the cities of Dew had emergency barracks. She had no idea what city they had come to at first, having missed the station signs. She didn't care. The kids needed looking after, and she was bone tired.

Not too tired, though, to know that the hours were counting quickly down to zero. She couldn't stand being cut off, she had to know Hammond's reply to her message, but there were no terminals in the barracks. She had to know he was all right.

She finally managed to convince some women to look after Judy and Alex, and set off to find a way out. There were several policemen loitering around the massive metal doors that separated the barracks from the city, and they weren't letting anyone pass. She walked briskly around the perimeter of the barracks, thinking. Barracks like this were usually at ground level, and were supposed to have more than one entrance, in case one was blocked by earthquake or fire. There must be some outside exit, and it might not be guarded.

Deep at the back where she hadn't been yet, she found her airlock, unguarded. Its lockers were packed with survival suits; none of the refugees would be going outside, especially not here on unknown ground. There was no good reason for them to leave the barracks, because going outside would not get them home. But she needed a terminal.

She suited up, and went through the airlock. Nobody saw her. Elise stepped out onto the surface of Dew, where she had never been except during survival drills. A thin wind was blowing, catching and worrying at drifts of carbon-dioxide snow. Torn clouds revealed stars high above the glowing walls of the city. This place, where ever it was, had thousands of windows; she supposed all the cities did now. They would have a good view of whatever happened in the sky today.

After walking for a good ten minutes, she came to another airlock. This one was big, with vehicles rolling in and out. She stepped in after one, and found herself in a warehouse. Simple as that.

From there she took the elevator up sixteen levels to an arcade lined with glass. Here finally were VR terminals, and she gratefully collapsed at one, and logged into her account.

There were two messages waiting. Hammond, it had to be. She called up the first one.

"You're gonna thank me for this, you really are," said Oliver. He looked smug. "I checked in on your work—hey, just doing my job. You did a great job on moving the ice, but you totally screwed up your trajectory on Prospector Six. Just a little error, but it added up quick. Would have missed *Chinook* completely if I hadn't corrected it. Guess I saved your ass, huh?" He mock-saluted, and grinned. "Didn't tell anybody. I won't, either. You can thank me later." Still smug, he rung off.

"Oh no. No, no no," she whispered. Trembling, she played the second message.

Hammond appeared, looking drawn and sad. His backdrop was a metal bulkhead; his breath frosted when he breathed. "Hello, Elise," he said. His voice was low, and tired. "Thank you for caring so much about me. But your plan will never work.

"You're not here. Lucky thing. But if you were, you'd see how hopeless it is. There's a handful of us prisoners, kept alive for amusement and because we can do some things they can't. They never thought we'd have a reason to go outside, that's the only reason I was able to get out to take over the message laser. And it's only because of their bragging that we got the video and data we did.

"They have a right to be confident, with us. We can't do anything, we're locked away from their part of the ship. And you see, when they realize you've mined space near Dew, they'll know someone gave them away. We knew that would happen when we decided to do this. Either way I'm dead, you see; either you kill me, or they do. I'd prefer you did it, it'll be so much faster."

He looked down pensively for a moment. "Do me the favor," he said at last. "You'll carry no blame for it, no guilt. Destroy *Chinook*. The worlds really aren't safe until you do. These people are fanatics, they never expected to get home alive. If they think their missiles won't get through, they'll aim the ship itself at the next world. Which will be much harder to stop.

"I love you for your optimism, and your plans. I wish it could have gone the way you said. But this really is goodbye."

Finally he smiled, looking directly at her. "Too bad we didn't have the time. I could have loved you, I think. Thank you, though. The caring you showed me is enough." He vanished.

Message end, said the mailer. *Reply?*

She stared at that last word for a long time. She signaled *yes.*

"Thank you for your music, Mark," she said. She sent that. Then she closed her programs, and took off the headset.

*   *   *   *   *

The end, when it came, took the form of a brilliant line of light scored across the sky. Elise watched from the glass wall of the arcade, where she sat on a long couch with a bunch of other silent people. The landscape lit to the horizon, brighter than Dew's artificial sun had ever shone. The false day faded slowly.

There was no ground shock. No sound. Dew had been spared.

The crowd dispersed, talking animatedly. For them, the adventure had been over before they had time to really believe in the threat. Elise watched them through her tears almost fondly. She was too tired to move.

Alone, she gazed up at the stars. Only a faint pale streak remained now. In a moment she would return to her children, but first she had to let this emotion fill her completely, wash down from her face through her arms and body, like Hammond's music. She wasn't used to how accept-ance felt. She hoped it would become more familiar to her.

Elise stood and walked alone to the elevator, and did not look back at the sky.

A number of years ago I picked up a book of unlikely coffee-table photography: At Work in the Fields of the Bomb, *by Robert Del Tredici. Its black-and-white treatments of the irradiated industrial wastelands of the nuclear age are astonishing and compelling, and it fired my imagination as no set of pretty landscapes could. Imagine the shoreline of a lake so toxic that wading there for an hour will kill you. Picture the strange labyrinthine mechanisms of the world's only atomic jet engine, abandoned on a flatbed railway car in the desert. Around these forlorn and shunned places, I began to picture a distant figure, an equally forlorn and lonely man walking the ruins with his Geiger counter . . . a man who can only be happy in such places. And so Gennady Malianov was born. "The Dragon of Pripyat" is my first story with him; there will be more.*

"Dragon" was another anthology sale, originally appearing in Tesseracts 8, *from Tesseract Books (Fall, 1999). It was subsequently picked to appear in* The Year's Best Science Fiction, Seventeenth Annual Edition, *edited by Gardner Dozois (St. Martin's Griffin, 2000), and was translated into French for* Bifrost No. 26 (April 2002).

★ ★ T H E   D R A G O N   O F ★ ★
P R I P Y A T

"There's the turnoff," said Gennady's driver. He pointed to a faded wooden skull and cross-bones that leaned at the entrance to a side road. From the pattern of the trees and bushes, Gennady could see that the corner had once been a full highway interchange, but the turning lanes had overgrown long ago. Only the main blacktop was still exposed, and grass had made inroads to this everywhere.

The truck stopped right at the entrance. "This is as far as I go," said the driver. He stepped out of the idling vehicle and walked around the back to unload. Gennady paused for a moment to stare down the green tunnel before following.

They rolled out some steel drums containing supplies and equipment, then brought Gennady's motorcycle and sidecar.

The driver pointed to the Geiger counter that lay on top of the heaped supplies in the sidecar. "Think that'll protect you?"

"No." Gennady grinned at him. "Before I came I did a little risk calculation. I compared the risk of cancer from radiation to that of smoking. See? Here the Geiger clicks at about a pack-a-week. Closer in, that's going to be a pack-a-day. Well, I'll just avoid the pack-a-minute spots, is all. Very simple."

The driver, who smoked, did not like this analogy. "Well, it was nice knowing you. Need anything else?"

"Uh . . . help me roll these behind the bushes there." They moved the drums out of sight. "All set."

The driver nodded once, and Gennady started down the abandoned road to Pripyat.

The tension in his shoulders began to ease as he drove. The driver had been friendly enough, but Gennady's shyness had made the trip here an uncomfortable one. He could pretend to be at ease with strangers; few people knew he was shy. It still cost him to do it.

The trees were tall and green, the undergrowth lush. It smelled wonderful here, better than the industrial area around Gennady's apartment. Pure and clean, no factory smell.

A lie, of course. Before he'd gone a hundred meters, Gennady slowed, then stopped. It all looked serene and bursting with health—a seductive and dangerous innocence. He brought out a filtered face mask he had last worn in heavy traffic in St. Petersburg. For good measure he wrapped his boots in plastic, snapping rubber bands over his pant cuffs to hold it on. Then he continued.

The view ahead was not of a straight black ribbon with sky above, but a broad green tunnel, criss-crossed at all levels with twigs and branches. He'd expected the road would be cracked and buckled from frost heaving, but it wasn't. On the other hand underbrush had overgrown the shoulder and invaded the concrete, where patches of grass sprouted at odd places. For no good reason, he drove around these.

Over the next half hour he encountered more and more clearings. Tall grass lapped like waves around the doors of rusting metal pole-sheds once used for storing farm equipment. Any houses made of lath and plaster had caved in or been burned, leaving only single walls with windows looking from open field to open field. When he spotted the giant lattice-work towers of the power line looming above the trees he knew he was getting close. As if he needed visual confirmation—the regular ticking from the counter in his sidecar had slowly become an intermittent rattle, like rain.

Then without warning the road opened out into a vista of overgrown concrete lots, rusted fences and new forest. Wildflowers and barley rioted in the boulevard of the now-divided highway, and further ahead, above patchy stands of trees, hollow-eyed Soviet-style apartment blocks stared back at their first visitor in . . . years, possibly.

He shut off the bike and brought out his Pripyat roadmap. It was thirty years out of date, but since it was printed a year before the disaster, the roads would not have changed—other than the occasional oak tree or fallen building blocking his path. For a few minutes he puzzled over where he was, and when he was certain he pulled out his phone.

"Lisa, it's me. I'm here."

"You okay?" She had answered promptly. Must have been waiting. His shoulders relaxed a bit.

"I'm fine. Place looks like a park. Or something. Very difficult to describe." There were actual trees growing on the roofs of some of the apartment blocks. "A lot of the buildings are still standing. I'm just on the outskirts."

"What about the radioactivity?"

He checked the Geiger counter. "It's not too hot yet. I'm thinking of living in a meat locker. Somewhere with good walls that got no air circulation after the Release."

"You're not near the reactor, are you?"

"No. It's by the river, I'm coming from the north-west. The trees hide a lot."

"Any sign of anybody else?"

"Not yet. I'm going to drive downtown. I'll call you when I have the satellite link running."

"Well, at least one of us is having an exciting day."

"I wouldn't exactly call it exciting. Frightening, maybe."

"Well." She said *well* in that tone when she was happy to be proved right about something. He could practically see her. "I'm glad you're worried," she said at last. "When you told me about this part of the job you pretended like it was no big deal."

"I did not." Well, maybe he had a little. Gennady scratched his chin uncomfortably.

"Call me soon," she said. "And hey—be careful."

"Is my nature."

*   *   *   *   *

Downtown was too hot. Pripyat was a Soviet modern town anyway, and had no real center aside from some monolithic municipal buildings and farmers' markets. The populace had been professional and mobile; the town was built with wide thoroughfares connecting large, partially self-contained apartment complexes. Gennady read the cultural still-birth of the place in the utter anonymity of the buildings. Everything was faded, most signs gone, the art overwritten by vines and rust. So he could only identify apartment buildings by their many small balconies, municipal offices by their lack of same. That was the beginning and end of Pripyat's character.

Gennady paused often to look and listen, alert for any signs of human habitation. There were no tire tracks, no columns of smoke. No buses passed, no radios blared from the high-rises.

He found himself on the outskirts again as evening reddened the light. Twelve-storey apartment blocks formed a hexagon here, the remains of a parkette in its center. The Geiger counter clicked less insistently in this neighborhood. He parked the motorcycle in the front foyer of the eastern-most tower. This building still had a lot of unbroken windows. If he was right, some of the interior rooms would have low isotope concentrations. He could rest there, as long as he left his shoes outside, and ate and drank only the supplies he had brought with him.

The sound of his boot crashing against an apartment door seemed to echo endlessly, but no one came to investigate. Gennady got the door open on the third try, and walked into the sad evidence of an abandoned life. Three days after Reactor 4 caught fire, the tenants had evacuated with everything they could carry—but they'd had to leave a black upright piano that once they might have played for guests who sipped wine here, or on the balcony. Maybe they had stood watching the fire that first night, nervously drinking and speculating on whether it might mean more work for renovators and fire inspectors.

Many faded and curled photos were pinned to the beige kitchen cupboards; he tried not to look at them. The bedroom still held a cot and chest of drawers with icons over it. The wallpaper here had uncurled in huge rolls, leaving a mottled yellow-white surface behind.

The air was incredibly musty in the flat—a good sign. The Geiger counter's rattle dropped off immediately, and stabilized at a near-normal level. None of the windows were so much as cracked, though the balcony door had warped itself to the frame. Gennady had to remove its hinges, pull the knob off and pry it open to get outside. Even then he ventured only far enough to position his satellite dish, then retreated indoors again and sealed the split frame with duct tape he'd brought for this sort of purpose. The balcony had swayed under him as he stepped onto it.

The sarcophagus was visible from here on the sixth floor. Twenty years ago this room must have looked much the same, but the Chernobyl reactor had still sported the caged red-and-white smokestack that appeared in all early photos of the place. The stack had fallen in the second accident, when Reactor Two went bad. The press referred to the first incident as The Disaster; the second they called The Release.

The new sarcophagus was designed to last ten thousand years. Its low sloping sides glowed redly in the sunset.

Gennady whistled tunelessly as he set up the portable generator and attached his computer, EM detection gear and the charger for his Walkman. He laid out a bedroll while the system booted and the dish outside tracked. As he was unrolling canned goods from their plastic sheaths, the system beeped once and said, "Full net connection established. Hi Gennady."

"Hi. Call Mr. Merrick at the Chernobyl Trust, would you?"

"Trying . . ."

Beep. "Gennady." Merrick's voice sounded tinny coming from the computer's speaker. "You're late. Any problems?"

"No. Just took a while to find a secure place. The radiation, you know."

"Safe?"

"Yes."

"What about the town? Signs of life?"

"No."

"The sarcophagus?"

"I can see it from here, actually." He enabled the computer's camera and pointed it out the window. "Well, okay, it's too dark out there now. But there's nothing obvious, anyway. No bombs sitting out in the open, you know?"

"We'd have spotted them on the recon photos."

"Maybe there is nothing to see because there is nothing there. I still think they could be bluffing."

Merrick grunted. "There was a release. One thousand curies straight into the Pripyat river. We monitored the plume. It came from the sarcophagus. They said they would do it, and they did. And unless we keep paying them, they'll do more."

"We'll find them. I'm here now."

"You stayed out of sight, I trust."

"Of course. Though you know, anything that moves here stands out like a whore in church. I'm just going to sit on the balcony and watch the streets, I think. Maybe move around at night."

"Just call in every four hours during the day. Otherwise we'll assume the worst."

Gennady sighed heavily. "It's a big town. You should have a whole team on this."

"Not a chance. The more people we involve, the more chance it'll get out that somebody's extorting the Chernobyl Trust. We just barely hold onto our funding as it is, Gennady."

"All right, all right. I know I come cheap. You don't have to rub it in."

"We're paying you a hell of a lot for this. Don't complain."

"Easy for you to say. You're not here. Good night, Merrick."

He stretched out for a while, feeling a bit put out. After all, it was his neck on the line. Merrick was an asshole, and Lisa had told him not to come. Well, he was here now. In his own defense, he would do a good job.

It got dark quickly, and he didn't dare show much light, so reading was out. The silence grew oppressive, so he finally grunted and sat up to make another call.

This time he jacked in to the net. He preferred full-sense interfaces, the vibrant colors and sounds of net culture. In moments he was caught up in a whirlwind of flickering icons and sound bites, all the news of the day and opinions from around the world pouring down the satellite link to his terminal. Gennady read and answered his mail, caught up on the news, and checked the local forecast. Good weather for the next week, apparently. Although rain would have helped keep the isotopes out of the air, he was happy that he would be able to get some sun and explore without inconvenience.

Chores done, he fought upstream through the torrent of movie trailers, whispers of starlet gossip, artspam messages and hygiene ads masquerading as real people on his chat-lines, until he reached a private chat room. Gennady conjured a body for himself, some chairs and, for variety, a pool with some sunbathers, and then called Lisa.

She answered in window mode, as she often did. He could see she was in her London apartment, dressed in a sweatshirt. "Hi," he said. "How was the day?"

"It was okay."

"Any leads on our mythical terrorists?" Lisa was a freelance Net hacker. She was well-respected, and frequently worked for Interpol. She and Gennady talked almost every day, a result of their informal working relationship. Or, he sometimes suspected, maybe he had that backwards.

She looked uncomfortable. "I haven't found anything. Where have you been? I thought you were going to call as soon as you arrived."

"I told you I'd call. I called."

"Yeah, but you're not exactly reliable that way."

"It's my life." But this was Lisaveta, not just some anonymous chat on the Net. He ground his teeth and said, "I am sorry. You're right, I make myself hard to find."

"I just like to know what's going on."

"And I appreciate it. It took me a while to find a safe place."

Her expression softened. "I guess it would. Is it all hot there?"

"Most of it. It's unpredictable. But beautiful."

"Beautiful? You're daft."

"No really. Very green, lush. Not like I expected."

She shook her head. "Why on earth did you even take this job? That one in Minsk would have paid more."

"I don't like Minsk."

She stared at him. "Chernobyl's better?"

"Listen, forget it. I'm here now. You say you haven't found our terrorists?"

She didn't look like she wanted to change the subject, but then she shrugged and said, "Not a whisper on the Net. Unless they're techno-Luddites, I don't see how they're operating. Maybe it's local, or an inside job."

Gennady nodded. "Hadn't ruled that out. I don't trust this Merrick fellow. Can we check into the real financial position of the Trust?"

"Sure. I'll do that. Meanwhile . . . how long are you going to be there?"

He shrugged. "Don't know. Not long."

"Promise me you'll leave before your dosimeter maxes out, even if you don't find anything. Okay?"

"Hmm."

"Promise!"

He laughed. "All right, Lisaveta. I promise."

Later, as he lay on his bedroll, he played through arguments with Lisa where he tried to explain the strange beauty of the place. He came up with many phrases and examples, but in the end he always imagined her shaking her head in incomprehension. It took him a long time to fall asleep.

∗　∗　∗　∗　∗

There was no sign that a large group of people had entered Pripyat at any time in the recent past. When Trust inspectors came they usually arrived by helicopter, and stayed only long enough to replace the batteries at the weather stations and radiation monitoring checkpoints. The way wildflowers and moss had begun to colonize the drifted soil on the roads, any large vehicle tracks should have been readily visible. Gennady didn't find any.

Despite this he was more circumspect the next day. Merrick might be right, there might well be someone here. Gennady had pictured Pripyat in black and white, as a kind of industrial dump. The place was actually like a wild garden—though as he explored on foot, he would often round a corner or step into an open lot and find the Geiger counter going nuts. The hotspots were treacherous, because there was no way to tell where they'd be.

A few years after the disaster, folk had started to trickle back into Pripyat. The nature of the evil was such that people saw their friends and family die no matter how far they ran. Better to go home than sit idle collecting coffin-money in some shanty town.

The Engine of Recall

When the Release happened, all those who had returned died. After that, no one came.

He had to remind himself to check his watch. His first check-in with Merrick was half an hour late; the second two full hours. Gennady completely lost track of time while skirting the reactor property, which was separated from the town by marshy grassland. All manner of junk from two eras had been abandoned here. Green helicopters with red stars on them rusted next to remotely piloted halftracks with the U.N. logo and the red, white and blue flag of the Russian Republic. In one spot he found the remains of a wooden shed. The wood drooped over matted brown mounds that must once have been cardboard boxes. Thousands of clean white tubes—syringes, their needles rusted away—poked out of the mounds. The area was hot, and he didn't linger.

Everywhere he went he saw potential souvenirs, all undisturbed. Some were hot, others clean. The entire evidence of late-Soviet life was just lying about here. Gennady found it hard to believe a sizable group could spend any time in this open-air museum, and not pry into things at least a little. But it was all untouched.

He was a bit alarmed at the numbers on his dosimeter as he turned for home. Radiation sure accumulated quickly around here. He imagined little particles smashing his DNA. Here, there, everywhere in his body. It might be all right; he would probably be perfectly healthy later. It might not be all right.

A sound startled him out of his worry. The *meow* came again, and then a scrawny little white cat stepped gingerly onto the road.

"Well, hello." He knelt to pet it. The Geiger counter went wild. The cat butted against his hand, purring to rattle its ribs loose. It didn't occur to him that it was acting domesticated until a voice behind him said, "That's Varuschka."

Gennady looked up to see an old man emerge from behind a tall hedgerow. He appeared to be in his seventies, with a narrow hatchet-like face burned deep brown, and a few straggles of white hair. He wore soil-blackened overalls, and the hand he held out was black from digging. Gennady shook it anyway.

"Who the hell are you?" asked the old man abruptly.

Was this the extortionist? Well, it was too late to hide from him now. "Gennady Malianov."

"I'm Bogoliubov. I'm the custodian of Pripyat." Bogoliubov sized him up. "Just passing through, eh?"

"How do you know that?"

"The Geiger counter, the plastic on your shoes, the mask . . . Ain't that a bit uncomfortable?"

"Very, actually." Gennady scratched around it.

"Well what the hell are you wearing it for?" The old man grabbed a walking stick from somewhere behind the hedge. "You just shook hands with me. The dirt'll be hotter than anything you inhale."

"Perhaps I was not expecting to shake hands with anyone today."

Bogoliubov laughed dryly. "Radiation's funny stuff. You know I had cancer when I came here? God damn fallout cured me. Seven years now. I can still piss a straight line."

He and Varuschka started walking, and Gennady fell in beside them. "Did you live here, before the disaster?" Bogoliubov shook his head. "Does anybody else live here?"

"No. We get visitors, Varuschka and me. But if I thought you were here to stay I wouldn't be talking to you. I'd have gone home for the rifle."

"Why's that?"

"Don't like neighbors." Seeing his expression, Bogoliubov laughed. "Don't worry, I like visitors. Just not neighbors. Haven't shot anyone in years."

Bogoliubov looked like a farmer, not an extortionist. "Had any other visitors lately?" Gennady asked him. He was sure it was an obviously leading question, but he'd never been good at talking to people. He left that up to other investigators.

"No, nobody. Unless you count the dragon." Bogoliubov gestured vaguely in the direction of the sarcophagus. "And I don't."

"The what?"

"I call it the dragon. Sounds crazy. I don't know what the hell it is. Lives in the sarcophagus. Only comes out at night."

"I see."

"Don't you take that tone with me." Bogoliubov shook his cane at Gennady. "There's more things in heaven and earth, you know. I *was* going to invite you to tea."

"I'm sorry. I am new here."

"Apology accepted." Bogoliubov laughed. "Hell, you'd have to do worse than laugh at me to make me uninvite you. I get so few guests."

"I wasn't—"

"So, why are you here? Not sightseeing, I assume."

They had arrived at a log dacha on the edge of the grassland. Bogoliubov kept some goats and chickens, and even had an apple tree in the back. Gennady's Geiger counter clicked at levels that would be dangerous after weeks, fatal in a year or two. He had been here seven years?

"I work for the University of Minsk," said Gennady. "In the medical school. I'm just doing an informal survey of the place, check for fire hazards near the sarcophagus, that sort of thing."

"So you don't work for the Trust." Bogoliubov spat. "Good thing. Bunch of meddling bureaucrats. Think they can have a job for life because the goddamn reactor will always be there. It was people like them made the disaster to begin with."

The inside of Bogoliubov's dacha was cozy and neatly kept. The old man began ramming twigs into the firebox of an iron stove. Gennady sat admiring the view, which included neither the sarcophagus nor the forlorn towers of the abandoned city.

"Why do you stay here?" he asked finally.

Bogoliubov paused for an instant. He shook his head and brought out some waterproof matches. "Because I can be alone here. Nothing complicated about it, really."

Gennady nodded.

"It isn't complicated to love a place, either." Bogoliubov set one match in the stove. In seconds the interior was a miniature inferno. He put a kettle on to boil.

"People die, you know. But places don't. Even with everything they did to this place, it hasn't died. I mean look at it. Beautiful. You like cities, Malianov?"

Gennady shook his head.

The old man nodded. "Of course not. If you were a city person, you'd run screaming from here. It'd prey on you. You'd start having nightmares. Or kill yourself. City people can't handle Pripyat. But you're a country person, aren't you?"

"I guess I am." It would be impossible to explain to the old man that he was neither a city nor a country person. Though he lived in a large and bustling city, Gennady spent most of his free time in the pristine, controllable environments of the Net.

Bogoliubov made some herbal tea. Gennady tested it with the Geiger before he sipped it, much to Bogoliubov's amusement. Gennady filled him in on Kiev politics and the usual machinations of the international community. After an hour or so of this, though, Gennady began to feel decidedly woozy. Had he caught too big a dose today? The idea made him panicky.

"Have to go," he said finally. He wanted to stand up, but he seemed to be losing touch with his body. And everything was happening in slow motion.

"Maybe you better wait for it to wear off," said Bogoliubov. Minutes or hours later, Gennady heard himself say, "Wait for what to wear off?"

"Can't get real tea here," said the old man. "But marijuana grows like a weed. Makes a good brew, don't you think?"

So much for controlling his situation. Gennady's anxiety crested, broke in a moment of fury, and then he was laughing out loud. Bogoliubov joined in.

The walk back to his building seemed to take days. Gennady couldn't bring himself to check the computer for messages, and fell asleep before the sun set.

*   *   *   *   *

Lisa shook her head as she sat down at her terminal. Why should she be so upset that he hadn't called? And yet she was—he owed her a little consideration. And what if he'd been hurt? She would have heard about it by now, since Gennady had introduced her to Merrick as a subcontractor. Merrick would have phoned. So he was ignoring her. Or something.

But she shouldn't be so upset. After all, they spoke on the phone, or met in the Net—that was the beginning and end of their relationship. True, they worked together well, both being investigators, albeit in different areas. She spoke to Gennady practically every day. Boyfriends came and went, but Gennady was always there for her.

But he never lets me be there for him, she thought as she jacked into the net and called him.

Though she didn't intend to, when he finally answered the first thing she said was, "You promised you'd call."

"You too? Merrick just chewed me out for yesterday." He seemed listless.

"Credit me with better motives than Merrick," she said. She wanted to pursue it, but knowing how testy he could be, just said, "What happened?"

"It's not like I'm having a picnic out here, you know. It's just not so easy to stay in touch as I thought." He looked like he hadn't slept well, or maybe had slept too well.

"Listen, I'm sorry," he said suddenly, and he sounded sincere. "I'm touched that you care so much about me."

"Of course I do, Gennady. We've been through a lot together." It was rare for him to admit he was wrong; somewhat mollified, she said, "I just need to know what's going on."

He sighed. "I think I have something for you." She perked up. Lisa loved it when they worked together as a team. He was the slow, plodding investigator, used to sifting through reams of photographs, old deeds and the like. She was the talker, the one who ferreted out people's secrets by talking with them. When they'd met, Gennady had been a shy insurance investigator unwilling to take any job where he had to interview people, and she had been a nosy hacker who get her hands dirty with field work. They made a perfect match, she often thought, because they were so fundamentally different.

"There's an old man who lives here," said Gennady. "Name's Bogoliubov. Has a dacha near the reactor."

"That's insane," she said.

Gennady merely shrugged. "That's where I was yesterday—talking to him. He says nobody's come through Pripyat in ages. Except for one guy."

"Oh?" She leaned forward eagerly.

"We had a long talk, Bogoliubov and me." Gennady half-smiled at some private joke. "He says he met a guy named Yevgeny Druschenko. Part-time employee of the Trust, or so he said." As he spoke Lisa was typing madly at her terminal. "He was a regular back when they still had funding to do groundwater studies here. The thing is, he's driven into town twice in the past year. Didn't tell Bogoliubov where he was going, but the old man says both times he headed for the sarcophagus with a truckload of stuff. Crates. Bogoliubov doesn't know where they ended up."

"Bingo!" Lisa made a triumphant fist. "He's listed, all right. But he's not on the payroll anymore."

"There's more." She looked at him, eyebrows raised. Gennady grinned. "You're going to love this part. Bogoliubov says it was right after Druschenko's first visit that the dragon appeared."

"Whoa. Dragon?"

"He doesn't know what else to call it. I don't think he believes it's *supernatural*. But he says something is *living* inside the sarcophagus. Been there for months now."

"That's ridiculous."

"I know. It's fatal just to walk past the thing."

Lisa scowled for a minute, then dismissed the issue with a wave of her hand. "Whatever. I'm going to trace this Druschenko. Are you through there now?"

"Not quite. Bogoliubov might be lying. I have to check the rest of the town, see if there's any signs of life. Should take a couple of days."

"Hmmf." She was sure he knew what she felt about that. "Okay. But keep in touch. I mean it this time."

He placed a hand on his heart solemnly. "I promise."

* * * * *

It was hard. For the next several mornings Gennady awoke to find Bogoliubov waiting for him downstairs. The old man had designated himself tour guide, and proceeded to drag Gennady through bramble, fen and buckled asphalt, ensuring he visited all the high points of the city.

There was a spot where two adjacent apartment blocks had collapsed together, forming a ten-story arch under which Bogoliubov walked whistling. In another neighborhood, the old man had restored several exquisite houses, and they paused to refresh themselves there by a spring that was miraculously clean of radiation.

What Bogoliubov saw here was nature cleansing a wound. Gennady could never completely forget the tragedy of this place; the signs of hasty abandonment were everywhere, and his imagination filled in vistas of buses and queues of people clutching what they could carry, joking nervously about what they were told would be a temporary evacuation. Thinking about it too long made him angry, and he didn't want to be angry in a place that had become so beautiful. Bogoliubov had found his own solution to that by forgetting that this was ever a place of Man.

Gennady was suspicious that the old man might be trying to distract him, so he made a point of going out on his own to explore as well. It was tiring, but he had to verify Bogoliubov's story before he could feel he had done his job. Calling Merrick or Lisa was becoming difficult because he was out so much, and so tired from walking—but as well, he found himself increasingly moving in a meditative state. He had to give himself a shake, practically learn to speak again, before he could make a call.

To combat this feeling he spent his evenings in the Net, listening to the thrum of humanity's great chorus. Even there, however, he felt more an observer. Maybe that was okay; he had always been like this, it was just cities and obligations that drove him out of his natural habits.

Then one night he awoke to the sound of engines.

It was pitch-dark and for a second he didn't know where he was. Gennady sat up and focused on the lunar rectangle of the living room window. For a moment he heard nothing, then the grumble started up again. He thought he saw a flicker of light outside.

He staggered to the balcony where he had set up his good telescope. The sound was louder here. Like an idling train, more felt than heard. It seemed to slide around in the air, the way train sounds did when they were coming from kilometers distant.

Light broke around a distant street corner. Gennady swung the telescope around and nearly had it focussed when something large and black lurched through his visual field, and was gone again. When he looked up from the lens he saw no sign of it.

He took the stairs two at a time, flashlight beam dodging wildly ahead of him. When he got to the lobby he switched it off and stepped cautiously to the front doors. His heart was pounding.

Gennady watched for a while, then ventured out into the street. It wasn't hard to hide here; any second he could drop in the tall grass or step behind a stand of young trees. So he made his way in the direction of the sound.

It took ten minutes to reach the spot where he'd seen the light. He dropped to one knee at the side of a filling station, and poked his head around the corner. The street was empty. The whole intersection had been overtaken with weeds and young birch trees. He puzzled over the sight for a minute, then stood and walked out into their midst. There was absolutely nowhere here that you could drive a truck without knocking over lots of plants. But nothing was disturbed.

It was silent here now. Gennady had never ventured this far in the dark; the great black slabs of the buildings were quite unnerving. Shielding the light with one hand, he used the flashlight to try to find some tracks.

There were none.

On impulse he unslung the Geiger counter and switched it on. It immediately began chattering. For a few minutes he crisscrossed the intersection, finding a definite line of higher radioactivity bisecting it. He crouched on that line, and moved along it like he was weeding a garden, holding the counter close to the ground.

As the chattering peaked he spotted a black divot in the ground. He shone the flashlight on it. It was a deep W-shaped mark, of the sort made by the feet of back-hoes and cranes. A few meters beyond it he found another. Both were incredibly hot.

A deep engine pulse sounded through the earth. It repeated, then rose to a bone-shaking thunder as two brilliant lights pinioned Gennady from the far end of the street.

He clicked off the flashlight but the thing was already coming at him. The ground shook as it began to gallop.

There was no time to even see what it was. Gennady fled through whipping underbrush and under low branches, trying to evade the uncannily accurate lamps that sought him out. He heard steel shriek and the thud of falling trees as it flung aside all the obstacles he tried to put between them.

Ahead a narrow alley made a black rectangle between two warehouses. He ran into it. It was choked with debris and weeds. "Damn." Light welled up behind him.

Both warehouses had doors and windows opening off the alley. One door was ajar. On a sudden inspiration he flicked on the flashlight and threw it hard through a window of the other building, then dove for the open door.

He heard the sound of concrete scraping as the thing shouldered its way between the buildings. The lights were intense, and the noise of its engines was awful. Then the lights went out, as it paused. He had the uncanny impression that it was looking for him.

Gennady stood in a totally empty concrete floored building. Much of the roof had gone, and in the dim light he could see a clear path to the front door.

Cinderblocks shuddered and crashed outside. It was knocking a hole in the other building. Gennady ran for the door and made it through. The windows of the other warehouse were lit up.

He ran up the street to his building, and when he got inside he pulled his bike into a back room and raced up the stairs. He could hear the thing roaring around the neighborhood for what seemed like hours, and then the noise slowly faded into the distance, and he fell back on his bedroll, exhausted.

At dawn he packed up and by midmorning he had left Pripyat and the contaminated zone behind him.

*   *   *   *   *

Merrick poured pepper vodka into a tall glass and handed it to Gennady. "Dosvedanya. We picked up Druschenko this morning."

Gennady wondered as he sipped how the vodka would react with the iodine pill he'd just taken. Traffic noises and the smell of diesel wafted through the open window of Merrick's Kiev office. Merrick tipped back his own drink, smiled brightly and went to sit behind the huge oak desk that dominated the room.

"I have to thank you, Gennady. We literally couldn't find anyone else who was willing to go in there on the ground." He shook his head. "People panic at the thought of radiation."

"Don't much like it myself." Gennady took another sip. "But you can detect and avoid it. Not so simple to do with the stuff that comes out of the smokestacks these days. Or gets by the filters at the water plant."

Merrick nodded. "So you were able to take all the right precautions."

Gennady thought of Bogoliubov's warm tea settling in his stomach . . . and he had done other stupid things there too. But the doctors insisted his overall dosage was "acceptable". His odds for getting cancer had gone up as much as if he'd been chain-smoking for the past six months. Acceptable? How could one know?

"So that's that," said Merrick. "You found absolutely no evidence that anyone but Druschenko had visited the sarcophagus, right? Once we prove that it was him driving the RPV, we'll be able to close this file entirely. I think you deserve a bonus, Gennady, and I've almost got the board to agree."

"Well, thanks." RPV—they had decided the dragon must be one of the Remotely Piloted Vehicles that the Trust had used to build the new sarcophagus. Druschenko had taken some of the stockpiled parts and power supplies from a Trust warehouse, and apparently gotten one of the old lifters going. It was the only way he could open the sarcophagus and survive.

Merrick was happy. Lisa was ecstatic that he was out of Pripyat. It all seemed too easy to Gennady; maybe it was because they hadn't seen the thing. This morning he'd walked down to the ironworks to watch someone using a Chernobyl-model RPV near the kilns. It had looked like a truck with legs, and moved like a sloth. Nothing like the thing that had chased him across the city.

Anyway, he had his money. He chatted with Merrick for a while, then Gennady left to find a bank machine, and prove to himself he'd been paid. First order of business, a new suit. Then he was going to shop for one of those new interfaces for his system. Full virtual reality, like he'd been dreaming about for months.

The noise and turbulence of Kiev's streets hit him like a wall. People everywhere, but no one noticed anyone else in a city like this. He supposed most people drifted through the streets treating all these strangers around as no more than ghosts, but he couldn't do that. As he passed an old woman who was begging on the corner, he found himself noticing the laugh lines around her eyes that warred with the deeply scored lines of disappointment around her mouth; the meticulous stitchwork where she had repaired the sleeves of her cheap dress spoke of a dignity that must make her situation seem all the worse for her. He couldn't ignore her, but he couldn't help her either.

For a while he stood at a downtown intersection, staring over the sea of people. Above the grimy facades, a haze of coal smoke and exhaust banded the sky a yellow that matched the shade on the grimy tattered flags hanging from the street lamps.

Everywhere, he saw victims of the Release. Men and women with open sores or wearing the less visible scars of destitution and disappointment dawdled on the curbs, stared listlessly through shop windows at goods they would never be able to afford on their meager pensions. No one looked at them.

He bought the interface instead of the suit, and the next day he didn't go out at all.

* * * * *

He was nursing a crick in his neck, drinking some weak tea and preparing to go back into a huge international consensual-reality game he now had the equipment to play, when Lisa called.

"Look, Lisa, I've got new toys."

"Why am I not surprised. Have you been out at all since you got back?"

"No. I'm having fun."

"How are you going to meet a nice Ukrainian girl if you never go out?"

"Maybe I like English girls better."

"Oh yeah? Then fly to England. You just got paid."

"The Net is so much faster. And I have the right attachments now."

She laughed. "Toys. I see. You want the latest news on the case?"

He frowned. No, actually, he didn't think he did. But she lived for this sort of thing. "Sure," he said to indulge her.

"Druschenko says he was just the courier. Says he never drove the dragon at all. He's actually quite frantic—he claims he was paid to bring supplies in and do the initial hook up of a RPV, but that's all. Of course, he's made some mighty big purchases lately, and we can't trace the money and he won't tell us where it is. So it's a stalemate."

Gennady thought about Merrick's cheerful confidence the other day. "Did the Trust actually make the most recent payment to the extortionist?"

"No. They could hardly afford to, and anyway Druschenko—"

"Could not have acted alone."

"What?"

"Come on, Lisa. You said yourself you can't find the money. It went into the Net, right? That's your territory, it's not Druschenko's. He's a truck driver, not a hacker, for God's sake. Listen, have they put a Geiger counter on him?"

"Why . . ."

"Find out how hot he is. He had to have been piloting the RPV from nearby, unless he had a satellite link, and there too, he's just a truck driver, not James Bond. Find out how hot he is."

"Um. Maybe you have a point."

"And another thing. Has the Trust put some boats in the river to check for another radiation plume?"

"I don't know."

"We better find out. Because I'll bet you a case of vodka there's going to be another Release."

"Can I call you right back?"

"Certainly." He hung up, shaking his head. People who lived by Occam's Razor died young. That, he supposed, was why he got paid the big bucks.

*   *   *   *   *

He spent most of the next week in the Net, venturing out for groceries and exercise. He smiled at a pretty clerk in the grocery store, and she smiled back, but he never knew what to say in such situations, where he couldn't hide behind an avatar's mask or simply disappear if he embarrassed himself; so he didn't talk to her.

In the platonic perfection of the Net, though, Gennady had dozens of friends and business connections. Between brief searches for new work, he participated in numerous events, both games and art pieces. Here he could be witty, and handsome. And there was no risk. But when he finally rolled into bed at night, there was no warm body there waiting for him, and at those times he felt deeply lonely.

In the morning the computer beckoned, and he would quickly forget the feeling.

Merrick interrupted him in the middle of a tank battle. In this game, Gennady was one of the British defending North Africa against the Desert Fox. The sensual qualities of his new interface were amazing; he could feel the heat, the grit of the sand, almost smell it. The whole effect was ruined when the priority one window opened in the middle of the air above his turret, and Merrick said, "Gennady, I've got a new job for you."

North Africa dissolved. Gennady realized his back hurt and his mouth was dry. "What is it?" he snapped.

"I wouldn't be calling if I didn't think you were the perfect man for the job. We need someone to make a very brief visit to Pripyat. Shouldn't take more than a day."

"Where's that bonus you promised me?"

"I was coming to that. The board's authorized me to pay you an additional twenty percent bonus for work already done. That's even if you turn down this contract."

"Ah. I see. So what is it you need?" He was interested, but he didn't want to appear too eager. Could lower the price that way.

"We want to make sure the sarcophagus is intact. We were going to do a helicopter inspection, but it's just possible Druschenko did some low level . . . well, to put it bluntly, got inside."

"Inside? What do you mean, inside?"

"There may be some explosives inside the sarcophagus. Now we don't want anybody going near it, physically. Have you ever piloted an RPV?"

"Not really. Done a lot of virtual reality sims, but that's not the same thing."

"Close enough. Anyway, we only need you to get the thing to the reactor site. We've got an explosives expert on call who'll take over once you get there and deactivate the bombs. If there are any."

"So he's coming with me?"

"Not exactly, no. He'll be riding in on a satellite link. You're to establish that link in Pripyat, drive the RPV to the reactor, and he'll jack in to do the actual assessment. Then you pull out. That's all there is to it."

"Why can't somebody pilot it in from outside the city?"

"It's only works on a short-range link. You'll have to get within two miles of the sarcophagus."

"Great. Just great. When do you want this to happen?"

"Immediately. I'm having your RPV flown in, it'll arrive tonight. Can you set out in the morning?"

"Depends on what you're willing to pay me."

"Double your last fee."

"Triple."

"Done."

Shit, he thought. *Should have gone for more.* "All right, Merrick, you've got yourself an RPV driver. For a day."

*   *   *   *   *

Gennady debated whether to call Lisa. On the one hand, there was obviously more to this than Merrick was admitting. On the other, she would tell him not to go back to Pripyat. He wanted to avoid that particular conversation, so he didn't call.

Instead he took a cab down to a Trust warehouse at six o'clock to inspect his RPV. The warehouse was a tall anonymous metal-clad building; his now practised eye told him it might remain standing for twenty or thirty years if abandoned. Except that the roof would probably cave in . . .

"You Malianov?" The man was stocky, with the classic slab-like Russian face. He wiped his hands on an oily rag as he walked out to meet Gennady. Gennady shook his hand, smiling as he remembered Bogoliubov, and they went in to inspect the unit.

"What the hell is that?" Whatever it was, it was not just a remotely piloted vehicle. Standing in a shaft of sunlight was an ostrich-like machine at least three meters tall. It sprouted cameras and mikes from all over, and sported two uncannily human arms at about shoulder level. Gennady's guide grinned and gave it a shove. It shuffled its feet a little, regaining balance.

"Military telepresence. Latest model." The man grabbed one of its hands. "We're borrowing it from the Americans. You like?"

"Why do we need this?"

"How the hell should I know? All I know is you're reconnoitering the sarcophagus with it. Right?"

Gennady nodded. He kept his face neutral, but inside he was fuming. Merrick was definitely not telling him everything.

That evening he went on a supply run downtown. He bought all the things he hadn't on his first trip out, including a lot more food. Very intentionally, he did not pause to ask himself why he was packing a month's worth of food for a two day trip.

He was sitting in the middle of the living room floor, packing and repacking, when Lisa phoned. He took it as a voice-only call; if she asked, he'd say he wasn't dressed or something.

"Remember what you said about how Druschenko would have to have had a satellite link to run the dragon?"

"Yeah." He hopped onto the arm of his couch. He was keyed up despite the lateness of the hour.

"Well, you got me thinking," she said. "And guess what? There's a connection. Not with Druschenko, though."

"Okay, I'll bite."

"Can you jack in? I'll have to do some show and tell here."

"Okay." He made sure the apartment cameras were off, then went into the Net. Lisa was there in full avatar—visible head to foot, in 3D—grinning like the proverbial cat with the canary.

"So I thought, what if Druschenko did have a satellite link to the sarcophagus? And lo and behold, somebody does." She called up some windows that showed coordinates, meaningless to Gennady. "At least, there's traffic to some kind of transceiver there. I figured I had Druschenko right then—but the link's still live, and traffic goes way up at regular intervals. During the night, your time. So we're dealing with a night-hawk, I thought. Except he wouldn't have to be a night-hawk if he was calling from, say, North America."

"Wait, wait, you're getting way ahead of me. What's this traffic consist of? You intercepted it, didn't you?"

"Well, not exactly. It's heavily encrypted. Plus, once it's in the net it goes through a bunch of anonymous rerouters, gets split up and copies sent to null addresses, and so on. Untraceable from this end, at least so far."

"Ah, so if he's from North America, that narrows it down a bit. To only about half a billion possibilities."

"Ah, Gennady, you have so little faith. It's probably a telepresence link, right? That's your dragon. Nothing big was brought in, so it's got to be an adaptation of the existing Chernobyl designs. So whoever it is, they should be familiar with those designs, and they'd have to know there were still some RPVs in Pripyat, and they should have a connection to Druschenko. And—here's the topper—they had a lot of start-up capital to run this scam. Had to, with the satellite link, the souping-up of the RPV, and the missiles."

"Missiles? What missiles?"

"Haven't you checked the news lately? One of the Trust's helicopters crashed yesterday. It was doing a low-level pass over the sarcophagus, and wham! down it goes. Pilot was killed. An hour after the news was released I started seeing all sorts of traffic on my secure Interpol groups, police in Kiev and Brussels talking about ground-to-air misssiles."

"Oh, shit," he said.

"So anyway, I just looked for somebody involved in the original sarcophagus project, on the RPV side, who was American and rich. And it popped out at me."

Gennady was barely listening, but his attention returned when she brought up a window with a grainy photo of a thin-faced elderly man. It was hard to tell, but he appeared to be lying on a bed. His eyes were bright and hard, and they stared directly out at Gennady.

"Trevor Jaffrey. He got quite rich doing RPV's and telepresence about twenty years ago. The Chernobyl project was his biggest contract. A while after that he became a recluse, and began wasting his money on some pretty bizarre projects."

"Dragons?"

"Well, Jaffrey's a quadriplegic. He got rich through the Net, and he lived through it too. When I say he became a recluse, he already was, physically. He dropped out of Net society too, and spent all his time and money on physical avatars—telepresences. I've got access to a couple of them, because he had to sell them when he couldn't pay his bills. Want to see one?"

"What, now?"

"I've got a temporary pass. This one's being used as a theme park ride now. At one time Jaffrey must have spent all his free time in it. The mind boggles."

She had his entire attention now. "Okay. Show me."

"Here's the address, name and password. Just take a quick peek. I'll wait."

He entered the commands, and waited as a series of message windows indicated a truly prodigious data pipe opening between his little VR setup and some distant machine. Then the world went dark, and when it came back again he was underwater.

Gennady was standing on the ocean floor. All around were towers of coral, and rainbow fishes swam by in darting schools. The ocean was brilliant blue, the sunlight above shattered into thousands of crystal shards by the waves. He turned his head, and felt the water flow through his hair. It was warm, felt silky against his skin. He could breathe just fine, but he also felt completely submerged.

Gennady raised a hand. Something huge and metal lifted up, five steel fingers on its end. He waggled them—they moved.

This is not a simulation, he realized. Somewhere, in one of the Earth's seas, this machine was standing, and he was seeing through its eyes and hearing through its ears.

He took a step. He could walk, as easily as though he were on land.

Gennady knelt and ran his fingers through the fine white sand. He could actually feel it. Black Sea? More likely the Caribbean, if this Jaffrey was American.

It was achingly beautiful, and he wanted to stay. But Lisa was waiting. He logged out, and as he did caught a glimpse of a truly huge number in American dollars, which flashed *paid in full* then vanished.

Lisa's avatar was smiling, hands behind her back and bobbing on the balls of her feet. "Jaffrey can't pay his bills. And he's addicted to his telepresences. You should see the arctic one. He even had a lunar one for a while. See the common thread?"

"They're all places nobody goes. Or nobody can go," he said. He was starting to feel tired.

"Jaffrey hates people. And he's being driven out of his bodies, one after the other. So he turns in desperation to an old, reliable one—the Chernobyl RPV. Designed to survive working conditions there, and there's still parts, if he can pay off an old acquaintance from the project to bring them in."

"So he does, and he's got a new home." He nodded. "And a way of making more money. Extort the Trust."

"Exactly. Aren't I smart?"

"You, Lisaveta, are a genius." He blew her image a kiss. "So all we need to do is shut him down, and the crisis is over."

"Hmm. Well, no, not exactly. American law is different, and the Net connections aren't proven to go to him. We can't actually move on him until we can prove it's him doing it."

"Well, shut down the feed from the satellite, then."

"We were about to do that," she said with a scowl. "When we got a call from Merrick. Seems the extortionist contacted him just after the missile thing. Warned that he'd blow the sarcophagus if anybody cut the link or tried to get near the place."

"A dead-man switch?"

"Probably. So it's not so simple as it looks."

He closed his eyes and nodded.

"How about you?" she asked. "Anything new?"

"Oh, no, no. Not really. Same old thing, you know?"

*   *   *   *   *

It was raining when he reached his apartment building. Gennady had driven the motorcycle in, leaving all his other supplies by the city gates. He wanted to try something.

The rain was actually a good thing; it made a good cover for him to work under. He parked his bike in the foyer, and hauled a heavy pack from the sidecar, then up twelve floors to the roof. Panting and cursing, he paused to rest under a fiberglass awning. The roof was overgrown with weeds. The sarcophagus was a distant gray dome in a pool of marshland.

He hooked up the satellite feed and aimed it. Then he unreeled a fiber-optic line down the stairs to the sixth floor, and headed for his old place.

Somebody had trashed it. Bogoliubov, it had to be. The piano had bullet holes in it, and there was shit smeared on the wall. The words "Stay away" were written in the stuff.

"Jesus." Gennady backed out of the room.

Scratching his stubble nervously, he shouldered his way into the next apartment. This one was empty except for some old stacking chairs, and had a water-damaged ceiling and one broken window. Radiation was higher than he would have found acceptable a week ago—but after he finished here he could find a better place. Then think what to do about Bogoliubov.

He secured the door and set up his generator and the rest of the computer equipment. He needed a repeater for the satellite signal, and he put that on the balcony. Then he jacked in, and connected to his RPV.

At first all he saw was dirt. Gennady raised his head, and saw the road into town, blurred by rain. He stood up, and felt himself rise to more than man-height. This was great! He flexed his arms, turned his torso back and forth, then reached to pick up his sacks of supplies.

It was a bit awkward using these new arms, but he got the hang of it after spilling some groceries and a satchel of music disks into the mud. When it was all hanging from his mantis-like limbs, he rose up again and trotted toward town.

The RPV drank gas to feed its fuel cells. Bogoliubov had shown Gennady some full tanks on the edge of town, enough to keep the thing going for months or years. Thinking of the old man, Gennady decided that as soon as they were done with Jaffrey, he would visit Bogoliubov with the RPV, and confiscate his rifle.

He jogged tirelessly through the rain until he came to his building. There he paused to hide the bike, in case the old man did come around today, then bumped his way into the stairwell and went up.

Gennady paused in front of the apartment door. He hadn't counted on the eeriness of this moment. He listened, hearing only the faint purr of the generator inside. Hesitantly, he reached to turn the knob with a steel hand, and eased the door open.

A man crouched on the floor near one wall. He was stocky and balding, in his late thirties. He was dressed in a teal shirt and green slacks. His eyes were closed, and small wires ran from his temples to a set of black boxes near the balcony door. He was rocking slowly back and forth.

Jesus, am I doing that? Gennady instantly cut the link. He blinked and looked up, to find the doorway blocked by a monstrous steel and crystal creature. Its rainbow-bedded lenses were aimed at him. Plastic bags swayed from its clenched fists. Gennady's heart started hammering, as though the thing had somehow snuck up on him.

Swearing, he hastily unloaded the supplies from its arms. After putting the stuff away he found himself reluctant to re-enter the living room. Under this low roof the RPV looked like a metal dinosaur ready to pounce. It must weight two hundred kilos at least. He'd have to remember that, and avoid marshy ground or rotten floors when he used it outside.

He linked to it again just long enough to park it down the hall. Then he shut the door and jammed a chair under the knob.

∗   ∗   ∗   ∗   ∗

The morning birds woke Gennady. For a long time he just lay there, drinking in the peace. In his half-awake state, he imagined an invisible shield around this small apartment, sheltering him from any sort of pain, aggravation or distraction. Of all places in the world, he had finally found the one where he could be fully, completely carefree. The hot spots of radiation could be mapped and avoided; he would deal with Bogoliubov in time; Jaffrey would not be a problem for long.

No one would ever evict him from this place. No one would come around asking after him solicitously. No noisy neighbors would move in. And yet, as long as he had fuel to run the generator, he could step into the outside world as freely as ever, live by alias in any or all of the thousands of worlds of the Net.

Be exactly who he wanted to be . . .

Feel at home at last.

But finally he had to rise, make himself a meager breakfast and deal with the reality of the situation. His tenancy here was fragile. Everything would have to go perfectly for him to be able to take advantage of the opportunity he had been given.

First he phoned Merrick. "You never told me about the helicopter."

"Really? I'm sure I did." It was only a voice line; Gennady was sure Merrick wouldn't have been so glib if they'd been able to make eye contact.

Gennady would feel absolutely no guilt over stealing the RPV from him.

"Forget it, except let me say you are a bastard and I'll join the Nazis before I work for you after this," he said. "Now tell me what we're doing. And no more surprises or I walk."

Merrick let the insult pass. They set the itinerary and time for the reconnoitering of the sarcophagus. Gennady was to use the RPV's full set of sensors to ensure there were no tripwires or mines on the approach. Druschenko had denied knowledge of anything other than Jaffrey's RPV. Certainly hearing about the missiles beforehand would have been nice.

"You're to do the initial walking inspection this afternoon at 2:00. Is that enough time for you to familiarize yourself with the RPV?"

Gennady glanced at the apartment door. "No problem."

With everything set, Merrick rang off and Gennady, stretching, stepped onto the balcony to watch the morning sun glow off the sarcophagus. It was an oval dome made of interlocking concrete triangles. Rust stains spread down the diamonds here and there from the heavy stanchions that held it all together. Around the circumference of the thing, he knew, a thick wall was sunk all the way to bedrock, preventing seepage of the horrors within. It was supposed to last ten thousand years; like most people, Gennady assumed it would crumble in a century. Still, one had to be responsible to one's own time.

Humming, he groped for his coffee cup. Just as it reached his lips the computer said, "Lisaveta is calling you."

He burned his tongue.

"Damn damn damn. Is it voice or full-feed? Full-feed. Shit."

He jacked in. He hoped she would match his laconic tone as he said, "Hello, Lisa."

"You asshole."

He found it difficult to meet her gaze. "Are we going to get into something pointless here?"

"No. I'm going to talk and you're going to listen."

"I see."

"Why the hell didn't you tell me you were going back?"

"You'd have told me not to go. I didn't want an argument."

"So you don't respect me enough to argue with me?"

"What?" The idea made no sense to him. He just hadn't seen what good it would do to fight. And, just maybe, he *had* been afraid she might talk him out of it. But he would never admit that to her.

"Gennady. I'm not trying to run your life. If you want to throw it away that's your business. But I'm your friend. I care about you. I just . . . just want to *know*, that's all."

He frowned, staring out the window. Dozens of empty apartment windows stared back. For an instant he imagined dozens of other Gennadys, all looking out, none seeing the others.

"Maybe I don't want to be known," he said. "I'm tired of this world of snoops and gossips. Maybe I want to write my memoirs in a private language. Apparently that's not allowed."

"Pretty ironic for you to be tired of snoops," she said, "inasmuch as that's what you do for a living. And me too . . ." She blinked, then scowled even harder. "Are you refering to—"

"Look, I have to go now—"

"*That's* what this is about, isn't it? You just want to be able to hang up on anybody and everybody the instant you start feeling uncomfortable." Lisa looked incredulous. "Is that it? It is, isn't it. You want to have your cake and eat it. So you found a place where you can hide from everybody, just poke your head out whenever you need someone to talk to. Well, I'm not a TV, you know. I'm not going to let you just turn me on and off when it suits you.

"Keep your empty town and your empty life, then. I'll have none of it."

She hung up.

"Bitch!" He yanked off the headset and kicked the wall. No neighbors to complain—he kicked it again. "What the hell do you want from me?"

He'd put a hole in the plasterboard. Dust swirled up, and he heard the Geiger counter buzz louder for a second.

"Oh, God." He slumped on the balcony, but when he raised his eyes all that met them was the vista of the sarcophagus, gleaming now like some giant larva on the banks of the river.

Unaccountably, Gennady found his eyes filling with tears.

How long has it been, he wondered in amazement, *since you cried?*

Years. He pinched the bridge of his nose, and blinked a few times. He needed to walk; yes, a long walk in the sun would bring him around. . . .

He stopped at the door to the apartment. There was the plastic wrap he should use to cover his shoes. And the face mask. And beside that the Geiger counter.

A horrible feeling of being trapped stole over him. For a few minutes he stood there, biting his nails, staring at the peeling wallpaper. Then the anger returned, and he kicked the wall again.

"I'm right." To prove it, he sat down, jacked in, and called up the interface for the RPV.

* * * * *

Gennady held his head high as he walked in the sun in a plaza where no human could set foot for the next six thousand years. He knelt and examined the gigantic wildflowers that grew in abundance here. They were *his,* in a way that nothing else had ever been nor could be outside this place. This must be how the old man felt, he marveled—but Bogoliubov's armour was a deliberate refusal to believe the danger he was in. With the RPV, Gennady had no need for such illusions.

He didn't take every opportunity to explore. There would be plenty of time for that later, after he reported the accidental destruction of the RPV. For now, he just sauntered and enjoyed the day. His steel joints moved soundlessly, and he felt no fatigue or heat.

Beep. "Merrick here. Gennady, are you on line?"

"Yes. I'm here."

"Gennady, let me introduce Dentrane. You'll hand the RPV off to him when you get in position, and he'll take it from there. If we're lucky, we'll only need to do this once."

"Hello, Gennady," said Dentrane. He had a thick Estonian accent.

"Good to hear from you, Dentrane. Shall I walk us over to the sarcophagus and you can take a peek at what all the fuss is about?"

Dentrane laughed. "Delighted. Lead on."

Time to be 'all business' as Lisaveta would say. He jogged towards the river.

∗   ∗   ∗   ∗   ∗

"It's American law," Lisa was saying to Merrick. They had met in a neutral room in cyberspace. Merrick's avatar was bland as usual; Lisa had represented herself as a cyber-Medusa, with fiber-optic leads snaking from her hair to attach to a globe that floated before her. "When you're dealing with the Net, you've got both international and local laws to worry about," she explained. "We can't guarantee our trace of the paths to the satellite signal. We can't shut it down on the satellite end. And unless we have proof that it's Jaffrey doing this, we can't shut it down at his end."

"So our hands are tied." Merrick's avatar was motionless, but she imagined him pacing. In a window next to him, the live feed from the RPV showed green foliage, then the looming concrete curve of the sarcophagus.

"You're going to have to trust me. We'll find a way to prove it's Jaffrey."

"I have sixteen military RPVs waiting in the river. The second I see a problem, Ms. MacDonald, they're going in. And if they go in, you have to shut down Jaffrey."

"I can't! And what if he's got a dead-man switch?"

"I'm relying on Dentrane to tell us if he does. And I'm relying on you to cut Jaffrey off when I order it."

She glared at the avatar. It must be ten times she'd told him she had no authority to do that. She knew how to, sure—but if they were wrong and Jaffrey wasn't the extortionist, she would be criminally liable. But Merrick didn't care about that.

He didn't seem to care about Gennady, either. And why should he? Gennady had chosen to plant himself right next to the sarcophagus. If it blew up he would have no one to blame but himself.

And that would be absolutely no consolation when she had to fly out to watch him die of radiation poisoning in some Soviet-vintage hospital ward. She had woken herself up last night with that scenario, and had lain awake wondering why she should do that for a man whom she knew only through the Net. But maybe it was precisely because their association was incomplete. Lisa knew he was as real a person as she; in a way they were close. But they would not have really met until she touched his hand, and she couldn't bear the thought of losing him before that happened.

Angrily she glanced at her ranks of numbers and documents, all of which pointed at Jaffrey, none conclusively. It all made her feel so help-less. She turned to watch the movement of the RPV instead.

The RPV had scaled the steep lower part of the sarcophagus, and now clambered hand over hand toward a red discoloration on one flank. With a start, Lisa realized there were some bulky objects sticking up there. The camera angle swerved and jittered, then the RPV paused long enough for her to get a good look. She heard Merrick swear just as she realized she was looking at tarpaulins, painted to resemble the concrete of the struc-ture, that had been stretched over several green metal racks.

Then one of the tarps disappeared in a white cloud. The camera shook as everything vanished in a white haze. Then—static.

The Engine of Recall

"What was that?"

"Holy mother of God," said Merrick. "He launched."

*   *   *   *   *

Gennady froze. He had stepped onto the balcony to let Dentrane get on with his work. From here he had a magnificent view of the sarcophagus, so the contrail of the rocket was clearly visible. It rose straight up, an orange cut in the sky, then leveled off and headed straight at him. He just had time to blink and think, *I'm standing right next to the RPV signal repeater* before the contrail leapt forward faster than the eye could follow, and all the windows of the surrounding buildings flashed sun-bright.

The concussion was a sudden hammer blow, nothing like the roaring explosions he heard in movies or VR. He was on his back on the balcony, ears ringing, when he heard the *bang!* echo back from the other buildings, and could almost follow its course through the abandoned city as the rings of shocked air hit one neighborhood after the next, and reported back.

A cascade of dust and grit obscured the view. It all came from overhead somewhere. He realized as he sat up that the explosion had occurred on the roof. That was where he'd set up the big dish necessary for Dentrane's data-feed.

The fear felt like cold spreading through his chest, down his arms. He leaned on the swaying balcony, watching for the second contrail that would signal the second rocket. The dish on the roof was the link to the Net, yes; but it fed its signal down here to the transmitter that sat a meter to Gennady's left, and that transmitter was the control connection to the RPV. It was the only live beacon now.

Nothing happened. As the seconds passed, Gennady found himself paralyzed by indecision: in the time it took him to rise to his feet and turn, and take three steps, the rocket might be on him—and he had to see it if it came.

It did not. Gradually he became aware that his mouth was open, his throat hurting from a yell that hadn't made it from his lungs to his vocal chords. He fell back on his elbows, then shouted "Shit!" at a tenth the volume he thought he needed, and scrambled back into the apartment.

He was halfway down the stairs when the cell phone rang. He barked a laugh at the prosaic echo, the only sound now in this empty building other than his chattering footsteps. He grabbed it from his belt. "What?"

"Gennady! Are you all right?"

"Yes, Lisa."

"Oh, thank God! Listen, you've got to get out of there—"

"Just leaving."

"I'm so glad."

"Fuck you." He hung up and jammed the phone back in his belt. It immediately rang again. Gennady stopped, cursed, grabbed it, almost pressed the receive button. Then he tossed it over the bannister. After a second he heard it hit the landing below with a crack.

He ran past it into the lobby, and pulled out the bike. He started it, and paused to look around the sad, abandoned place he had almost lived in. His hand on the throttle was trembling.

The release could happen at any moment. There would be an explosion, who knew how big; he imagined chunks of concrete floating up in the air, exposing a deep red wound in the earth, the unhealing sore of Chernobyl. A cloud of dust would rise, he could watch it from outside. Quiet, subtle, it would turn its head toward Kiev, as it had years ago. Soon there would be more ghosts in the streets of the great city.

He would get away. Lisa would never speak to him, and he could never walk the avenues of Kiev again without picturing himself here. He could never look the survivors of the Release in the eye again. But he would have gotten away.

"*Liar!*"

The sound jolted him. Gennady looked up. Bogoliubov, the self-pro-claimed custodian of Pripyat, stalked towards him across the courtyard, his black greatcoat flapping in the evening breeze.

"Liar," said the old man again.

"I'm not staying," Gennady shouted.

"You *lied* to me!"

Gennady took his hand off the throttle. "What?"

"You work for the Trust. Or is it the army! And to think I believed that story about you being a med student." Bogoliubov stopped directly in Gennady's path.

"Look, we haven't got time for this. There might be another release. We have to get out of here. Hop on."

Bogoliubov's eyes widened. "So you betrayed him, too. I'm not sur-prised." He spat in the dirt at Gennady's feet and turned away. "I'm not going anywhere with you."

"Wait!" Gennady popped the kickstand on the bike and caught up to the old man. "I'm sorry. I didn't mean to hurt you. I came here because of the dragon. How could I know you weren't involved?"

Bogoliubov whirled, scowling. He seemed to be groping for words. Finally, "Trust was a mistake," was all he said. As if the effort cost him greatly, he reached out and shoved Gennady hard in the chest. Then he walked rapidly away.

Gennady watched him go, then returned to the bike. His head was throbbing. He shut the bike down, and walked slowly back to the entrance of the apartment building. He stopped. He waited, staring at the sky. And then he went in.

*   *   *   *   *

"Lisaveta, I'm linking to the RPV now."

"Gennady! What?" He smiled grimly at the transparent surprise in her voice. She who liked to Know, had been startled by him. Gennady had linked the cell-phone signal to the RPV interface. She would get voice, but no video this way.

He adjusted the headset. "Connecting now." He took a deep breath, and jabbed the *enter* key on his board.

Vision lurched. And then he was staring at a red tarpaulin, which was tangled up in the fallen spars of a green metal rack. Several long metal tubes stuck out of this, all aimed at the ground. A haze like exhaust from a bus hung over everything.

The missile rack shook. Gennady cautiously turned his head to see what might be causing the motion. Directly beside him was the black, rusted flank of a thing like a tank with legs. Several sets of arms dangled from its sloped front, and two of these were tearing the tough fabric of the tarp away from the collapsed rack.

"Gennady, talk to me!" He smiled to hear the concern in her voice. "Where are you?"

"Dentrane's out of the loop, so I've taken over the RPV. I've got it on the side of the sarcophagus."

"But where are you?"

"Lisa, listen. *Someone else is here.* Do you understand? There is another RPV, and it's trying to fix the missile rack."

"Jaffrey . . ."

"That his name? Whatever." The black dragon had nearly unravelled the tarp. If it succeeded in realigning the missile tubes, it would have a clear shot at the balcony where Gennady now sat.

"It's ignoring me. Thinks I've run away, I guess." He looked around, trying not to turn his head. There was nothing obvious to use as a weapon—but then his own RPV was a weapon, he recalled. Nothing compared to the hulking, grumbling thing next to him, but more than a match for—

—the missile tubes he pounced on. Gennady felt the whole structure go down under him, metal rending. He flailed about, scattering the tubes with loud banging blows, winding up on his asbestos backside looking up at the two spotlight eyes of the black RPV.

He switched on the outside speaker. "This isn't your private sandbox, you know."

Two huge arms shot out. He rolled out of the way. Metal screamed.

A deep roaring shook the whole side of the sarcophagus. He could see small spires of dust rise from the triangular concrete slabs. The dragon had leaped, and utterly smashed the place where Gennady had just been.

Just ahead under the flapping square of another gray tarp Gennady saw a deep black opening in the side of the sarcophagus. "This your home?" he shouted as he clambered up to it.

"Stay away!" The voice was deep and carrying, utterly artificial.

"What was that?" Lisa was still with him.

"That would be your Jaffrey. He's pissed, as the Yankees would say."

"Why are you doing this?"

"Lisa, he's going to make a release. We both know it. Only a fool wouldn't realize there's a backup plan to me being here. If I fail, the men in the choppers come in, am I wrong? You and I know it. This guy knows it. Now he's got nothing to lose. He'll blow the top off the place."

"Merrick's ready to send the others in now. You just get out of there and let them handle it."

"No." The monster was close behind him as Gennady made it to the dark opening. "I can't avoid this one. You know it's true."

She might have said "Oh," and he did imagine a tone of sad resignation to whatever she did say, but he was too busy bashing his way into the bottom of a pit to make it out. Gennady rolled to a stop in a haze of static; his cameras adjusted to the dark in time for him to see a huge black square block the opening above, and fall at him.

"Shit!" He couldn't avoid it this time. Something heavy hit him as he staggered to his feet, flicking him into a wall as though he were made of balsa wood. He didn't actually feel the blow, but it was an impossibly quick motion like a speeded-up movie; sensation vanished from his right arm.

He managed to cartwheel out of the way of another piston blow. Gennady backed up several paces, and looked around.

This was sort of an antechamber to the remnants of one of the reactor rooms. Circles of light from the headlamp eyes of the dragon swooped and dove through an amazing tangle of twisted metal and broken cement under the low red girders of the sarcophagus's ceiling. Here were slabs of wall still painted institution green, next to charred metal pipes as thick as his body. The wreckage made a rough ring around a cleared area in the center. And there, the thing he had never in his life expected to see, there was the open black mouth of the obscenity itself.

Jaffrey, if this was indeed he, had made a nest in the caldera of Reactor Four.

Gennady bounded across the space and up the rubble on the other side. He clutched at a cross-beam and pulled himself up on it while the dragon labored to follow. When he reached with both arms, only one appeared and grasped the beam.

"Come down," said the dragon in its deep bass that rattled the very beams. Its bright eyes were fixed on him, only meters below.

"What, are you crazy?" he said, instantly regretting his choice of words.

The dragon sat back with a seismic thud. It turned its big black head, eerily like a bear's as it regarded him.

"I've been watching you," it said after a long minute.

Gennady backed away along the girder.

"When I was a boy," said the dragon of Pripyat, "I wrote a letter to God. And then I put the letter in a jar, and I buried it in the garden, as deep as I could reach. It never occurred to me that someone might dig it up one day. I thought, no one sees God. God is in the hidden places between the walls, behind us when we are looking the other way. But I have put this letter out of the world. Maybe God will pass by and read it."

"Gennady," said Lisa. "You have to find out who this is. We can't cut Jaffrey's signal until we have proof that it's him. Can you hear me?"

"I watched you walking in the evenings," said the dragon. "You stared up at the windows the same way I do. You put your hands behind your back, head down, and traced the cracks in the pavement like a boy. You moved as one liberated from a curse."

"Shut up," said Gennady.

"Do you remember the first photos from the accident? Remember the image of this place's roof? Just a roof, obviously trashed by an explosion of some kind. But still, a roof, where you could stand and look out. Except you couldn't. No one could. That roof was the first place I had ever actually seen that had been removed from the world. A place no one could go or ever would go. To stand there for even a moment was death. Remember?"

"I was too young," said Gennady.

"Good," said Lisa. "We know he's old enough to remember 1986. Keep him talking."

Gennady scowled, wishing the RPV could convey the expression.

"Later I remembered that," said the dragon. "When I could no longer live as a person in the world of people. Remember the three men in the Bible who were cast in the belly of the furnace, and survived? Oh, I needed to do that. To live in the belly of the furnace. You know what I mean, don't you?"

Gennady crawled backward along the beam. The horrible thing was, he did know. He couldn't have explained it, but the dragon's words were striking him deeply, wounding him far more than its metal hands had.

"So look." The dragon gestured behind it at the pit. It had arranged some chairs and a table around the black calandria. A bottle on the table held a sprig of wildflowers. There was other furniture, Gennady now saw—filing cabinets, bookshelves, and yes, books everywhere. This monster had not merely visited this place; it lived here.

He saw another thing, as well. On the back of the dragon, under a cross of bent metal spars, was a small satellite dish. This spun and turned wildly to keep its focus on some distant point in the heavens.

"Lisa, he's linked directly to the dragon. No repeaters."

"That a problem?"

"Damn right it's a problem! I can't stop the thing by pulling any plugs."

"You and I have had the same ambition," the dragon said to Gennady. "To live in the invisible world, visit the place that can't be visited. Except that I was forced to it. You're healthy, you can walk. What made you come here?"

"Don't," said Gennady.

The searchlights found and pinned him again. "What hurt you?" asked the dragon.

Gennady hissed. "None of your business."

The dragon was now perfectly still. "Is it so strong in you that you can never admit to it? Tell me—if I were to say I will hunt your body down and kill you now unless you tell me why you came here—would you tell me?"

Gennady couldn't answer.

The dragon surged to its feet. "You don't even know what you have!" it roared. "You can walk. You can still make love—really, not just in some simulation. And you *dare* to come in here and try to take away the only thing I've got left?"

Gennady lost his grip on the beam and fell. A bookshelf shattered under him.

The dragon towered over him. "You can't live here," it said. "You're just a tourist."

He expected a blow that would shatter his connection, but it didn't come. Instead the monster stepped over him, making for the exit.

"I can run faster than your little motorbike," it said. Then it was gone, up the entrance shaft.

Gennady tried to rise. One of his legs was broken. One-legged, one-armed, there was no way he was getting out of here.

"Gennady," said Lisa. "What's happening?"

"He left," said Gennady. "He's gone to kill me."

"Break the link. Run for it. You can get to the motorcycle before he gets to you, can't you?"

"Maybe. That's not the point."

"What do you mean?"

He raised himself on his good elbow. "We haven't got our proof, and we don't know if there's a dead-man switch. Once he's done with me he's just going to come back here and tear the roof off. Are Merrick's commandos on their way?"

"Yes."

"Maybe they can stop him. But I wouldn't count on it."

"What are you saying?"

"I'm in his den. Maybe I can find what we need before he gets to me."

For a moment her breath labored in his ear, forming no words. Gennady told himself that he, in contrast, felt nothing. He had lost, completely. It really didn't matter what he did now, so he might as well do the decent thing.

He bent to the task of inspecting the dragon's meager treasure.

*　*　*　*　*

"Talk to me," she said. Lisa sat hunched over her work table, out of the Net, one hand holding the wood as if to anchor herself. All her screens were live, feeding status checks from her hired hackers, Merrick's people, and all the archival material on Jaffrey that she could find.

"There's no bombs here," he said. His voice was flat. "But there's three portable generators and fuel drums. They're near entrance shaft. I guess dragon could blow them up. Wouldn't be much of an explosion, but fire would cause release, you know."

"What else is there? Anything that might tell us who this is?"

"Yes—filing cabinets." That was all he said for nearly a minute.

"What about them?" she asked finally.

"Just getting there—" Another pause. "Tipped them over," he said. "Looking . . . papers in the ashes. What the hell is this stuff?"

"Is it in English or Russian?"

"Both! Looks like records from the Release. Archival material. Photos."

"Are any of them of Jaffrey?"

"Lisa," he snapped, "it's dark, my connection's bad, and I only saw that one photo you showed me. How in God's name am I to know?"

"There must be something!"

"I'm sure there is," he said. "But I don't have time to find it now."

She glanced at the clock. The dragon had left five minutes ago. Was that enough time for it to get to Gennady's building?

"But we have to be sure!"

"I know you do," he said quietly. "I'll keep looking."

Lisa sat back. Everything seemed quiet and still to her suddenly; the deep night had swallowed the normal city noises. Her rooms were silent, and so were her screens. Gennady muttered faintly in her ear, that was all.

She never acted without certain knowledge. It was what she had built her life on. Lisa had always felt that, when a moment of awful decision came, she would be able to make the right choice because she always had all the facts. And now the moment was here. And she didn't *know.*

Gennady described what he saw as he turned over this, then that paper or book. He wasn't getting anywhere.

She switched to her U.S. line connection. The FBI man who had unluckily pulled the morning shift at NCSA Security sat up alertly as she rang through.

Lisa took a deep breath and said the words that might cost her career. "We've got our proof. It's Jaffrey, all right. Shut him down."

The Engine of Recall

* * * * *

Relief washed over Gennady when she told him. "So I'm safe."

Her voice was taut. "I've given the commands. It'll take some time."

"What? How much?"

"Seconds, minutes—you've got to get out of there now."

"Oh my God Lisa, I thought this would be instant."

Gennady felt the floor tremble under him. Nothing in the den of the sarcophagus had moved.

"Now!" She almost screamed it. "Get out now!"

He tore the link helmet off: *spang* of static and noise before reality came up around him. Sad wallpaper, moldy carpet. And thunder in the building.

Gennady hesitated at the door, then stepped into the hallway. Light from inside lit the narrow space dimly—but it was too late to run over and turn out the lamp. From the direction of the stairwell came a deep vibration and a berserk roar such as he had only ever heard once, when he stood next to an old T35 tank that was revving up to climb an obstacle at a fair. Intermittent thuds shook the ceiling's dust onto Gennady's shoulders; he jerked with each angry impact.

Gennady shut the door, and then the end of the hall exploded. In the darkness he caught a confused impression of petalling plasterboard rushing at him, accompanied by a gasp of black dust. The noise drowned his hearing. Then Jaffrey's eyes blazed into life at ceiling level.

He was too big to fit in the hallway—big as a truck. So Jaffrey demolished the corridor as he came, simply scooping the walls aside with his square iron arms, wedging his flat body between floor and ceiling. The beams of his halogen eyes never wavered from pinioning Gennady as he came.

Into the apartment again. The dial on the Geiger counter was swinging wildly, but the clicking was lost now in thunder. The windows shattered spontaneously. Gennady put his hands over his ears and backed to the balcony door.

Jaffrey removed the wall. His eyes roved over the evidence of Gennady's plans—the extra food supplies, the elaborate computer setup, the cleaning and filtering equipment. A deep and painful shame uncoiled within Gennady, and with that his fear turned to anger.

"Catch me if you can, you cripple!" he screamed. Gennady leapt onto the balcony, put one foot on the rail and, boosting himself up, grabbed the railing of the balcony one floor above. He pulled himself up without regard to the agony that shot through his shoulders.

Jaffrey burst through the wall below, and as Gennady kicked at the weather-locked door he felt the balcony under him undulate and tilt.

The door wouldn't budge. Jaffrey's two largest hands were clamped on the concrete pad of the balcony. With vicious jerks he worked it free of the wall.

Gennady hopped onto the railing. Cool night air ruffled past and he caught a glimpse of dark ground far below, and a receding vista of empty, black apartment towers. He meant to jump to the next balcony above, but the whole platform came loose as he tried. Flailing, he tried a sideways leap instead. His arms crashed down on the metal railing of the balcony next door.

He heard Jaffrey laugh. This platform was already loose, its bolts rusted to threads. As he pulled himself up Jaffrey tossed the other concrete pad into the night and reached for him.

He couldn't get over the rail in time, but Jaffrey missed, the cylinders of his fingers closing over the rail itself. Jaffrey pulled.

Gennady rolled over the top of the railing. As he landed on the swaying concrete he saw Jaffrey. The dragon was half outside, two big legs bracing him against the creaking lintel of the lower level. He was straining just to reach this far, and his fingers were now all tangled up in the bent metal posts of the railing.

Gennady grabbed the doorknob as the balcony began to give way. "Once more, you bastard," he shouted, and deliberately stepped within reach of the groping hand.

Jaffrey lunged, fingers gathering up the rest of the metal into a knot. The balcony's supports broke with a sound like gunshots, and it all fell out from under Gennady.

He held onto the doorknob, shouting as he saw the balcony fall, and Jaffrey try too late to let go. The bent metal held Jaffrey's black hand, and for a second he teetered on the edge of the verge. Then the walls he'd braced his feet against gave way, and the dragon of Pripyat fell into the night air and vanished briefly, to reappear in a bright orange flash as he hit the ground. Rolling concussions played again through the streets of the dead city.

The doorknob turned under Gennady's hand, and the door opened of its own accord—outward.

Trying to curse and laugh, hearing wild disbelief in his voice, he swung like a pendulum for long seconds, then got himself inside. He lay prone on some stranger's carpet, breathing the musty air and crying his relief.

Then he rose, feeling pain but no more emotion at all. Gennady left the apartment, and went downstairs to get on with his life.

* * * * *

Lisa sat up all night, waiting for word. The commandos had gone in, and found the violated sarcophagus, and the body of the dragon. They had not found Gennady, but then they hadn't found his bike either.

When the FBI cut off Jaffrey's signal, the feed to the dragon had indeed stopped. They had entered his stronghold apartment minutes later, and arrested him in his bed.

So her career was safe. She didn't care; it was still the worst situation she could have imagined. For Gennady to be dead was one thing. For her not to know was intolerable. Lisa cried at 4:00 A.M., standing in her kitchen stirring hot milk, while the radio played something baroque and incongruously light. She stared through blurred eyes at the lights of the city, feeling more alone than she could have prepared herself for.

It was midmorning when Gennady called. Her loneliness didn't vanish with the sound of his voice. She started crying again when she heard him say her name. "You're really all right?"

"I'm fine. At a gas station near Kiev. Didn't feel like sticking around to be debriefed, you know. Sorry I lost the cell phone, I'd have called earlier." There was a hesitancy in his voice, like he wasn't telling her everything.

"Merrick says there was no release. Were you irradiated?"

"Not much. Ten packs or so, I guess." Despite herself she laughed at his terminology. She heard him clear his throat and waited. But he said nothing else.

She held the phone to her ear, and glanced around at her apartment. Empty, save for her. Lisa felt a sadness like exhaustion, a deep lowering through her throat and stomach. "You're just a voice," she said, not knowing her own meaning. "Just a voice on the phone."

"I know." She wiped at her eyes. How could he know what she meant, when she didn't?

"Look," he said, "I can't go on like this." His voice faded a bit with the vagaries of the line. "It's not working."

"What's not working, Gennady?"

"My—my whole life." She heard the hesitant intake of breath again. "I can't control anything. It's just . . . beyond me."

She was amazed. "But you did it. You got Jaffrey for us."

"Well, you know . . ." His voice held a self-conscious humor now. "It was your hand on the switch. I just kept him busy for you. It doesn't matter. I don't know what to do."

"What do you mean?"

"I can't just go back to Kiev. Sit around the flat. Jack into the Net. It's not enough."

"You don't have to," she said. "You have money now. I'll make sure Merrick comes clean."

"Yeah. You know . . . I've got enough for a vacation, I figure."

Lisa leaned back in her work chair. She toyed nervously with a strand of her hair. "Yeah? Where would you go?"

"Oh . . . Maybe London?"

She laughed. "Oh yes! Yes, please do."

"Ah." His shyness was such a new thing, and charming—but then, he wasn't falling back on the safety of the Net this time. "One condition?" he ventured.

"Yes?"

"Don't ask me too many questions."

For a second an old indignation took her. But she recognized it for the insecurity it was. "All right, Gennady. You tell me what you want to tell me. And I'll show you the city."

"And the Tower? I always wanted to see the Tower."

Again she laughed. "It figures. But we go only once, okay? No more castles for you after that. Promise?"

"Promise."

What goes on under the shroud of smog that hides Titan's surface? Ironically, by the time this collection comes out we may know the answer: the Cassini *probe is scheduled to send back pictures from the surface in early 2005. But whatever it finds, I hope some mystery remains—some dim and fog-shrouded valley, perhaps, or a polar ocean where I can continue to imagine Ari Bolan and Allan Barron sitting on the ice, talking about life, death, and all the lost places of their pasts.*

"The Cold Convergence" first appeared in Figment *magazine, Spring 1993 issue, and was reprinted in the July 1997 issue of* Cosmic Visions *(Volume 2, Number 5). This story also won the* Context *'89 fiction contest, sponsored by the Context '89 SF convention in Edmonton, Alberta.*

✷ ✷ T H E   C O L D ✷ ✷ C O N V E R G E N C E

"He lives alone," Murray said. "In that." He gestured to the window. Outside, orange thunderclouds lay piled up, lightning skittering around their bases. A drizzle of supercooled gasoline fell on the plains around Titan Commerce Camp Six.

Ari Bolan shivered, though she saw through the director's dramatism. She couldn't look at the landscape of this winter moon without feeling uneasy.

"Alone?" she asked. "Why? And why didn't I hear about this case before?"

"You've had your hands full with the other dislocals," he said. "The ones who simply refuse to work and those damn secessionists. A big job. This guy's different, though. He's plain crazy." Murray shrugged. "There's no understanding these people. Not for me, anyway. I guess you do, you're the psychologist."

She looked again at the ethane storm. She specialized in treating the men and women who broke under the strain of spacer life. A significant number did, a fact repugnant to people like Murray. On their first meeting she had sized him up by the cut of his suit, the expensive glitter of his Comwatch. They told her he was a born-again worshipper of the Meritocracy. Nothing he had said or done in the six weeks since that meeting had changed her impression.

She was sure he had never felt the gaze of the ice on him when he walked past a window here.

"We're quite pleased with the work you've done for us, Ari," he was saying. "The drop-outs you've treated seem to be coming around. We think your methods can be generalized now, once the computers have fully learned them."

She toyed nervously with her comp bracelet. "I'm glad. But really, what works is just a little respect and attention. And I can't tell how much has been due to me, and how much to the other incentive programs you've started."

He nodded dismissively. "Of course. We want to test the versatility of your therapies for that reason. I'd like you to consider working your magic on this man. This dislocal."

Ari shifted in the deep plush chair. He quickly turned to take a folio card from his desk top, and handed it to her. She pressed the card's surface, and a picture of the loner appeared there.

"Allan Barron," said Murray, hovering over her. "They call him the Bear. Used to, anyway, when he was a specialist in orbital transfers. Flipped his lid two years ago, and walked off into the blizzard. Usually they do it to commit suicide, but Bear kept going. He didn't join the dislocals; couldn't take their socialist-regressive philosophy, I guess. Can't say as I blame him for that. He's been out there, somewhere in the Templeton Rill, ever since."

"How does he survive?"

"He stole a symbiot. They always do unless they're killing themselves."

She'd seen men and women in the bulky symbiots, monster shapes in the lifeless Titanian hills. "It must be living death to be locked in one of those."

Murray laughed. "Some of the guys grow attached to their symbiots. You never know." He leaned down to press the card. "Here are his stats."

As she examined the card, Murray retreated to his desk, to sit with his hands steepled. He watched her. "What do you say, Ari? We have a major problem there, and I'm dedicated to the fast track to a solution. If you can prove your techniques with the Bear, I can guarantee a budget sufficient to expand your project. Maybe give you your own department."

Ari looked up quickly, but past him, at the storm. Murray noticed, and turned in his swivel chair to regard the bleak scene. "There is that . . ." he said after a time. "We can't find Bear usually, much less convince him to come in. If you take this project on, you'll have to meet him on his own ground."

She twisted the card in her fingers, staring out the window. *No way,* she thought, even as she said, "I'll think about it."

*   *   *   *   *

In full daylight, it was dark as night. Ari faced the wastelands of the Templeton Rill. Her back and shoulders were warm, but her face and the front of her body felt a fearsome cold she hadn't yet experienced on Titan, although she knew it was the norm. She shuffled her feet to prevent them from sinking into the soil, and a dramatic nimbus of volatized gas erupted around her, like angelic wings. Behind her, deep pits—footsteps—led back to the Tether lander.

She wore only a skin suit for this expedition, which was to familiarize her with the conditions in the Rill. Her Symbiot wasn't ready yet; she'd gone to see it that morning. Watching it grow inside a jar in the Biology Division, she felt like the mother of a monster, coming to the viewing room for the first time.

She could go no further in the skinsuit. True space-suits were expensive, and the Commerce division wouldn't spare one for this jaunt. She was dependent for body heat on the masers mounted on the lander. They bathed her with microwaves from behind, but all that heat was being lost through the side facing the Rill.

Kasmi, her pilot, watched her appreciatively. "You don't need training, Ms Bolan. Where'd you learn to be comfortable with disecologies?" He was grotesque in his symbiot, a furred round bulk with a squat head and a looping tail. The tail moved by itself, grazing on the hydrocarbon slush that covered the ice.

"I spent three years on Mars." She turned around, to let the masers warm her front. "This place reminds me of why I left. I'd forgotten what real cold feels like."

"You don't like it here?"

"Do you?" She began walking back to the lander, past the remains of her demonstrations of survival skills: the igloo, the ice mirror.

"I hate it. Why'd you come?"

"Money, Kasmi. Same as everybody else."

He laughed. "You're going after the Bear, eh?"

"Yes." She watched his inhuman form lope toward the lander. "Do you know about him?"

"Everybody does. Some know more than others. I met him. Seemed like a regular guy."

"How could he survive this?" She gestured at the lowering red mist, the greenish sponge hills and muddy, hydrocarbon bogs.

"I don't think anything human could, frankly," said Kasmi in a somewhat defensive tone. "What's out there is just shreds, if you know what I mean. I think it's his symbiot runs him. Just animal sense. Nobody home in it."

His hairy bulk clambered up the lander's ladder, shedding frigid liquids. Billowing vapor, she followed.

"The other dislocals aren't like him," added Kasmi as he settled behind the controls. "Some people just crack, but when you crack out here, it's a billion miles to go home. No way you can. Murray thinks you can change all that."

"And you?"

"I don't think. But maybe I hope, sometimes."

She knew how he felt. Mars had been a desert, almost Earth-like except for the pink sky. But this horrid world, its oceans so cold a human hand dipped in one would freeze instantly, so ugly its topography had been named after ancient maps of hell, could strip even the hardiest spirit. And once so broken, where could you go? Everyone who came here was condemned to a term of years by the laws of celestial mechanics.

She was glad to be back in the lander. This was a great place for breakdowns, madness. She had survived the Tharsis outpost on Mars, hellhole that it was. Though that made her a veteran, she still felt unready for this assignment.

As they flew back, they passed one of the harvesting machines. Its scoop buckets dragged tonnes of muck from the silicone bogs. Men were needed to determine the unpredictable location of the 'rich bogs', which contained deposits of tholins, astonishingly complex hydrocarbons which could not yet be produced in laboratories. Kasmi banked them over the mottled yellow wasteland. "It's all produced by lightning," he said, pointing to a distant storm. "The storms follow a line around the equator, which is why we only dig here. Too bad; the atmosphere is richer in the stuff that makes these tars nearer the poles, like over Templeton Bay. But no lightning there. Have to take what Titan gives us. Tightfisted bitch—just like the Corporation."

The tiny, regular points of the Commerce Six domes appeared ahead. Kasmi laughed. "People always want what they can't have. Can't go home again, can't make it rain." He shrugged monstrous shoulders. "Can't have everything."

*   *   *   *   *

Her boat had stalled in the middle of Templeton bay. Ari looked around herself uneasily. It was midmorning, the air was calm and she shouldn't worry, but this was just the kind of thing she'd been afraid would happen. The ethane ocean was a waveless roiling plain stretching away into haze; layers of aerosols in colored bands made the sky into a giant tiered cylinder with her on the inside bottom. The layers were different colors, blue, mauve, brown—smog upon smog piled up. Strange froth moved through the ocean, not rising, but running in submerged currents. And the boat perched on top of the liquid like it was about to take flight.

The radio wasn't reassuring. "It's Tuesday," the announcer was saying, "and a balmy 95 degrees Kelvin out there, so let's get out and shovel that acetylene! God knows nobody else is going to." Static was starting to degrade the signal.

The motor seemed dead, but Ari refused to call for help. She had to prove she could cope with Titan. The boat was drifting further off course, though. Clumsy with the symbiot paws, she had dropped her only map overboard. If she entered a radio shadow they'd be forced to send a lander if she didn't report in, but she knew this dismal sea extended past the horizon and she'd been told landers couldn't come close to these oceans; their engine heat would cause explosive evaporation.

Obviously, the infrared blip she'd taken to be Bear (on an island, she'd presumed) had been spurious.

Something reared out of the ocean at the stern of the boat. Ari gasped and drew back, almost capsizing. Two long arms clutched the gunwales, and a bedraggled symbiot hauled itself into the boat. It dropped Ari's map by the motor.

"Who are you?" she squeaked. The figure didn't reply, but bent over the motor. "What on earth were you doing, swimming in *that?*"

"Easier," grunted the ape-like figure. Seconds later the motor started, and they steered back toward shore. She watched the creature as they went, wondering what to do now.

When they'd dragged the boat onto shore she said, shakily, "Thanks. I guess I owe you one for this. Damn that motor, anyway. How did you fix it?" He turned and started walking away without a word. "Hey," she called, "you're the Bear, aren't you?"

"Lady, go home," said the symbiot-muffled voice.

"Is this *your* home, Bear?" she asked, more quietly.

He stopped. She hurried on with, "I need your help. This bit with the boat has me rattled. And I lost some of my supplies in the ocean. Which way is Commerce Six?"

"Call in."

"They'll take away my symbiot license if they think I can't hack it. Come on, Bear, help me out. Maybe I can do something for you."

"Nothing *you* can do. She left. It's all that matters."

"Who left, Bear?"

"What do you care?" His torso turned, as though he were watching the scene around them—like there was something to watch. To her, their surroundings appeared as still as a death-mask.

She stood her ground. "I came here to see you."

"Charming." His voice over the bioradio was strange, a soft baritone, slightly hoarse. It took dips and slides of tone inconsistent with his actual words. The overall effect was unnerving, coupled with the inhumanity of his appearance. "You can do what you want, means nothing to me."

"Why were you swimming? I could never do that here. Was it just to rescue me?"

Bear gave a metallic laugh. "Everybody talks about me, don't they? Listen, you think I'm stupid? I know what happened, and you know. She wouldn't wait for me. I volunteered for the Tether project. To stay on an extra term. I did it for her. And she wouldn't wait. That's all."

"You mean your wife." He didn't reply. "That can't be all, Bear," Ari insisted quietly. "Why did you run here? I could see running *away* from this place—but not into it."

"I know." He turned slowly away. "You're not as smart as you think. Doesn't matter if it happened to somebody else, or to everybody. It happened to me!" He swung his arms, huffing. "She left me. Not just anybody, you know. Me.

"What else, you know, where else could I go?"

Ari rose and went over to him. "Bear, when was the last time you were out of your symbiot? The last time you breathed real air?"

"The air is locked in the ground," he said as if to explain. The blank eyes of his symbiot turned to her. "You know I came here to make money? You take the cold muck and make money with it, and with the money you make a life with you and her and that's what makes sense. Only she wouldn't wait. So the sense went."

Sadly, Ari said, "But why *here*, Bear? You have to come away from this . . . pit."

"But it's mine. My homestead."

"What?"

"My own place." His voice took on an unctuous tone. "You know I own this land? It's my homestead. A very special kind of homestead. You want to buy it? Maybe I'll sell it to you."

Looking around, Ari began to feel afraid. This was hell, yet Bear was projecting some paradisal fantasy—some might-have-been—onto it.

"I want the real thing, Bear. Real land, on the real Earth. And I think you do too."

He turned and walked away from her. She should follow, but something held her back. Maybe respect. Looking at the lifeless hills ahead of him, she only said, "Don't you, Bear?"

* * * * *

"Hey, brain-lady!" someone shouted at her. Ari was crossing the floor of the station hangar, brooding. She stopped to frown at whoever had cat-called—but the voice was familiar.

A small group of laborers was playing poker with plastic cards on the upturned surface of an iron tholin-scoop. She looked from face to face, finally settling on one under black curls, with long-lashed dark eyes, mahogany skin. ". . . Kasmi?"

"The very same. You never saw me without my symbiot, eh? Like what you see?"

"I think you'd better put it on." Everybody laughed. Kasmi grinned, and moved over on his makeshift seat. "Sit. You play poker?"

"I do." She sat. The men smirked boyishly at her, which made her feel a bit self-conscious about only dressing in faded coveralls today. She was short and slim; the workers hulked over her, perfectly at home with their heavy machinery while she looked out of place, more suited for an office than this hangar. "How are you?" she said.

"We're great. Hear you saw the Bear."

"Yes." She watched the thin youth across from Kasmi deal.

"How is he?"

Something in Kasmi's tone surprised her. Ari chose her words with care. "I don't think he's beyond hope."

"Does he talk? Did he talk about . . ."

"About what?"

Kasmi shrugged. "What he used to talk about." He picked up his hand and hid behind it. "About the sky, and his wires."

"No. He tried to sell me the land he lives on." She watched Kasmi frown at his cards, waiting for him to continue. Finally, Ari asked, "Did you know him well? You said you met him. Did you work together?"

"Yeah. In Orbits. For almost a year."

"Tell me about it. What about these wires?"

"Bear loved tethers. A tether is just a long wire in orbit around a planet or moon. Around Earth they call them skyhooks, and use them for orbital transfers; attach a cargo to the bottom of one, in low orbit, and pull it up to the a higher one. Out here, though, there's been some experimenting with using them for producing electricity. Saturn has a magnetic field. A wire orbits Saturn, it's a wire moving in a magnetic field. Which is your definition of an electric generator. Bear was obsessed with the idea we could get all the power we needed from tethers."

"But we use solar power satellites, right?"

"Yes. The sun's so weak out here, it's expensive. Anyway, the point is Saturn's field is too weak, the wires had to be incredibly long to get any current. They'd break under tidal strain. We had a couple of near misses with his experiments . . ."

Kasmi vividly described doing a close orbit of the giant planet with the Bear in a two-seater orbital transfer vehicle. One of the Bear's wires trailed out behind them, coils unfurling into night, while a wall of beige—Saturn—came straight towards them. Whirlpools the size of continents beckoned. Kasmi waved his hands exuberantly as he told the enthralled players how his hair stood on end with the charge accumulating off the tether. They let it go at the last minute, and lightning dissolved the wire as the current peaked. The Bear gave a whoop of triumph as they swung, almost too low, around the night side of Saturn. In the clouds below, dim lightning flashed so frequently it was like the static snow on a TV screen.

Some exaltation had gripped the Bear, Kasmi said, when he contemplated the orbital dynamics of his tethers. They moved with cold, platonic precision through the emptiness around Saturn, cutting a crop of electrons. This was a world without Man, yet it was not Nature here, either. No one could mistake Titan and the other shepherds of the rings as natural, Bear told him, not like trees and lakes and storm clouds were natural. They were something else, outside of the cozy face-to-face world of Man/Nature everyone was brought up on.

"He scared the hell out of me. So cocksure. But by God, he was the sort who gave you things to talk about, you know stories to tell your grandchildren." Kasmi seemed somewhat put out, as though the Bear's exile had been a slight directed solely at him.

He slammed the cards down and turned to her. "What really is your interest? Huh? Do you care about Bear? You told me you're in this for the money."

Caught off guard, Ari said, "But I do care. I have to. I . . . maybe I'm as vulnerable to this place as the people I'm treating. There's something here that invades, like the cold . . ." She foundered. How could she explain that Bear frightened her? They had all thrown away their pasts to stay in this hell, but Bear had given up his future too. He was the mirror of her own anxieties about Titan. For her own reassurance now, she had to bring him out of his exile.

"Maybe," she finished, "if you *do* care for him, Kaz, you'll help me."

*   *   *   *   *

Murray's answer was surprising. "He certainly does own that land. Bear bought an entire ten-degree latitude of Titan, thousands of kilometers of useless ice, just before he walked out. He's not really a squatter, you see. It's his homestead." He smiled brightly across the polished desk top. "If he wants to sell, why don't you buy?"

"Don't joke, Murray." She tightened her grip around the coffee mug.

"I mean it. If he's offering to sell, it can only be because he finally wants to leave. I want you to look good in this; why don't I allocate some funds to you so you can buy the land. Then you can sign it back to us later." He laughed. "I assume you don't actually want it for yourself."

"Hmm." She sipped. "I doubt he was serious. Why should he want to sell now? After all this time?"

"Who knows? If he isn't serious, it does us no harm. We keep trying until something works, right?"

That afternoon they went over the details and got the allocation. Ari made sure it was enough to buy Bear passage back to Earth and then some. Her opinion of Murray went up several notches. Even if he was doing this for his own ultimate advantage, his choice of tactics was disarming. She did up her black hair and put on the one good dress she'd brought from Earth, and let him take her out for dinner that evening. They had a pleasant time, and she began to think she might like Titan, after all.

Early in the morning she rose to prepare to visit the ice again. She collected her things, inventoried everything, then crawled into the warm symbiot.

Kasmi was waiting for her at the hangar. "You sure he's not going to run away when he sees there's two of us?" he asked.

"Not completely. But he was willing to talk to me, and you were his friend." She tossed her pack into the waiting lander. "Anyway, I wanted to ask you more about him."

She watched the ocher ground fog drop away as Kasmi talked. Bear, he remembered, had talked about his wife incessantly . . . was always talking about his plans for their reunion after his term here . . . had a big picture of Earth on his stateroom wall. His breakdown had been a shock to everyone because he was viewed as one of the most stable men at the camp.

"Why should an orbital specialist spend his time on Titan?" she asked. "I never got that quite clear."

"He called it the 'right spot,'" said Kasmi. "You know, the old idea of if you had a long enough lever and found the right spot to put it, you could move the world? The thing was, he had this genius ability with orbits. He calculated them all relative to Titan, and stayed here to have the latest, most accurate data on Titan's rotation around Saturn."

"He sent the ice cargoes back into the inner system, right?"

"Yeah, was good at it. We should have seen something coming though, when he got obsessed with this tether power idea. He started wasting money, and there was a lot of pressure for him to give up."

"Wasting money? On flights like the one you were telling me about?"

"And on wire." They banked through a green cloud. "Millions of klicks of wire, and it's still up there. There isn't enough of a magnetic field around Saturn to light a pocket computer, but he said he'd figured out a set of orbits of wires—different wires, going at different speeds—that would all go into synch at some point and form one long line from within the rings out past it, all the way to here. A single wire that long would break under the stress. This 'transitory wire' would only exist for a few seconds, but a big current would flow along it in that time."

Spokes in spokes around Saturn, each set turning at a different speed. They would all line up, like a planetary conjunction, and Bear claimed a spike of high-energy plasma would be drawn out from the rings and the whole thing would feed back to produce more power. "But what good would that do?" said Kasmi ruefully. "Who needs too much power, for too short a time, and just once? His project was cancelled. Nobody understood it anyway."

He'd enlisted a lot of money and reputations in an idea that turned out to be crazy and unworkable. Bear found himself shunned by former companions, and the bureaucracy pressuring him. Then his wife left him.

"That did him in. He couldn't leave Titan, and he couldn't stand it here either. He ran to his land. God knows what he saw there."

Kasmi set the lander down expertly by Templeton bay, not far from where she had first met Bear. They unloaded enough gear for a week-long stay, and headed into the dim hills. Ari broadcast calls at regular intervals, but in that first day there was no reply.

They made camp in a forest of ice stalagmites. Only the shifting clouds seemed alive to Ari; she struggled to keep images of Earth in mind as she slipped into sleep. Not memories of the garish cities and pollution, but the wilderness, where farms and estates could still be built, by those wealthy enough. Only the kind of money she was paid here could ever give her that.

Strange, to have to leave in order to really come home . . .

*   *   *   *   *

"Today's the day, and I just don't care."

Ari sat up, suddenly wide awake. Bear's voice . . . a symbiot was sitting on a truncated ice pillar near the portable kitchen. Kasmi still slept beside her.

"You're the social worker lady," said Bear. He sat very still, a mound of tangled fur. "Why did you come back? You should leave Titan." He pointed at the lump Kasmi had become. "And who's that?"

Kasmi sat up slowly. "It's me, Bear."

The Bear was silent for a long time. Then he said, "Varun Kasmi. Why are you here? Why haven't you left?" His voice sounded strained.

"I had the option," said Kasmi simply. Ari silently cheered him on. "Since I could I said, well, why not go for one more round, Kaz? Double you money. This is like roulette, only all you lose is time."

"That's what I said too." Bear hunched over, and actually kicked at the snow. "You should be there now. You should be on a beach somewhere." He looked up. "When was the last shuttle out of here?"

"Five weeks. There's another due in three months, they're making them more frequent 'cause the muck is becoming so valuable."

"Be on it."

"Bear. I am not going. You are."

Silence. Bear rose and began walking away. Kasmi pursued him. "You're not getting away from me that easily, Bear! You owe us all an explanation, you know. Why the hell'd you do this? I was depressed for weeks, we all were. When we came to talk to you, you ran away. Like we were a plague you didn't want to catch." Ari followed them both quietly, hoping Kasmi wouldn't go too far.

"I didn't know what else to do. Because . . ." Bear turned. "The way it is, our life together was in the things we could do, they were in the money, and the money was in the clouds here, in the ground. So what's important, her and me and what we could have had, was in the ground. The air is locked in the ground, the trees, the forests, Earth and lakes and houses and movies, were locked in the ground. And I found the key to get them out. Look!" He pointed at the cold wax mounds and frozen foam lying abandoned to the horizon. "It's all in there, everything. Where else could I go?"

"I don't understand, Bear."

"I do," said Ari. She shuddered. "I came here too because I thought this place could buy my happiness back home."

"Lady. Do you want to buy my land?"

"Yes."

"No, you don't. Law says you can't own land unless you live on the world it's part of. You don't want to be here, you want to go home."

"What I want isn't the issue here. If you sell me the land, Bear, you can finally leave. Think about it."

"You're not a Titanide," Bear said. "Kasmi is. You want to make your pile and get out, but he's fallen in love with the ice. Haven't you Kasmi?" The two of them were standing very close, their symbiots sizing one another up.

Bear coughed. His voice was strained. "All this time I was frozen here too. I waited, waited for today. I—actually believed I could bring her back by this. But I woke up. You woke me up, lady, you sounded so determined to make it here, and I said to myself, *why?* No, she has to leave! Who could stay here? How could I have . . .

"Okay, I'll sell my land. Maybe I'll even go. But I won't sell it to you. Only Kasmi."

Tensely, she watched Kasmi, who'd crossed his arms. After almost a minute, he said, "Conference time, Bear. Just a minute." He switched channels to a private link with Ari.

"Now what? This looks like our big chance. But he's gonna charge me my whole income for this, I can see it coming."

"Come on, Kaz, you can afford it. We'll reimburse you later."

"Fat chance."

"Sure they will. You care about Bear, don't you?"

"You want a yes-no answer? Well . . ."

"Do it!"

"Okay." Kasmi tuned Bear in again. "If I agree to buy your land from you, Bear, will you agree to leave for Earth on the next shuttle?"

Bear hemmed and hawed. "I . . . guess so."

"Yes or no?"

"You don't trust me?" Kasmi waited. Finally Bear said in a tired voice, "Oh, God, all right, yes."

Ari was preparing to shout in triumph; then Bear named his price. It was well beyond what Murray had given her, almost a year's wages. Twenty times what the land had cost to begin with.

Kasmi cursed and shook a fist at Bear. "You cheat! You're driving a bargain you know I can't keep! This just so you can have an excuse to stay here and feel like you could, oh yes, you could have left, but tight-fist Kasmi wouldn't let you. Well, I'm not buying that and I'm not buying your land at that price either!"

"Wait, Kasmi," she said, "let's try Murray at least. Maybe we can work something out. Just five minutes, Bear. And we'll hold you to what you said."

She called Murray on the satellite link. His voice sounded calmly in her ears, muzak behind it. "Has he agreed to our offer, Ari?"

"Yes, but only if Kasmi buys him out."

"What?" Murray's voice took on a flat tone. "Is Kasmi with you?"

"Yes, and what we're wondering is if we can allocate the funds to him, so he can—"

"Out of the question."

"What?" Ari hadn't even explained the higher price. "It'll work the same this way."

"Not a chance. That money can't go any further than you, Ari. That's final."

"Well, that's nuts if you don't mind my saying so. Look, maybe Kasmi and I should throw in together if you don't want to, after all the price has gone up anyway—"

"No! Ari we don't want you using your own money for this. You don't want that kind of involvement."

"Call it an investment—"

"What do you mean the price has gone up?"

Angrily, Ari told him Bear's offer. In the background Kasmi was trying to bargain him down, but Bear just turned his back.

"That much?" Murray definitely sounded upset. "He's got us, then. Say yes, Ari. But only if you do the buying."

"You're kidding!"

"You heard me."

There was something very strange about this. Bear wanted more than the present yearly operating budget Ari was allocated. Murray was willing to pay that, just to get Bear out of the dislocality immediately?

"Well, all right Murray, if you say so that's the way we'll do it." She broke the link, and tuned to Kasmi to explain the new situation to him.

"I don't like this, Ari. He's up to something." Kasmi tuned in Bear. "Bear, why would Murray want your land?"

"Oh, he wants it, does he? Thought he might be behind your offer, lady."

"Why?" she asked.

Bear raised his arms, gesturing around at the stalactite forest, the low slush hills, the banks and clouds of gas. "The beauty!"

"Give us a break, Bear—" began Kasmi. Bear laughed.

"You buy this land, Kaz, you'll be the richest man on Titan. Richer than the Corp! What's the time?" Puzzled, Kasmi told him. Bear rocked on his heels, amused. "Only hours away. This is nothing, now. Empty, like me. In three, four days it'll be the richest piece of land in the solar system. Good old Murray knows that. Why do you think he sent you, lady social worker? Out of the goodness of his heart? I bet he said he'd give you funds out of some budget or other. No way, it's his own money. He wants to buy those forests, those lakes off me. My home, and my future. Not a chance."

"You really are crazy," said Kasmi sadly.

Bear bounded up the hillside through the ice forest. "He's not buying that! I sacrificed everything to stay here, for the future. And now that my wires are almost in their places, ready to rain wealth on this land, all I can see is that I also sacrificed everything I might have filled my future with. Yes, I'll sell! But never to him!"

"Wires?" As one Ari and Kasmi leapt after him. "Bear, wait!"

*   *   *   *   *

They sat in the lander and watched the sky catch fire. The perfect calculations Bear had made, years before, had brought his tethers into an exact line stretching from Saturn to Titan. Current flowed, and charged particles began to stream along the cable.

"Imagine that long spoke," said Bear. "A fishing line to draw electric plasma up out of Saturn's nearer belts. The plasma fountains up; soon it's all along the wire, and soon there's more of it than there is wire. Current flows. A long wire connects Saturn and Titan, and sweeps the space between like the loop of a generator . . ."

Lightning stuttered from zenith to horizon. It would go for days, Bear predicted. And each strike, here in the rich atmosphere near the pole, sent a rain of priceless tholins down onto the Templeton Rill. Nucleotides impossible to manufacture elsewhere, strange amino acid variants, all the essential tools of Earth's burgeoning biological science, pattered onto the snow.

"Look at it fall," Bear whispered. "This is what makes life, the work of time, our work. Look at your future."

Late on the third day, as the plasma flux tube tore up in tidal disarray and the lightning began fading, a lander edged down beside theirs. A figure in a vacuum suit climbed down and waded through the carbonate muck to their ladder.

"The radio has been out," said Murray as they pulled him into the lander. "I've been trying to contact you since this started."

"Wonderful, isn't it?" said Kasmi lightly. "No more digging in the muck. We can just harvest it right off the ground."

"Yes." Murray paused awkwardly. He looked at Bear for a long time. They had pressurized the lander's cabin, and all wore skinsuits with the face-masks off. Bear's face was pinched, narrow and the eyes strangely vacant; but his symbiot had kept him clean and healthy all this time. "Listen," Murray said at last, turning to Ari. "You filed for the purchase of Templeton Rill just before this let loose. The Corp won't tell me any of the details . . ."

Kasmi laughed. Ari said, "That's probably because they're mad at you."

"Then . . ."

"We bought it, Kasmi and I. We pooled our resources. Once we realized what you were up to it was the only sensible thing to do." She laughed at the expression visible through his face mask. "Just revenge, dear. You were using me to get what you wanted. You'd be rich, and I'd still be like Bear—struggling for some future happiness I hoped to buy with Titan's blood."

"You wouldn't have agreed to it." Murray turned in the narrow cabin. "Damn you! All I wanted was to get out of here. I was never sure Bear's scheme would work; I was lucky to remember it at all. How could I tell you about it, it was such a hare-brained idea . . . But I had to take the chance. All I wanted was to buy my future. God knows Bear had no use for his."

Silently, Murray went down the ladder and stalked back to his lander.

"We'd better go," said Kasmi after a while. They dogged the hatches and strapped in.

As they lifted, Bear spoke very quietly. "When I realized what I had done to myself, that this could never make things up for me, I almost died. He's right. I had no use for the future. I'm so glad I was able to give it to you."

Kasmi looked away, out the windshield. Bear continued. "What will you do now? You can't keep the land if you go home. You'll have to sell, and Murray is the only buyer."

"That's not important," Ari said. "Really, the temptation to stay and make more money . . . it's a trap. And we'll all make enough at current prices to retire for life. I might give some of my land to the dislocals, though . . ."

Kasmi turned back, grinning enthusiastically. "You know what I'm doing, Bear? I'm going someplace *warm*." He looked at Ari. "Really though, what will you do?"

"Go home," she said. "And have my place in the country, and my peace and quiet, and pretend the blue sky and the trees and lakes weren't bought with money." She looked out at Titan, a little sad. "Pretend they were always free."

If you ask the wrong question, no answer will satisfy you. This is the idea behind the Zen koan, *for instance the famous "what is the sound of one hand clapping?" I think that most of the questions we ask about the nature of consciousness are like koans. "Making Ghosts" is an attempt to point this out—bearing in mind, as the Zen monks say, that "the finger that points at the moon is not the moon."*

"Making Ghosts" first saw print in On Spec's *"Hard SF" theme issue (Spring 1994). It has subsequently been published in French in* Solaris *(no. 145, Printemps 2003).*

* * M A K I N G   G H O S T S * *

What stands out in memory is that first picture of Maier's idea. I am standing at her right shoulder, and she leans forward over the RISC station and taps the mouse a couple of times. The nineteen inch monitor lights up with a three-dimensional image like a mist of caged light.

"See there," says Maier. "That's a thought."

"It's pretty," I say, quite uncomprehending. "This is 24-bit color, right?"

"Forget the screen, Graham. Look at what's in it." And she tells me what I'm seeing: a picture of her brain's synaptic activity, taken while she thought about her husband.

"We did it at the Med-Sci building. Ran through it fifty times. I pictured his face in my mind each time, and the magnetic resonance machine picked out the electrical activity that goes on when I do that. This is a picture of a thought, my own thought about Frank." She smiles at it lovingly. "Kind of like a portrait. Maybe I'll will it to him when I go."

*   *   *   *   *

The next time I met Maier, I didn't recognize her until she greeted me. "There you are, Graham! How've you been?" She had told me she'd meet me in the lobby of the Computer Science building at the University, and here we both were, but we nearly missed each other anyway.

"I'm pretty good," I lied. I couldn't think of what else to say. She looked like hell. Two years ago she had been a large-boned, solid woman who radiated health. This woman was frail and thin, and her eyes were over-bright, like liquid.

"I'm glad we found you," she said, waving a hand in the direction of the labs. "We need a very specific talent, and only you seem to have it. Did you bring your program?"

"Right here." I was flattered—more than flattered. As we walked, I thought about ways to keep her from seeing how desperate I was to get this job. Even if I didn't know what the job was yet, it had to be better than the advertising agency I had ended up in after grad school.

We retired to the 'padded cell' they used to test Virtual Reality. It was a featureless room with foam on the floor, and no other contents. Maier and I put on 'eyephones' and pulled data gloves up our arms. For a while I stared at test patterns on the little eyephone screens while they fired up the program, then the office appeared in stereo 3D.

A desk had appeared from nowhere. Two chairs. A lamp. Posters on the walls. All as believable as the real thing, especially because when you turned your head, the eyephones picked up the movement and adjusted the image accordingly.

I heard Maier take a quick breath. "Beautiful," she said.

In VR, everything was normally bright and sharp, made of Platonic objects which followed their own strange laws. My Ph.D. thesis was to take the perfect blues and oranges, and the glossy shapes, and drag them out of Plato's heaven into our own gritty world. When I was done with them, the blocks and clouds of VR had texture and could even look dirty. This office Maier and I stood in was as real to the people wearing the eyephones as the room we were actually in. But everything—down to the gum stuck under the desk—was computer-generated. Only Maier and I were unreal, stick-figure ghosts the program couldn't really simulate.

Maier walked over to my desk, reaching tentatively to touch it. The galvanic pads in the data gloves gave her full sensation as she drew her hand along the blotter and wood grain.

"You wanted to work on direct nerve stimulation to replace these gloves," she said. "What are you doing at an advertising agency?"

"It's all there was," I said bitterly. "The field is full. I'm still applying, but everybody says, 'maybe next year.'"

"I have a job for you," she said. I let out the breath I hadn't known I was holding.

"I'll take it."

"You don't even know what it is, yet."

"Doesn't matter. I have to get out of that place."

Maier chuckled. Her cartoon-version nodded a little. "I can relate to that."

* * * * *

"There's two phases to this project . . ." she was saying. I barely listened.

Maier's lab was wonderful. One of the newest small-scale Nuclear Magnetic Resonance scanners sat in one corner. It was hooked straight into a teraflop computer and some VR stuff that made my mouth water. Things change a lot in two years, in this field.

"The first phase is nearly done," she went on. "That's been to perfect synaptic photography and modeling."

"Like the frozen thought you showed me once?" I paced over to examine the NMR machine.

"Yes," she said. Maier sat in a deep armchair, and didn't seem inclined to move. Several pill bottles sat on the table near her hand. "If you remember that, maybe you remember I was working on taking 'snapshots' of the brain at work. First we were able to catch data on all the synapses. There's gigabytes of it, all in George, here." She gestured at the supercomputer. "Then we were able to trace the interconnections of those synapses, and reproduce the network in Barley's neural nets. Barley, show him one of your boards."

Barley, her lab assistant, looked a bit like a Viking. He came over carrying a circuit board with some big black chips on it. "Here," he said, pointing them out. "Million by a million memory circuit."

"Hmm?" I took it and turned it over in my hands. It was heavy, and smelled of solder. "What's it do?"

"Those blocks," he pointed to the big chips, "are spin-glass chips. They're a kind of neural net. What we've been able to do is take the data from George, there, and program these to the same pattern."

It took me a second to understand. "You're mapping a brain into these circuit boards."

"Yes. Wouldn't have been possible five years ago. These holographic memories can work as neural nets, though. Slow, but adequate."

"Where's the brain?" I said, half-joking.

Maier pointed to her own head. "Right here."

I felt that sliding discomfort you get when a joke goes bad. "You're the subject?"

"Why not?" Her sunken eyes challenged me. "We had to use someone. Pointless to use Rhesus monkeys or rats. The idea is to fire the thing up, and talk to it."

"Talk to it . . ."

"And that's where you come in." She turned awkwardly in her chair, gesturing to the VR system. "The system works perfectly. It just lacks the interface. The brain takes in colossal amounts of data every second. Our problem is we have the brain modeled. But we don't have senses for it."

"You want a feed to the simulation?"

"I want you to give eyes and ears to the homunculus," she said, smiling slightly. "Make it live in your VR."

Barley was standing behind her chair. He had dropped the friendly facade. They both looked very serious.

"Why?" I asked. "Why do it all at once? This whole project is leaping so far ahead of itself. How are we going to get any credibility?"

"We're doing it now because I'm dying," Maier said flatly. "Is that a good enough reason for you?"

That derailed me. "I'm . . . sorry," I said. "What . . .?"

"Cancer," she said tersely. "Do you realize what we're doing here?" She propped herself up. She didn't appear upset in any way, though Barley was glowering. "We're developing real immortality, Graham. That's what this experiment is all about."

I decided to say what I thought. "It's just a program."

"So is your mind, Graham. Remember that picture I showed you once? A picture of a thought. Haven't you ever wondered what was going on in that computer, when the program was running? Was it really thinking of Frank, like me, over and over again? I want to know that, Graham. You can help me find out."

"What does Frank think of this?"

"He died last year, Graham. Car accident."

"I'm sorry. I've been out of touch. I didn't know."

Maier was trying to make herself immortal. Cynically, I wondered to myself what her grant proposals said.

I thought the idea was sick, because I didn't believe it could work. But you don't deny the dying; I might as well view it as an old woman's conceit, like believing in angels. And some good might come of it, because if I could get her data feed working, I could probably design a working artificial vision interface. And *that* would be worth something.

"Are you interested?" she said hoarsely.

"Yes," I said. "All right, I am. Not in your Phase 1 stuff. But the interface, yeah. I'll do it."

She seemed to shrink back into her chair. "Good. Good. Thank you Graham. I knew you'd come through."

Now I felt bad at resisting her. I went and leaned on George. Barley went back to his workbench. I didn't know how to carry the conversation forward, but it didn't matter. Maier wanted to talk.

"You know, the Buddhists say death is what happens at the cessation of thought," she said. "And rebirth is what happens at the beginning of thought. There's this zen koan I heard once. It nags at me."

"What is it?"

"There was this zen master watching a funeral procession. And he said, 'how many ghosts there are following every man here!'"

"I don't get it," I said.

Maier looked up at me in amusement. "Good answer. I don't get it either. Yet."

∗   ∗   ∗   ∗   ∗

It was probably the most productive year of my life, but not the happiest. Strange, that—how, when you get what you want, it doesn't satisfy. I worked late hours in the lab, working on digital-to-synaptic translation. Vision was the easiest; Maier wanted touch and strength-feedback as well, which was insanely difficult. While I was at work I was in the flow of things and felt fine. But when I got home, sometimes as the sun was starting to rise, the nagging dissatisfaction would surface again. It was just like being asked a question and not having the answer.

Maier became weaker and weaker. She took to her office, surrounded by shelves of dishevelled paper, with the only light coming from her monitor screen. She slept and ate there. As the weeks passed she seemed to fade, becoming more a voice from the darkness, than a real person.

But the project flourished. Since vision was what I finished first, we used it on our first test. Maier and I donned eyephones and stepped into the platonic world of VR with Barley watching on an "outside" monitor. We appeared to be standing on an infinite gray plain, with a sky full of rotating spheres and cubes. Odd objects cruised through the air around us—toasters and oranges, books and Eiffel Towers.

"Connect it up," Maier said shakily. Her stick-shape here in VR had a kind of vibrant, electronic energy to it (it was a neon-green glowing wire-frame somewhat resembling a person). I knew she was really sitting down, hands folded in her lap, in the dark office, moving the body with a joystick. I paced, trying to keep the dimensions of the lab in my mind so I didn't bump into anything. Finally Barley said, "It's up and running. You should see it any second."

Sure enough, there it was: a pair of eyes had appeared, at about my shoulder height, in the air between Maier and me. The eyes were Maier's, bit-mapped from an old videotape. Nothing else of the simulated sensory or motor nervous systems existed yet.

Maier and I approached the eyes. They stared back, first at me then her. Then, in a gesture eerily like Maier's own, they closed, turned, and opened to look up at the child's-block sky.

"It's her," Maier whispered. She moved up close.

The feeling of *presence* was almost too much for me. The eyes examined Maier's wireframe again, then turned to me. Maier turned as well, and for a moment they were both motionless—the eyeless green outline of a head, and the textured, mask-shape of the eyes floating ten inches beside it. Both appraising me. Then they turned back to face each other.

"You've done good work, Graham," Maier said, her voice weirdly flat. "We're going to make it."

Later, after Barley and I had badgered her into going home for a decent sleep, I unloaded on him: "Why are we letting her do this to herself? It's like her version of the miracle cures in the *National Enquirer*. Or those old people who throw money at televangelists."

"You were always down on this," he snapped back. "Your problem is, you're beginning to see that it's working. And it scares the hell out of you."

"Bullshit. I think she's pinning her hopes on a miracle cure. What are we gonna do? Scan her dying moments? What she has there—at best—is a map of her mind taken months ago. Does she think her consciousness is somehow going to hop from her body when she dies, into *this*?" I slapped George. "Face it: for all she says, she believes she's got a soul. She believes she'll wake up in George after she dies."

Barley shrugged sourly. This part of the debate had been going on for a long time now. "And what do you believe, Graham?" he asked.

"Let's say for a second you're right, and we make a new Maier. It's not her, it's a copy of her from months ago. And as a program, she'll have no rights. She'll be at the mercy of whoever owns the computer after she dies. They're just as likely to wipe her, or do some software version of vivisection on her. Do you really want that?"

"It won't happen," he said, smiling smugly now. "Didn't she ever tell you she owns all this equipment? It's not part of her grant. And when she dies, it'll be part of her estate, and it'll go to me."

I was horrified. "And what're you? The keeper of the sacred relic? Barley, are you seriously planning to spend the rest of your life tending a memorial to Maier? Whether it talks to you or not isn't the issue."

"You totally lack imagination, you know that?" he said angrily. "This is just a first step—for all of us. Think it through."

"Get a life, Barley," I said, and left.

I couldn't sleep that night. Every time I drifted to the edge of unconsciousness, a little voice in me asked, "Where are you going when you do this?"

Where are you going?

At 5:00 A.M. sleep became impossible anyway, because the phone rang, and when I answered, Barley's voice said, "She's gone."

* * * * *

"I didn't get there in time," he said the next afternoon. Barley played with his shot glass, glancing nervously around the bar. "She phoned me and said goodbye. I called the police, but they didn't find her at home. Thought she was at work, so we went there. No, but her computer was on. I found a message for me on it. She'd checked into a hotel and taken an overdose of sleeping pills. The delay was just enough that when we got there, she was already dead."

"Jesus." I couldn't believe she had done it. And yet, she had been facing death for months. I would never have been capable of the kind of grim calculation she'd made, but really, it was just like her. Keep it neat and elegant, and always according to a plan.

I ordered a beer. "That's it then," I said. "What are you going to do now, B?"

He narrowed his eyes over the oily rim of the shot glass. "Just what I said. Execute the estate. Finish the project. There's enough money for that. After, it'll just be hydro costs to keep the computer running."

"You're crazy," I said. "She's dead, B."

"I know that!" He slammed down the glass. "But the project's alive. Look, you want to get down to brass tacks, here? I don't know what we've got in that computer, Graham. I don't really care whether it's her or not. Or whether it's really conscious, even. But it's important. Can't you see that?"

"I know it's important to you, B," I said a little more cautiously. "Some of it's important to me, too—but not in the same way. We've learned enough from this project to build a real synaptic interface— to let even completely paralyzed people walk, or give sight to the blind. We should be modeling the visual cortex so we can build one for people who were born without a working lobe. *That's* what's important here."

"That's a spin-off, and you know it." He sat back heavily. "Look, Graham, I'm going ahead with it, whether you're with me or not. I'll just hire somebody to finish your work, is all."

"Now wait," I said, but he had me in a corner and he knew it. There was no way I was going to let somebody else take credit for my work—and we both knew this whole project had been so close to crack-pot from the beginning, that I couldn't reasonably expect to use it to get another job. Like it not, we had to follow it through to the end.

* * * * *

I felt worse and worse in proportion as the project looked better and better. I started getting migraines, not surprising considering the long hours I spent staring at the computer screens. I was fatigued all the time. Barley, damn him, never noticed. There was no particular deadline to our work—Maier had left us plenty of money—but I felt driven anyway.

Every time we perfected part of the interface we had to test it. My anxiety peaked whenever I put on the eyephones to confront some version of Maier's ghost. Although it would be easy, I refused to hook up the speech centers of the brain model. Barley didn't press. When he came into VR with me, he was as uneasy as I around the eyes and ears, and then hands, of Maier which moved through the block-world, touching, listening and watching. And always returning to stare at us.

Several times, working late at the lab, I would look up with a start and realize hours had passed, and that I was in the middle of some part of the program I didn't recognize, fingers poised to type some line of code I couldn't for the life of me remember. Time to go home—and lie in bed picturing Maier's thought, bouncing against the sides of its cage of light.

The day came when it could be put off no longer: the interface was finished. I met Barley at the lab after a breakfast of cold pizza and Pepsi. I'd had a hard night and my head still ached. We didn't say a word to one another as we went round the lab turning everything on. We ended up at the eyephones at the same time. Barley picked up his and hefted them, looking at me. "What are you going to say to her?" he asked.

"I hadn't even thought about it. What I want to know is, what is she going to say to us?"

We went in. The block-world of VR had been fleshed out recently with an expansion of my 'office' module: a small cottage with a garden. Outside the garden was a blurry vastness, with blocky outlines that might have been office towers in the distance. Barley and I had made VR versions of ourselves for the occasion. We were both in tuxedos—his idea, not mine.

Together, we walked up the path and entered the house. "Maier?" Barley called.

A curiously slow and listless voice called out, "In here."

She was in the kitchen, looking out the window. She turned to us, very slowly, even blinking in slow motion, and gradually smiled at Barley. Maier's hand rose slowly and extended to him.

Barley looked at it as if it were a snake.

"I," she said. "Thought. For a. While. I. Had passed. Out. After the. Scanning session. But those. Towers out. There are. Not real. Are. They?"

"The hardware's too slow for her," Barley whispered to me. "Thought that might happen." He took her hand and said, "We did it, Maier. You're here. In George."

"Speak. Slower. Barley!" She gave a strange, hesitant laugh that went on for a long time. "You. Sound. Like. Mickey. Mouse." Withdrawing her hand from his, she rotated her head to look at me. This was Maier as she had been years ago—healthy and solid. We had given her the loose shirt and slacks she was used to. "We. Did. It. Then . . . .I'm dead."

Barley looked down, then at her. "Yes. Out there you are. But . . . do you feel dead?"

She laughed in slow motion again. "What. A. Question!" She looked at me again. "And. Who is. This?"

I felt a stab of disappointment. Of course she didn't know me—the map of her brain had been taken months before I was hired. There was so much to say, about what Barley and I had done and how we were— and no way to say it to someone who no longer knew me.

"Graham Glyde. He was a grad student of Mitsou's, remember? You wanted to hire him for the interface."

"Of. Course. Then. I. Guess. I did. Hire. Him."

"Tell me," Barley said urgently to her. "How do you feel? Is it . . . like you imagined? Like we talked about?"

"Different. I. Don't know. Give. Me time." She moved slowly to the window again, and stared out at the towers again.

"I'll be right back," I said, and switched off the eyephones. I was in the lab again, with Barley standing beside me blind and deaf, hands groping with the gloves. "Graham?" he said. "What's wrong?"

Not what I expected, I thought. I sat down gingerly on George—or rather on Maier, and for a while watched Barley have a slow, one-sided conversation with something only he could see. They talked about prosaic things, like the slowness of the system and her estate. She didn't ask how she died. I studied Barley for clues about my own unease—or was it disappointment? I became aware of growing tension in him, too, as the conversation wandered. Maybe it was that no revelations were forthcoming from Maier. It seemed to be her inside George, all right, but she had no insights for us. Gradually, I warmed to the feeling; it was good to disappoint Barley. He needed it.

Of course I went back in after a while, and often over the next several weeks. You got used to Maier's slowness eventually. She alternated between lethargy—watching the virtual TV I had made for her—and depression, for the first while. Her only comment about it to me was, "It's going to take me a while to get used to eternity, I guess." She didn't really know me, though; my visits were more formal than Barley's, but even he began spacing them further and further apart. Of course I did hook up a pair of stereo cameras in the lab to give Maier her own, reverse version of VR, and put an image of her cottage on TV so we could interact with her as though she was behind a window. But the time-lag was a constant reminder that her reality was different from ours.

I had thought at first that the strange disappointment Maier's ghost had raised in us (like most longed-for things that turn out to be real, it quickly became prosaic) would discourage Barley from his mission to be Maier's Anubis. When I brought the subject up in the pub though, he just laughed.

"The problem is it worked too well, Graham. The next generation board will be fast enough to keep up with the neural processing, and then what? Her mental states will be indistinguishable from the original."

He leaned forward. "*That's* the problem. She'll be indistinguishable, but how do we prove that? If she wasn't dead she could go in there and interrogate herself, and then we could find out if our Maier's really faithful to the original, or just a superficial copy. But nobody's gonna give us the Nobel prize until we can prove what we've done."

"I never thought of that," I said. It was obvious, in retrospect. "We needed a control, and she died."

"Right." He shifted uncomfortably in his chair, looking at me almost askance. "I've been thinking about it. We need to do it again."

"What?!" He winced. "What do you want to do? Wipe her and run another test? We can't do that, what about your promise? You're her guardian now."

"We don't *wipe* her, Graham. We remove the spin-glass modules from the boards and store them safely until we're done the new experiment. I put new modules on the boards and we record someone else, that's all. Someone alive. So we can send him in to find out if the ghost is really him."

"I get it," I said cynically. "You want to make your own ghost now, because who knows, you could be run over by a truck tomorrow. Safety first, huh?"

"I'm not going to do it," he said, sitting up quickly. "No way. It's going to have to be someone else."

I was surprised. "But I thought you were convinced the process works."

"I am, and that's why I won't do it. How am I going to cope with another me?" He gave a forced laugh. "No. It'll have to be somebody else. Somebody who doesn't believe in it."

"Like me?"

"Yeah, Graham. Like you."

$$* \quad * \quad * \quad * \quad *$$

Barley talked to Maier about it, and she agreed to let him put her on the shelf for a month or so. Later when the news broke, they figured we'd be able to afford a separate machine for my own map ("If I let it live," I told them) so she wasn't worried. Rebuilding the boards gave Barley an opportunity to speed the system up a bit, too.

Aside from building my VR body, I had little to do. The time preyed on me. And I wasn't feeling well. It felt like the flu, but went on and on. There was no way I could work as late in the lab as I used to, but I didn't want to anyway, after the blackouts started.

If you have never blacked out, randomly and unexpectedly, you have no idea how it makes daily life impossible. There's no uncertainty like being unsure whether any simple act you start—like standing up, or picking up a knife—will be seen to completion. Not that I ever fell down; the blackouts were more like memory lapses. I came to myself once standing in the hall outside my apartment with a book in my hand. I had been sitting on the john last I remembered. Somebody down the hall was just closing their door, cutting off some remark. Had they been speaking to me? What did we say? It scared hell out of me.

My car was never safe at the best of times, but I refused to drive it now. Barley asked a couple of probing questions, but I didn't tell him what was going on. I hadn't admitted it to anybody, not even myself. *It'll stop if you give it time,* I thought. *You've just been overworking.*

Drinking was an activity I could feel safe with, so I began doing that in earnest. I'm sure Barley thought I was worried about meeting myself. The truth was, I was barely thinking about the project any more.

Finally, as we sometimes do, I bared my soul to someone who hardly knew me: Maier's ghost. She listened patiently to my high-speed rant, then said the one sensible thing I had not said to myself: "See a doctor, Graham."

Sometimes these things are far easier said than done. By the time I did pluck up the courage, I was losing whole chunks of my day. Apparently I continued to function normally during these "blackouts"; I had several at the lab and Barley didn't notice.

So I made an appointment with a neurologist Maier had introduced us to during the project. He sent me to be strapped onto a rack much like the NMR machine in our lab, only bigger and old, all beige plastic curves and humming power. They couldn't tell me anything at the time; the pictures had to be processed and looked at by the doctor. I left feeling like Barley's bushman, with my soul photographed out of me.

Two days later Barley phoned, to tell me the new modules were in place, and we could do my brain mapping at any time. That night I got completely drunk, so that if I forgot the evening, at least I wouldn't have to worry about why.

I awoke to wan morning light and the ringing of the phone. Barley sounded cheerful. "It's all set, Graham. Come on down and we'll drain your brain."

"Yeah, right, thanks," I said, and put down the phone. My head hurt. That's the last thing I remember.

* * * * *

I've gone over it a hundred times, so by now I know what happened. I put the phone down, got dressed, ate a healthy breakfast, and went to the lab. Barley greeted me, we talked for a while, and then I sat down in the NMR machine.

Even if it's a down-scaled model, the NMR is still intimidating. Especially after the scan I took at the doctor's office, I can imagine how I must have felt, with the white donut vibrating past my head, back and forth, over and over again. Trying to read my mind, and me wondering whether it could pick up the waves of hostility and fear coming off me. Maybe I wondered if that would characterize the 'new me'—this moment of fear and anger.

I imagine I felt like that; I just don't know. The next thing I remember after putting down the phone in the morning, is stepping out of the way of a bus on Yonge street, blocks away from the University. The transition was so startling I looked down to see if I was still naked from bed.

A kind of wall of shock hit me. I felt like I was dying right there. Nobody seemed to notice; the crowd parted around me like I was invisible. I wanted to scream, or run, but was terrified that if I even moved, I would lose myself again. So I stood in desperate silence for many long minutes, until my pulse started to settle. Then I walked gingerly to a pay phone and called the neurologist.

"Check yourself in," he said. "I'll call you tonight with the test results."

"Okay," I said, perversely calmed by his callousness. But I didn't go to the hospital. I went to the lab.

Barley was there, and George, and Maier on a shelf at the back gathering dust. Barley looked surprised when I came in.

"Couldn't stay away, huh? I told you it'll be a couple of days before George's done mapping you into the spin glass. Or do you want to watch? There's nothing to see."

"Was I here?" I blurted.

Barley gave me a funny look. "Huh?"

"Was I here? Today? Did we do the scan?"

"Jesus, Graham, join A.A. or something."

"Fuck you!" I went over to George and glared at it, as if I could some-how see the process going on inside it. Was my identity being folded, mutilated and spindled in there? Had the NMR machine really stolen a day from me? Maybe that was why Maier had killed herself—the process had really stolen her soul. Was she losing hours and days towards the end, like I was?

"Go home and sleep it off, Graham," Barley called from his work bench. Supportive to the last.

I couldn't bring myself to tell him I didn't remember being here. Maier knew the problems I was having, and so did the doctor; I felt an obscure shame at the idea of telling Barley. It would be some sort of admission of failure. "Okay," I said. I threw up in the john down the hall, and left the lab.

On my way home I thought about smashing George. There was no way I was checking myself into the hospital until I found out what Barley's computer was assembling.

The doctor didn't seem to care that I hadn't admitted myself. "It's your life," he said when he phoned. "But listen, I've got the test results. Are you sitting down?"

"Give me a break," I answered.

"Graham, you have a tumor in the left temporal lobe of your brain. I think that's what's been causing your blackouts."

I didn't answer—to tell the truth I didn't know how to feel. Relieved that I wasn't going crazy? —or that my soul wasn't being stolen? Or frightened that I had cancer?

"We'll have to do more tests to find out whether it's operable," he said. "I'd like you to come in Friday."

"Okay," I croaked, and put down the phone. At least I knew what it wasn't.

The emptiness of the apartment was oppressive that night. Around 4:00 A.M. I got up and took a taxi to the lab. I brought a shaving kit and a towel, and made myself comfortable in Maier's armchair next to the warmth of George. Then I could sleep.

$$* \quad * \quad * \quad * \quad *$$

"It's up and running," said Barley. "You sure you want to go through with this?" He was treating me like I was made of glass since I told him about the tumor.

"Yeah." I'd missed my new set of tests. Too bad. I had my own test to perform. I put on the eyephones with a fairly steady hand, and sat down. With the tumor and all I didn't trust VR standing up, so I would use the joystick to move. It reminded me uncomfortably of how Maier had moved, towards the end.

The eyephones were reassuringly blank for a while, as Barley fussed with the computer. "Sure you don't want me in there too?" he asked.

"This is personal, B," I snapped. "You know what I mean?"

"All right then. You're on." The eyephones came to life. I saw the blurry cityscape we'd created, then as I turned my head, Maier's cottage.

Though I had rehearsed this so many times, doing it was almost impossible. This was worse than brain surgery, it was the exposure of my own Self for examination and dissection. Somehow, this act was diabolical; something in me was screaming *no* to it the way your body will if you accidentally start to drink Javex.

I moved into the cottage, stomach fluttering. This place was familiar now, and I half-expected Maier to come out to greet me.

But the cottage had another occupant now. He was waiting for me in the living room, sitting on the couch and turning a pen over in his fingers. He sat up and quickly put down the pen when I entered.

"Hi," he said in my voice.

I sat down warily across from him. Barley had prepared me for this moment by sometimes using my body-program when we were in VR together. I was used to seeing myself from the outside. But with Barley the body had seemed like a puppet, since his character shone through and it was obviously not me. This was different; it made me self-conscious just to watch this version move.

"This is the great meeting," he went on. "Where I tell whether I'm you or not. We were going to ask a whole bunch of questions, right? I remember them. The answers are: yes, yes, no, Shirley, grade six, and, taped under the couch." He picked up the pen again. With a start, I realized he was nervous—at least as nervous as I was.

When I didn't reply, he said, "Well? Those are the answers, aren't they? We were going to ask—"

"I know," I said. "But . . ." He stared at me, fidgeting. I had been thinking about what to ask, all along, to find out if its memories were complete, or just simulated. Barley and I had worked out a version of the Turing test for this moment, but the blackout during the scan had changed everything. "Do you remember the NMR session the other day?" I asked.

The other me sat back, visibly relaxing. "The other day? It was only a few minutes ago to me, remember? Of course I remember."

"What did Barley and I talk about? Before you sat down for the scan?"

"Well, let's see . . . Maier. We talked about Maier." He smiled again, confidently now.

I closed my eyes, feeling sick. Barley had just told me about the NMR session. We had talked about Maier.

"Then I only have one question," I said. "Are you me?"

He only looked surprised for a second. Then he nodded thoughtfully. "It really comes down to whether I *feel* it, doesn't it? We avoided dealing with that. I realized that, the moment I woke up here. It was pretty scary, believe me. Because I realized there was no way I could ever convince you, out there, of who I was. No amount of logic could do it. I couldn't argue you into it. I know myself too well. So: yes. Like it or lump it. I'm you."

I yanked off the eyephones. Barley looked up from his console as I stripped off the gloves. "Well?"

"It's not me," I said, as I walked out.

*   *   *   *   *

Maier got a bit strange there, towards the end. I can sort of sympathize with that. You tend to get maniacal about stupid questions. You lie there in your bed, alternating between unresolvable issues, and noticing simple things you haven't paid attention to since you were a kid.

That's how it seems, anyway, on the eve of the operation. I keep staring at the flowers on the windowsill, marveling that I can see them at all. Then I wonder about that other me, sitting on his couch in the world I created for him. I know he's thinking much the same thing. He knows about this operation. I wonder how he's taking it.

I feel cheated. Even up to my meeting with the other me, I had sort of hoped Barley was right—though I would never admit it to him. Maybe, I hoped, this was the secret of immortality. But it doesn't matter in the least that I have a second self out there. *I'm* the one who's maybe going to die today. When I close my eyes, his may open in that other world, but mine will not.

Maier was fascinated by the zen koan, "How many ghosts there are following every man." I think I understand that koan now, since I have made and met my own ghost.

That ghost, like my understanding, fades as I try to grasp it. I am left to gaze at these ordinary, badly arranged flowers, entranced, enlivened by their glowing sides and cups.

Sometimes stories come about from the collision of seemingly unrelated ideas. For several years I'd had two entirely separate (or so I thought) stories I wanted to write. One was about the temporary downloading of personalities into artificial bodies, the other about a mysterious object orbiting a burster neutron star. The problem was, neither story "caught fire" until one day Leo Modest appeared to me and I realized that the two ideas were really the two sides of one coin—this story, "The Engine of Recall."

"The Engine of Recall" was first published in the Winter 1997 issue of Aboriginal SF.

✷ ✷ THE ENGINE OF ✷ ✷
RECALL

"Mr. Modest? Is your ghost for hire?"

The spell of Leo Modest's self-indulgence broke. Annoyed, he turned from the plate of oysters he'd been sampling and looked his two visitors up and down. "What?" he said.

"Mind if we join you?" asked one of the men. He was a ascetic, worried-looking fellow. Leo shrugged.

"Dr. Alan Tarski." Leo shook the thin hand. The other man grinned in a falsely friendly manner and put his hand out too. "Will Kapleau."

"Hmmph." Leo dropped his gaze to the plate, and began bobbing his two-tined fork over it, searching for the next morsel. "What do you want with my ghost?" he asked distractedly. "I hardly use it."

"The answer to that is right behind you," said Tarski.

Leo had chosen a table next to the huge picture window that dominated this restaurant. It ran floor-to-ceiling and stretched sixty feet, and the management had assured him it was real, not a TV screen. It gave an excellent view of comet Blye and various colony cylinders and factory complexes orbiting it.

He followed Tarski's gaze past all that, to the rainbow-hued curls and shells of nebula that enshrouded the pulsar named Cobra. As he looked, the pinpoint in the core of the nebula brightened into a blazing sun and quickly faded again—as it did every few seconds, as it had for millions of years.

The Engine of Recall

This comet was as close as anybody got to Cobra. If the pulsar had ever had planets, they had been incinerated aeons ago. Comet Blye was an interstellar wanderer, and had never approached within thirty AU of the pulsar. It was the nearest thing to a world here; anyway it would do for Leo until a better destination presented itself.

"It's pretty," he said. Turning back to his visitors, he said, "You want my software ghost as a pilot? How'd you find me?"

"Another veteran spotted you," said Kapleau eagerly. "He said you're the best. We'll need the best to do a close orbit around Cobra for us."

Leo laughed. "Who's 'us'? The Dangerous Sports club? Do you know what you're asking?"

"We do," said Tarski. He nervously keyed an order into the table top; Leo noticed it was for a drink he hadn't tried yet. "We study Cobra. I'm the acting director of the Cobra Research Group here at Blye. We need data from a close orbit of the pulsar, and you're the best freelance pilot here. We're wondering if you want the job?"

The oysters were forgotten now. Leo looked from one man to the other. "What do you want a pilot for, live or ghost? It doesn't sound like much of a job; why not drop a dumb probe on the trajectory and pick it up on the other side? I mean, the radiation from that star blows hell out of anything within ten AU. I'd just toss cheap probes in until one of them came out the other side."

"A probe won't do for this job," said Tarski. "You'd be piloting a real ship, with full amenities, and we'd be expecting you to come out the other side intact."

"What the hell? It makes no sense."

Tarski's drink arrived. He sipped it delicately. "Mr. Modest, if we were able to convince you that only a conscious pilot, and not a computer, could do the job, would you consider it?"

"Ha!" Leo took Tarski's drink and downed it in one gulp. "I'll consider anything before I turn it down. Go ahead: convince me.—That's good, try this." Leo put his own tumbler in front of Tarski.

Kapleau looked at Tarski. Tarski looked at his empty glass. Finally Kapleau cleared his throat, and said, "There's one very good reason why we'd want your ghost to come out the other side intact, Modest." The searchlight beam of Cobra swept past again. The glow lit Kapleau's face a ghastly white. "We'd be going with it," he said. "Our real, physical selves."

*   *   *   *   *

Later, Leo drifted through the freefall area of Roth Colony, thinking about Tarski's offer. They were to meet again tonight, and he would give his answer. Below him now, vast banks of cloud reflected the fusion lamps at the colony axis. Above he had much the same view. The air swarmed with hang gliders and people like Leo, wearing foot-wings, coming and going between buildings suspended in the sky. He flapped lazily along, watching the legs of some young women as they passed. People gave him a wide berth; Leo was a large man, and moved through freefall like a battleship.

Leo spotted a spherical building apparently resting on the lip of a cloud bank. He flapped stolidly in its direction. Of course he was going to show up for the meeting, if only to find out what was so pressing at Cobra that it demanded human presence. And he did need the work; Blye was as far as his money had been able to get him this time. But he didn't have to go in unprepared.

The Memory Library's surface gleamed like spilled oil. People landed or embarked delicately from the branches of trees that grew out of its main doors. Inside, he headed straight to the chamber known mysteriously as the "Chinese Room."

Leo had come here to collect a ghost. Some people—those rich enough, and those addicted—lived via their ghosts, having tens or hundreds out collecting experience all the time. Leo preferred what he could get with his own hands, eyes and lips. He'd made this ghost only because he couldn't afford to visit the planet Revus in person.

The Engine of Recall

The "Chinese Room" was packed with people having their ghosts' memories implanted in them. He hesitated a moment in the doorway—the sight was familiar. People sat silently. Here and there one raised the headset from his or her brow, and emerged from trance smiling. The gesture was familiar to Leo, the smile was not; he remembered rooms like this full of men and women in uniform, and their expressions when coming out from under the helmets had been of horror or sadness.

Leo shook off a sudden feeling of melancholy. He found a free harness and adjusted the headset to fit his large skull. A warm muzziness descended on him, then the machine registered his account and sought out the memory file.

The ghost had returned the night before, but Leo hadn't had time to get down here until now. More important things, like drinking, sleeping and eating had intervened. Now, though, he needed to find out what his trip to Revus had been like.

*   *   *   *   *

Ten minutes later, Leo left the Library. The Revus ghost had cost him 15,000 Labor Units; a physical visit would have cost more like half a million. He'd paid another 50 Units to have an Agent ghost research the Cobra Institute, and now as he glided towards a cluster of restaurants, he pondered everything that had happened.

Revus was a habitable world, covered with rolling hills and low, sinuous seas. Its primary vegetation was grass, and while human cities had sprung up all over the world in the past century, Leo had come to see something else.

He had made this software ghost four days ago. Minutes after its creation, its pattern had been beamed through superspace to Revus, and activated. Two hours after that, the robot his ghost had rented walked to the lip of a large excavation under the warm Revus sun. Men and women in tough shorts or sarongs labored down there, brushing delicately at the outlines of ancient buildings.

"The Aknitari lived here," said a voice in his ear. Leo turned to find a pretty, frank-eyed woman smiling up at him. She wore the same kind of dusty shorts as the workers below. Her outline shimmered briefly; she, too, was a ghost, projecting the holographic image of its owner on the surface of a robot.

"I'm Leo," he said, offering his hand. "Where do you go around here to celebrate, when you find something?"

She laughed. "That's a fresh question!" She turned to gaze out over the excavation. "We have our places. My name's Galil Aurean. I'm the head curator here, but I like to ghost and serve as guide too. Call it a perk."

He raised an eyebrow. "Not an eccentricity?"

"It lets me watch other people discover the place for the first time. Reminds me of what discovery's all about."

"Yeah?" He hooked his ghost-hair back with one thumb. "What's that?"

"Well, look at you. You must have a keen interest in the Aknitari, Leo. You probably paid a lot for this visit, when you could have just taken the VR tour."

He nodded, guardedly. "I've always wanted to meet an Aknitari." Let her think he was just curious; Leo had learned to keep his obsession with the aliens to himself.

But Aurean sighed with open longing. "Me too." She walked away along the lip of the pit. "Come on! I'll give you the tour."

They wandered the ruins for hours. She delighted in showing off the oddities in the pits, and Leo followed along like a child at a fair. He really couldn't hide his deep fascination with the ancient aliens. Aurean sensed his excitement, and it did seem to kindle a flame of enthusiasm in her.

This dig, like most, held only a few outlines of buildings, a bone or two, and the corroded remains of incomprehensible machines. There was just enough here to tantalize, and Leo found himself sharing old fantasies and legends about the aliens with Aurean. It was all speculation, for nothing was really known of the Aknitari, but somehow that made the stories better.

They dreamed aloud of colorful cities and starships, populated by a peaceful and wise race whose culture, languages, origin and demise were obscure. In the shade of that mystery, Leo could forget, if only for a few hours, the legacy of pain in his own, human past.

As the sun set over the ruins, he said, "I'd like to stay here. Sleep under the stars."

"Really?" She shot him a complicitous smile. "I've done it."

"What did you dream about?"

She looked at him. "What do *you* think I dreamed about?"

He sighed. "I don't know. I dream about the war."

"War? Hmm. You dream about it; do you talk about it?"

He shrugged. "Not now. But another dream . . . would be nice."

She put her hand on his arm. The robot touched metal to metal, but his ghost felt her warm skin on his. "You have my permission," she said seriously, "to sleep under the stars here. And dream of something . . . else."

They were lovers by moonrise. Their robots stood abandoned, dew beading on their metal limbs, while the ghosts of Leo and Galil Aurean made a nest, invisible to all, in Virtual Reality.

These memories, and more, were now Leo's for life.

* * * * *

The Roth Institute was a collection of low, grass-covered buildings on the edge of a forest. Leo smelled pine and fresh water as he came up the front walk from the subway kiosk. Kapleau was waiting for him at the doors.

"Glad you could come, glad you could come," he enthused, pumping Leo's hand. "This way; we're all set to begin."

Leo sighed, following reluctantly. The scientist led him to a darkened screening room whose far wall was eclipsed by a large hologram of

Cobra. Lounging in chairs below the multi-hued star were several men of Tarski's ilk: severe and focused. Leo eyed them as he levered himself into a leather-bound armchair.

"Good to see you," said Tarski as he stood up. He made to introduce the others, but Leo waved a hand impatiently.

"Get on with it," he suggested. "What's the big deal about Cobra?"

"Well . . ." Tarski made to sit down, thought better, and pointed at the hologram overhead. "Cobra is a rarity among collapsed stars, Leo. It was right on the edge of the mass limit when it collapsed. Most massive stars that supernova collapse into neutron stars. But this phase normally only lasts a few seconds before the star converts by relativistic combustion into a quark star, composed of 'strange' matter. Most supernova remnants are quark stars.

"Cobra got stuck in the neutron star stage because of its low mass. Eventually it'll accumulate enough material from its companion to move to quark star form, but that won't be for millions of years. It could be pushed over the edge by any addition of quark matter, too, but there just isn't any in this system. So for all intents and purposes, Cobra is a stable neutron star. It's interesting for that reason, but it became more than just interesting when we found this."

Tarski touched the arm of his chair, replacing the holo of the two stars with one showing an indistinct smudge in false color on a yellow background. Leo heard or sensed the others in the room leaning forward or sitting straighter. Nobody spoke for a moment.

"What's that?" he asked finally, as he supposed he'd been expected to.

"We've been observing Cobra for years," said Tarski. "Watching the dynamics of the starquakes, the infall from its stellar companion, and the radiant beam. We weren't looking for anything like this. We hardly believed it when we first saw it."

"Yeah, yeah." Leo waved his hand. "Forget the melodrama. What is it?"

"Perhaps it would be better if I let the expert on this subject take over, now that she's arrived." Tarski waved to the door, which Leo realized had just opened.

"Sorry I'm late," said Galil Aurean as she trotted down to the level of the couches. "Hello," she said to Leo, obviously not recognizing him.

"Ah huh," Leo managed to say. He felt winded suddenly, as if he'd just run a mile.

"When you showed me the holos, I didn't believe it either," she said to Tarski. There was no holographic shimmer around Aurean this time. She turned to Leo, pinning him with her very real gaze. "But there's no doubt at all," she said. He barely heard her. "Something is flying—orbiting is the wrong word—around Cobra. It is very close, close enough to be vaporized if it gets caught in the radiant beam. Somehow, it steers clear of the infalling debris, and manages to avoid the beam. Only an intelligent, self-powered object could do this."

Leo began to recover his composure. *Intelligent object?* "Wait a minute—" he began. He wanted to ask what it was, but was suddenly afraid to. "How—how big is it?"

Aurean nodded as though he'd asked the right question. "Under a kilometer in diameter. That's all we really know. It's also massive—would have to be, to survive in there. We won't know any more about it until we can get close."

"But you think . . ." He decided to commit himself to the thought: "You think it's Aknitari."

She blinked, then grinned. "You're quick. I can see why Tarski wants you." He flushed, hoping it wouldn't be visible in the dark. "Yes, we think it's Aknitari. And not just a ruin, or a stripped asteroid, but a *device* which is, in a sense, alive. Alive even after all this time." Her eyes were shining.

"And we want to go in and get it," said Kapleau.

Leo let all his breath out in a whoosh, focusing on the strange blob overhead. "You don't even know what it looks like, or what it's made of. You say it avoids the radiation beam; what's to prevent it from avoiding us?"

Aurean looked to Tarski, who shook his head slightly. "We have a solution," she said to Leo.

"What about our ship? It's going to have to be pretty big—and tough. What do you have?"

Tarski changed the holo to show a mirrored egg-shape hanging in space. There were no visual referents to show its size, but Leo recognized the profile. "Who gave you a battleship?"

"The *Pall*," said Tarski. "It's decommissioned, which is how we could buy it—not cheaply, I might add. It's similar to the type you piloted against the Individualist uprising of '64, am I correct?" Tarski's hands were steepled in front of him, and his face was in shadow. The leather armchair began to feel confining to Leo. He glanced at Aurean, but her face was neutral.

"Yeah. You do know a lot about me," he said. His Agent this afternoon had discovered no link between the Institute and the military. He looked at Aurean again. She must be the link.

"We know what kind of piloting background you have, and that you're good." Tarski waved his hand dismissively. "That's all we need to know. Are you with us? This ship is big enough to collect the anomaly—that's what we're calling it, by the way—and bring it home. It's also strong enough to withstand the tidal forces at the orbits we'll be taking."

He thought about it. They were holding something back, but maybe he'd be able to learn what from Aurean. "So you want my ghost to take you physically to Cobra, where you will try to reel this *anomaly* into our hold, and then we scram back here?"

Tarski nodded. "That's right. That's all."

"Why your physical selves? You're letting me send a ghost, after all. Why don't you do the same?"

Tarski and Kapleau exchanged an almost unnoticeable glance. Kapleau smiled easily and said, "We don't know what an Aknitari machine is capable of. If we board it—and we might have to—we don't think we should trust our robots to do it, even if they do have our ghosts in them. You're different, you'll be on the bridge for the duration."

"Hmmph." Kapleau was a bad liar, Leo decided. Still, he'd let them get away with it—because to tell the truth, there was probably nothing they could say at this point to get him to turn them down. The instant he'd learned the anomaly was Aknitari—or was it the instant Aurean had walked in?—Leo had decided. No need to let them know that, though. "I can do it," he said. "But not for under twenty million."

"Twenty five million," Tarski said instantly.

Leo opened his mouth to haggle, then paused, brows knitting as he realized Tarski had *upped* the price, not lowered it. "Oh," he said. "Okay."

Tarski laughed. "It means that much to us, Modest. Price is no object. You're the best pilot, so we want you. It's that simple." The others were rising from their seats. Tarski flipped the holo off, plunging the room further into darkness.

"When do we do it?" Leo said to the moving shadows.

"Two days, Modest. We're ready. We just need to get your ghost in condition, and that won't take long."

"I suppose not." By the light of the opening door he made out Aurean's slim form, and made his way after her. "Sounds fine," he shot over his shoulder as he elbowed aside one of the other scientists, and came up behind the curator.

He experienced a delicious moment of indecision as they stepped into the well-lit corridor together. Dalliances between ghosts were common enough, and there was always the chance of meeting the original afterwards. That was bound to be awkward, and—had Leo not been in the situation before—he might have found himself at a loss for words now. Before they turned their separate ways, he touched

Aurean's elbow and leaning close, said, "You might want to attend to your mail from Revus."

Surprised, she turned, a question on her lips. Leo nodded brusquely and walked away.

* * * * *

Leo was still awake late that night when the doorbell chimed. He sat in his bathrobe in the living room of a rented apartment, worrying over some flight plans. He hadn't had time to try the simulations himself, but had given Tarski a ghost. The ghost had itself been split into several clones and its time-sense distorted, so Leo remembered seven days of intensive flight simulation around Cobra. Recurring images of fire and deathly light made him too uneasy to sleep.

The ring at the door didn't surprise him; he automatically smoothed back his hair, started to smile, then looked down at himself. He was no longer the strong young man whose gray eyes had such a usefully magnetic effect on others. He knew without tracing them the deep lines around his mouth, and the thickening of his flesh from self-indulgence. The need to bury himself in sensation was as ineradicable as a scar. It had made him ugly.

He flinched his frown away and opened the door. "Hello," said Galil Aurean, somewhat bashfully. Leo smiled, then saw the glimmer of holographic light around her blue silk skirt. It wasn't really her; she had sent a ghost instead.

He held the smile gallantly, and waved her inside. "I checked on my ghosts, like you suggested," she said as she walked in. She looked around herself, eyes wide. "So this is how you live."

"Not really," he said. "It's rented." That she had sent a ghost meant she was not personally interested in him. One sent ghosts to cleanly end relationships, to do snubs or make scenes; in short, to do the dirty work. Leo stifled his disappointment and moved to the bar. "I thought you should know," he said. "After all, we'll be working together." He began to mix himself a martini.

"Yes," she said. She seemed at a loss for words, and sat down on the couch. When he came over and sat as well, she looked down, knit her hands, and said, "Look, Leo, I—"

The doorbell rang again. Leo and Galil looked at one another in annoyance. Then he said, "Moment, please," and went to answer it.

Galil Aurean was standing in the hallway outside. No shimmer: this was the real one. "Sorry," she said. "Look, I just . . . sorry." She slipped past him inside.

The two Galil's blinked at one another for a moment. Then the first one, the ghost, flickered and vanished, leaving behind a featureless white robot. It stood quickly and walked out.

Leo watched it go, arms crossed. The real Galil Aurean closed the door gently behind it. "That was quite an entrance," he said.

She winced. "I changed my mind, but it was too late. I owed you more than a brush-off. Especially because of the—" she stopped herself. "Leo, everything was fine until this afternoon."

"Until I came along?" He smirked and handed her the martini. "I seem to remember you liked these." He went to make himself one.

"I have something to tell you," she said. "About the mission."

"You're going along, aren't you?"

"It's not that. Although I appreciate your concern."

They sat together, much as he and the ghost had moments before. "Nobody knows better than I how dangerous this is going to be," he said. "Take my advice: ghost it. Your chances of getting killed otherwise are pretty good."

"I can't. I did make an insurance ghost of myself, though; I have enough for a new body if, you know, mine is destroyed . . ."

He laughed harshly. "Backup copies are no good. I know, we used 'em in the war. Ghosts aren't your complete self, just a partial cognitive map. *They* don't have your memories, just your habits. Only *you* have real memories. Leaving a ghost behind as insurance is useless. If you die you lose the experiences that ground your identity. Who cares if the backup preserves the current you, if you lose the rest?"

"Leo, I don't want to hear it! It's too late for me to back out. Just listen for a minute, will you?" He glowered, but shut up.

"Tarski's not getting you to ghost pilot just out of concern for your life, Leo. And we're not going along physically just because of some uncertainty about machine reliability."

"Go on." He sat back, sipping quietly.

"We can't send our ghosts along, and couldn't bring you physically, for the same reason," she said. "Because we're not coming back here with the anomaly."

It wasn't one of the alternatives he'd considered, but Leo had to admit it fit the facts. He nodded. "They're going to wipe my ghost afterwards, right?"

"Yes." She cradled her drink, not looking at him. "Tarski and the others owe big to the neo-Individualists, who've supported the Institute for years. They want the anomaly badly—badly enough to kill for, certainly badly enough to use their connections to force Tarski into this scheme."

"What about you?" he said quietly. "How did they get you?"

"Simple." She laughed humorlessly. "They told me about the anomaly, then told me it was going to be given to the Individualists whether I helped them or not. At least if I go along I have the chance of examining it before they hand it over."

"They think it's an angel, don't they?" Leo chuckled. "I can see why, the way it flutters around Cobra like a moth. Good propaganda material."

"But only as long as they preserve its mystery," she said. "They want it, but they need to control it. That's why they can't just leave it alone.

"Tarski and Kapleau have sold out, but they agree with me we have to study it first. So I'm going along."

"And I'm not?" He stood up suddenly. "The bastards want to cheat me of the experience!" He paced, shrugging his shoulders angrily.

"Yes. Until this afternoon, Leo, I agreed with them. Our pilot's ghost was expendable. He, like everyone else, would see us leave but not return. Nobody would know we'd actually stolen the anomaly until it was too late. He wouldn't get his memories from the ghost, but what of it?"

She put her drink down and came to him. "So I had to know, Leo, were you serious there on Revus? Do the Aknitari mean so much to you?"

"They did, once." He took her hand, carefully. "Childhood enthusiasms die, you know. But what they were to me once—like dreams of a former life, something sacred, I mean—that hasn't changed. I fought the Individualists because I thought they were enemies of what's really sacred: experience, and memory. You were right to tell me this, Galil. I wouldn't have taken losing this ghost easily."

Her shoulders slumped, and tension drained from her face. "You are the same man I met on Revus," she said. "I'm glad."

"I can't take the job now," he grumbled. "Worse, I'll have to tell the police about this."

She shook her head. "Tarski and the others will deny the neo-Individualist thing. So will I, for that matter. I don't want yet another group involved in this thing. The government's just as likely to use the anomaly to serve its own purpose."

"So what's the alternative?" he burst out. "I'm out of it, you find yourself another pilot, and where does that leave me?"

Galil smiled ironically. "I hoped you'd react like that. I could just say, 'too bad, Leo', and leave it at that, you know. But then, I could have just not told you to begin with."

"What's your point?" he growled. He tossed back his drink and went to pour another.

"There's an alternative," she said. Galil curled up on the couch, watching him attentively. He thought about that, hiding behind the mixer, but finally shrugged at her helplessly.

"Tell me."

"You pilot the ship, but not as a ghost."

He laughed. "You want to smuggle me aboard physically?"

She nodded. "The software signal won't wipe a real pilot, and since you'll be on the bridge and really in control, you'll be able to bring us back."

". . . Or to Revus, say?"

She looked innocent.

"Okay." He started to pour himself a drink, thought better, and took the whole jug with him. He sat next to her. "How are you going to get me on board physically without them finding out?"

"Leave it to me."

"And what do I get out of it?"

She looked at him levelly. "You help save the most important Aknitari treasure we've ever found."

Leo tilted back the jug and drank. She had him figured out pretty well, he decided. "You're upping the ante something fierce," he said. "If it was dangerous before, this will double it. Or triple it."

"Scared?"

He put down the jug and leaned in close to her. "Of course. But I'll do it. My question right now is:" he ran his fingers up her arm, "are *you* scared?"

"Of you, Mr. Modest?" She put her arms around his neck, sighing in resignation. "It's far too late for that, isn't it?"

*　*　*　*　*

He watched the shuttle approach from a real window near the command center. Leo wore a helmetless space suit against the cold; the battleship was powered down. It would have been suspicious for him to turn any of the systems on, so he had spent his time in frosted corridors lit only by trouble lights, waiting. The last thirty hours had not been easy.

Leo knew this kind of ship too well. It was impossible to escape memories of the war here; he regretted accepting the job for that reason, not because of the danger. He had joked with Aurean on the way over here, but then she'd left, and without an audience Leo could not indulge himself in extravagant gestures. He was left with his thoughts.

The shuttle containing Aurean and the others turned and began breaking. It would dock shortly. Time for him to hide.

Leo drifted into the command center. The half open clam-shapes of the gravitics-beds arrayed in arcs here would normally be full of reclining men whose eyes and ears were hidden beneath chrome helmets, their minds one with the sensors and weapons of the ship. Holograms and hissing voices should be flickering around him, but he only saw the mist of his own breath as he opened the g-bed he'd chosen. He remembered one ship he'd served on, where the custom was to put a coin on your bed before going into battle. Whoever found his coin first afterwards won a drink.

He climbed in, glancing out once at the cold stillness. He'd found his coin exactly once. It had been embedded in the metal ceiling. Leo shivered, and lowered the lid.

He had stenciled a sign on the shell of the bed: INTERNAL FIRE. SEALED. The bed's outside status lights were blinded, but Leo had left himself full access to the ship's systems.

He pulled on his command helmet, and let partial ghosts of his personality split off to inhabit the many subsystems of the ship. Computers throughout the metal body took on Leo's instincts for acuity and movement, replacing a human crew. None were sentient; they were enhanced agents of Leo himself, servants so familiar with their master that they need never consult with him. One of them gave him a feed to Aurean's headset. "Ready," he told her.

He heard a faint, shuddering sigh from her. "We're docked," said Tarski's voice in his other ear. "Leo, are you awake?"

If he and Aurean had rigged it right, Tarski's readouts should show Leo to be a ghost, mapped into the ship's computer. "Right here," said Leo laconically. The ghost would sound and act like Leo himself; carrying out this pretence was easy. "You all brought your barf bags and prayer books, I hope?"

"Don't joke, please, Leo," said Aurean. "It's easy for you: you're not really here."

He smiled in complicity. "True," he said. "Find your stations and cocoon yourselves. We're going to pull a lot of g's shortly."

The shuttle disengaged. Humming the *Ride of the Valkyries*, he set the *Pall* in motion.

The ship was now his body. His consciousness was layered with overlapping shades, each whispering its status in his voice. Leo loved the sensuality of piloting; the ship was a perfectly responsive body, requiring no effort to move through all its degrees. His ghosts saw and interpreted the whole electromagnetic spectrum, giving him beautiful second sight. He could hear the faint vapor of solar wind from Cobra sighing around him. Momentarily, he forgot his passengers.

But as he took the ship through its short superspace hop to the vicinity of Cobra's companion star, Leo was reminded of other flights in ships like this. There were too many such memories; Leo had only been a military pilot for two years, but the weight of a decade of war oppressed his memory. He had lived and relived horrors he had never prepared for; the pre-war Leo had been an innocent. At some point in it all he had stopped merely flying, and begun fleeing. He had been running ever since, his memories pursuing him everywhere except into the refuge of his five senses, and the refuge of his daydreams of Aknitari peace and wisdom.

So it seemed that the hands of many ghosts reached with his to grasp space-time and draw the *Pall* into Cobra's knot of fire. More voices than Leo's own echoed in his ears, and those voices were of men and women who were truly dead.

The mist of virtual particles around the ship decided their reality and a blazing wall of sun-fire appeared in front of him. The light and heat were overwhelming, and the roar of the solar wind deafened him. Instinct and old training took hold: Leo roared back, reaching for non-existent weapons through his ghosts, though he knew he had not stumbled into a battle.

"Leo!" Aurean and Tarski shouted simultaneously.

He shut down the interface for a second to get his bearings. "Tone it down, will you?" he snapped. "I'm fine." He had not lost control of the ship; they were already coasting into their planned close-orbit around the companion star. Even so, Leo's stomach was fluttering with unexpected nervousness. He damped the sensors down to an acceptable level, and peered through the stellar corona, hunting for Cobra.

The neutron star was behind the horizon, but evidence of it was everywhere—in the distorted, shocked pyres of stellar prominences and gusts of hard radiation pouring from malformed sunspots like tortured mouths. The sky of the star was alive with whipped scarves of light from tidal upheavals.

"Hell," shouted Leo. "You people are insane! This place will eat us alive."

"Shut up," said Galil tensely. In Leo's other ear, Tarski asked, "Are you saying it can't be done, Leo? Should we turn back?"

He thought about it while he watched a line of brightness on the horizon thicken into a band of churning fire. The *Pall* wasn't feeling the heat yet. They had full power and the flight plan was simplicity itself—as simple as stepping off a cliff.

He had to admit it wasn't Cobra that frightened him, but the intensity of remembrance. This place, the sights and sounds, were so like a battle he'd ghosted and remembered. He suddenly recalled seeing a cloud of human bodies like struggling midges erupt from the side of a shattered troop-craft.

Get me out of here! He had seconds to decide whether to abort. That bright wall of fire on the horizon was resolving into thunderheads of radiation-blasted stellar material, and a ring of light like the eye of the devil was rising beyond it.

He was trapped. Leo had lied to Galil. His wandering might have originally been to find something nebulous, like the Aknitari. But after the war, he had wandered not to find, but to escape. To avoid facing memory. And it had followed him here.

He reached to abort as thunderheads reared up and passed to either side and, through the cleft, Cobra appeared. In that vortex, in the very immolation of heat, some Aknitari machine was dancing. It had spun and glided there since before Leo's ancestors invented war. As he thought this, Leo closed his fists and let the moment pass.

They were now committed to their trajectory.

"Here we go," he said to his passengers. His voice sounded calm to him now. Cobra's whirlpool stood overhead, reaching in impossible size to the zenith. And ahead of the *Pall,* the horizon itself lifted in plateaus and curtains of light, ascending like Jacob's ladder to touch and join that vast spiral. Leo felt the call of Cobra's gravity, and let the *Pall* rise as well, steering only to keep outside the core of the ladder.

For a while he was completely absorbed in piloting. When he finally had a few instants of grace, he convened the memories of all his shipboard ghosts. It was as if he had flown this exact course many times, now; this star was now familiar territory. He had also watched Galil in her g-bed, these last minutes. She'd hugged herself, gritting her teeth with tears starting at the edges of her shut eyes, and a part of Leo had descended to murmur comfort in her ear. Her left hand had reached out, fingers wide, to touch him, and come up against the soft resilience of the bed's force fields. He had wanted to take that hand, and could not. But, "I am here," he had said.

They were accelerating. With sensors battle-damped, Leo saw Cobra's approaching accretion disk as a torus of light, much bigger than a planet, turning slowly at its periphery, with dizzying speed further in. Only the outside edges of the ring were visible to the human eye; near the neutron star only gamma rays were given off. Intense beams of radiation flickered from the poles of the pulsar, thin and bright as lasers.

The Engine of Recall

Leo let the *Pall* be drawn into the outermost ring, and suddenly time seemed to speed up: they were pulled in faster and faster to fall turning within radiant and iridescent streamers of cloud, in a long arc into the inner rings.

Leo relinquished command to a ghost whose time-sense was accelerated. The *Pall* shot through galleries and pavilions of fire, cork-screwing around thickenings of gas and ducking currents that threatened to pull them down. Leo felt the engines firing in seemingly random bursts, and the ship toppled end over end, and spun and darted within a delirious blur of color and noise.

A long, powerful pressure built under him, and the wind of fire died down. The ghost-pilot dumped its memories back into Leo. He coughed in awe as he realized three hours' worth of clever piloting through the accretion disk. When the shock receded a bit, he said to his passengers, "We've arrived."

They spun deep in the ultraviolet layers of the disk. The *Pall*'s shielding rang with a deep thrumming, as if they were under attack from all sides. The engines were on full, keeping them level and matching speeds with the anomaly.

"There it is!" Galil shouted.

"What the—" echoed Tarski. Kapleau was shouting too; they weren't making sense, so Leo shifted frequencies to see the thing himself. For a moment after he spotted it he felt only puzzlement and, very nearly, disappointment.

It was not a ship; it didn't seem to have any large structure that could contain something. The anomaly was a tangle of incandescent threads, looping through and around itself with demented urgency. It was also much smaller than expected—just over a hundred meters in radius.

In lower frequencies, it broadcast a ceaseless, wavering scream into the sky of fire.

The others had stopped yelling. Leo cleared his throat and said, "Okay, people, what the hell is that?"

"Leo, break out the probes," said Tarski. Leo felt his ghosts move to comply. Bright arrow shapes moved to circle around the anomaly. They dashed back like hounds whenever the threads snapped too close.

"The rotation's not random," said Kapleau. The other Institute researchers spoke, their voices turning professionally bland as they moved to analyze the incoming data. "Subject is radiating at a temperature of eight thousand degrees." "Rotation velocity of thread appears to be six hundred meters per second." "Thread thickness is only three millimeters."

Leo took a look through the camera on one of the probes. The radiant thread oscillated around a central thickening of about ten meters' radius. He couldn't see inside it because of the whirl of glowing lines. "Is something in there?" he asked.

Galil's voice was slurred, whether from concentration or awe, he couldn't tell. "They're registering a mass in the core, Leo. An object."

He moved the probe in for a closer look. Suddenly one of the bright wires looped up and out, straight at him. Leo was plunged into static as the probe died.

He switched back to the view from the helm. "Did you see that?" Kapleau was shouting. "It cut it in half!"

". . . Definitely knows we're here," muttered Tarski. "And it's not happy."

"Maybe it's a defense mechanism," Galil said doubtfully. "Against solid debris?"

"Doing an impact analysis," said Kapleau. "Looks like . . . the thread didn't slow down at all when it went through the probe. Consistent with the thread being made of high-density degenerate matter. Not quite neutronium."

"Oh, great!" Leo wanted to wave his arms in frustration, but the bed's fields wouldn't allow it. "How much does this thing *weigh*?"

"Could be . . . millions of tonnes," said someone.

"Those threads will go through anything," said Tarski. "We built up the ship's hold to take solid bodies made of neutronium, but this stuff's got an edge to it. It would cut us to ribbons."

A moment of silence told Leo everyone was staring at the anomaly, and thinking the same thing.

He said it for them. "So how are we going to get it home?"

* * * * *

Tarski called a quick conference in Virtual Reality to decide what to do. The crew's images sat in outer space like gods, with the anomaly a runaway bonfire between them. Galil sat next to Leo; he could sense her excitement, and kept his public image frozen while putting a virtual hand on hers. "See this," she said, pointing at the core of the tangle. "There's a mass in there all right. It's fully protected by the thread-ball, but we know it's there because the whole thing pivots around it."

"Hmmph." Tarski leaned forward, his image illuminated by thread-light. "It begins to make sense. You were right after all, Galil."

She beamed. "What?" Leo asked roughly.

"It's a strongbox," she said. "A treasure-chest, if you like. Why else would the Aknitari build such elaborate armour, and store it where no one could get it?"

Leo stared at the anomaly. He was starting to get over the panic of the flight in, and now excitement was taking over. She was right. This could be the legacy of the Aknitari.

"It's priceless," said Tarski. "Possibly the most important find in human history. So we have to get it home. Agreed?" They all nodded. "How long have we got, Leo?"

"The ship can't take more than forty-five minutes of this." He shrugged. "I think we should come back, now that we know what we're up against."

"Not an option," snapped Tarski. "This is our only chance, and we have to take it."

Leo cast a sidelong glance at Galil. She was glaring at Tarski, and not hiding the fact behind any VR mask. "What are you saying?"

"The threads are armor, we're agreed on that," said Tarski. "So—"

"We're not agreed!"

"You said it yourself, Galil: the strongbox is at the center, hidden by the thread. Now apparently there's only *one* thread, which is knotted around the strongbox. So to get the strongbox out . . ."

"All we have to do is cut the thread!" Kapleau finished for him.

"No!" Galil stood up. "We don't know what it is! The thread could *be* the strongbox. It may even be alive, for all we know! You can't just gut it and take the hide home! We're not after trophies here."

"We're not after the same things, Galil," Tarski said bluntly. "If you won't help us, at least don't get in our way." He gestured, and Galil's image vanished; they had cut her out of the conversation.

Leo leaned over the anomaly. "You little shit, what do you think you're doing?"

Tarski blinked at him. "We need the strongbox, Leo. We're going to put an antimatter burst through the thread. When it unravels we'll take the strongbox and get out of here. All very easy."

"A million-tonne whip-lash going amok is *easy*? You really are crazy. I'm taking us out of here."

"No you're not." Tarski did something, and the whole scene vanished. Leo found himself back in his own body, inside the dimly lit womb of the g-bed.

"Damn damn *damn!*" He pounded ineffectually against the restraining fields. "Okay, calm down," he muttered to himself, hugging his chest tightly. He breathed hard for a few seconds, then flicked the switch to connect his mind directly with the body of the ship.

Nothing happened.

The anger washed away. "Umm." Leo stared blankly at his hands for a second. Tarski had cut him out of the communications loop. Probably, he'd given some command to shut off the conscious part of the primary ghost-Leo. That would be fine if Leo really were a ghost; the ship would still have access to his piloting skills. But the ship's core wasn't a ghost, it was Leo himself.

Tarski had just decapitated the ship. Leo wondered whether he knew it yet.

He tried to manually re-establish the connection for a few minutes, but he couldn't even get an outside visual. He had cleverly adjusted the ship's manifest to show this g-bed as inoperative. The adjustment had been done from here; his connection had remained open because the manifest only controlled future sessions. Tarski had shut down his session, and any new one would have to check the manifest. Which registered this bed as dead . . .

He would have to leave the g-bed. But doing that now, under hightide conditions, would probably be fatal.

Leo cast about for an appropriate curse, but there was no one to hear it anyway, so he stayed silent, and became still, hands pressed against the inside of the coffin.

* * * * *

"Leo?"

Galil's voice. Leo gave a gasp of relief. Fifteen minutes had passed, during which his imagination and memory had had free play. He was terrified now, and shouted, "Galil! Get me out of here!"

"Leo? What's happening?"

"Tarski shut me out! There's nobody conscious piloting the ship. Listen, you've got to go into the manifest and—"

"Leo? Can you hear me?"

He felt a chill like steel on his spine. She couldn't hear him. The connection was one-way, because his bed was down and wouldn't transmit.

"What have they done to you, Leo? You're not registering anywhere! Tarski's about to fire his shot, Leo, we have to stop him! He'll destroy the strongbox."

"Us too," he said bitterly.

"Your ghosts won't help me, Leo; they're so stupid! We've got one chance, but they can't do anything. There are manual over-rides for the weapons systems, right? Well, if we can't stop him through the computers, we'll have to do it from there."

"No!" he bellowed. "Don't open your bed! The tide'll kill you!"

"I'm going to leave my bed, and disable the controls from outside. It's our only chance to save the Aknitari, Leo! If you can help me, I need it now. Here goes."

"Galil, stop!" It was too late. He heard the alarms in her bed go off. Then silence.

Leo cursed his own cowardice. He should have opened his own bed when Tarski shut him out. If he'd succeeded in getting to another bed then, Galil wouldn't be leaving hers now.

He took several deep breaths, and hit the switches to kill the gravitics field. Deep red light pulsed around him as the siren wailed. The upper half of the clamshell lifted away and Leo fell into pain and the sound of Galil's screams.

She lay on the air a few meters away. Galil twisted tautly with her arms straight over her head and her feet pointed down. The air was being forced from her lungs in short spasmodic yelps, and her eyes were wide and blank. Her face was dark with blood, and her bare arms and legs were swelling. As Leo rolled out of the bed, he felt the same invisible force trying to stretch him straight. With a bone-cracking effort, he rolled himself into a ball.

Gravity had gone insane. There was no way to gauge his trajectory accurately. He kicked against the g-bed, and fell in a wobbling arc towards one of the empty ones. Demonic suction grappled at him, making his joints pop and his vision brown out. Galil had stopped screaming.

His knotted hands clutched the edge of an empty g-bed. He lost a fingernail as he was yanked down. A mad lofting sensation possessed his shoulders and head while his ankles turned against the metal flooring. Gasping, he pivoted his body around the lip of the bed and collapsed into it. Blindly, he punched at the keypad to close the lid.

This g-bed was registered in the manifest. He booted his command session and quickly re-entered Virtual Reality.

A flood of memories told him what Tarski and the others had been up to. All the ship's antimatter armaments were firing on a moving section of thread. It was too late for him to stop them, and he no longer cared. He had to save Galil.

First he nudged the ship ever so slightly, to bring Galil down to the floor with minimum impact. Then he rotated the *Pall* around the pivot-point of the command center, and fired the engines.

"Leo? What the hell are you doing?" shouted Tarski.

"Dropping us," he said. "Bastard."

"No! We're almost . . . Oh my God."

The thread had parted. Bright lines were flailing madly into the sky. Leo let the *Pall* fall past a lashing cord that could cut the ship in half. Radiation sang in his ears as the ship dropped straight at Cobra.

Twenty seconds. That was how long he had before Cobra's gravity took them irrevocably. He told his ghosts to wait fifteen seconds before firing the engines on a trajectory out of here. Then he opened the lid of the g-bed.

They were no longer orbiting, but falling, so the tidal forces had lessened. Leo still felt the dual pull on his head and feet as he emerged, but it was manageable.

Galil lay sprawled, arms and legs out, in the middle of the floor. She was turning like a human dial registering the rotation of the falling ship.

My coin, he thought. He staggered over and gathered her up, wheeling back to his bed.

He tripped. Galil fell up and slid along the ceiling, moaning and coughing weakly. She pushed off, thrusting him away blindly when he moved to grab her again. He got her but she mashed her elbow into his nose. He saw stars; disoriented, he lunged at what he thought was the bed.

They fell in and a murderous weight came down. The lid of the bed dropped like a guillotine, bringing darkness.

* * * * *

Galil lay limp and cold against him as Leo put on the interface helmet. He wrapped one arm around her and entered the command session.

They had picked up momentum in the close-orbit of Cobra and were rising in a long arc. They should pass right by the anomaly; when he looked, though, Leo couldn't find it.

The scientists were shouting in confusion and terror. For a few seconds it must have looked like Leo was killing them all. He ignored them; his first priority was getting Galil and himself out of here alive. The others could go to hell.

Their close orbit had done a lot of damage from tide and radiation. The *Pall* was limping now, but their trajectory formed a loop that would allow them to pick up the strongbox if it was free.

"Now hear this," Leo said. "We've got exactly one chance to net the fish on our way by. I want no arguments from anybody. Man your posts. If we don't get it on the first pass we're not coming back for a second."

The broken thread had unraveled and echoed only faintly in radar. Leo looked for an object a few meters in diameter on the anomaly's former orbit. Nothing registered.

"Where is it?" muttered Tarski. "It couldn't have been destroyed . . ."

"Sure it could," retorted Leo. "Idiot."

There was a signal, though, faint but in the right position. Whatever it was, it was tiny—only a few centimeters across. And it was falling.

"I see it!" crowed Tarski. "Guide us in, Leo."

"Wait." Something was wrong. The sensors showed Leo a sphere small enough to hold in his hand, mirror-bright and perfectly round. Not what he'd expected.

He called up the ship's guns and ordered a volley of conventional fire against the object.

"Leo, stop!" shouted Tarski.

"What are you going to do, crash my session again? We'll never make it back then." He fired the volley.

The rounds of degenerate matter, small bullets each weighing tonnes, flew silently out to impact against the sphere. Or, he thought they impacted; Leo could see the quick blips intersect the mirrored ball, but other than a flash of radiation there was no reaction. The ball didn't even tremble much less change course.

Nobody said anything, but the implication was clear. That sphere massed far more than their own ship.

"Neutronium . . . ?" Tarski said after a while.

Leo watched it fall, fighting back anger and disappointment. The sphere would hit Cobra in a few minutes, and the orbit of the thread was decaying too. They had come, and seen, and destroyed the last active Aknitari relic.

"Well, what the hell was it for anyway?" he asked aloud. "Why go to all that trouble to protect a chunk of neutron star? It's crazy!"

It didn't fit his idea of the Aknitari. He had believed they would somehow provide for their inheritors; it had to be accidental that their cities were so thoroughly effaced, their records lost. They were like wise parents, dead before their time but capable of providing for the humans who came after. But this didn't fit with that safe image at all. As he watched the bead fall, his hackles rose. For the first time, he found the anomaly itself frightening, even though that tiny sphere was doomed to do nothing more than splat against the surface of Cobra, without leaving so much as a dent.

It was perverse. Almost as if it was intended to do that . . .

". . . It wasn't a strongbox," he said aloud, and as he said it he realized what, in fact, it was.

"What do you mean, not a strongbox?" growled Tarski.

"That's not neutronium," said Leo. "This thing isn't a strongbox at all. It's a *mine!*"

He didn't wait for a reply. Leo calculated another close orbit of Cobra, and fired the engines. The *Pall* groaned around him as they looped down into the heart of the accretion disk.

"Leo!" "Stop!" He paid no heed to them. There was no time left. He dropped them to the edge of the death zone while his ghosts cried like mourners in his ears, reporting growing damage. Several fell silent as the systems they were in were torn apart. But the *Pall* held together through a pirouette around Cobra that took only a few seconds. Leo used Cobra as a gravitational slingshot to fling them under the accretion disk and back along the course they had taken on the way in.

The ship was out of control; everything was happening too fast for his human reflexes, and he should have spawned a time-dilated ghost to pilot, but panic drove Leo now. He had been betrayed by the Aknitari. Lulled by his own need to believe them better than humanity, he had come too close, and now they were going to kill him.

Leo fled through flaming skies, surrounded by his own ghosts and pursued by memories remade as engines of destruction. The stellar gas falling in from Cobra's companion hit the *Pall* as hard radiation, and he drew a bright contrail of fusing hydrogen as he climbed out of the neutron star's gravity well. The corona of the companion seemed a cool haven now.

"What's going on?" whined Kapleau. As Leo ran a diagnosis on the Transit drive, Tarski answered: "The anomaly was protecting a ball of quarkonium. If that stuff touches neutronium it instantly converts it to quarkonium too. Relativistic combustion of Cobra's neutronium will convert the whole pulsar in two or three seconds. It'll be like a second supernova. The gravity waves alone could kill us!"

The Transit drive would need full engine power for two minutes to charge it. The mine would hit Cobra before then. Their only chance was to get to the other side of the companion before the blast. Cobra's gravity weakened slowly as Leo aimed them at the companion's horizon.

He counted the seconds as Cobra lowered behind the star's white horizon. When it finally disappeared, Kapleau shouted, "Made it!"

"Not yet," said Leo. "The blast could tear the companion apart, us with it." He checked their trajectory; satisfied, he diverted power from the engines to charge the Transit drive. He felt the power building like warmth in the pit of his stomach, but knew it wouldn't be in time. He watched the horizon, sensors damped all the way down.

A flicker, then another. A ramp of light lifted into the sky—a knife blade cutting up from the horizon. The ceiling of heaven had appeared and was toppling slowly down on them as Cobra's explosion ate away the mantle of the star. A demonic howl filled Leo's ears as the radiation sensors overloaded. His damage monitors panicked as one.

The warmth in his gut had become heat. He readied himself to release it in transition to superspace, but had to glance out once more.

A tidal wave of tortured stellar material rose, peaking under the flat line of annihilating light, and fell at him.

He didn't remember giving the command, but suddenly they were in superspace. The ship groaned and popped as gravity and heat ended. An astonishing silence swept in, and he saw only the gray static of virtual particles; but an afterimage of that cresting wave of fire stayed with him for a while.

"Leo? Where are we going?" Tarski sounded very tired.

"Blye. We have to get an evacuation going before the explosion reaches them."

"Oh." There was a pause. Leo watched the instruments begin conjuring up the virtual map of Blye. "It'll all be destroyed, won't it?" said Tarski finally.

"You're the expert." Leo didn't want to talk anymore. He closed the connection, and retreated from command to let his ghosts complete the flight. For a while he drifted with the static, then he remembered Galil. Immediately he dropped out of the command session—and into dark warmth and the touch of her. She was breathing steadily, curled against him. He reached to open the bed and carry her to the medicomp, but she groaned and put her hand on his.

"I hurt," she said thinly.

"You need treatment."

"No, not yet. Just hold me for a while . . . Did we get it?"

He lay back, feeling Galil carefully move to rest her head on his chest. He thought of all the things he could tell her, truths and lies, but none seemed adequate.

"Leo?" she asked sleepily.

"I'm sorry, we lost it," he said.

In this silence and comfort, all else seemed to recede. Leo knew he would never clearly remember the past few hours, only moments and flashes, and that he would remember much of it wrongly. What he'd believed to be the Aknitari, had been a fantasy of his own, a comforting alternative to those crowding memories taken from the lives of machines. He had walked with that crutch for too many years. He was grateful it had been taken away. At least for now, and at least here, he touched the real, and nothing pursued him.

"Maybe," he said, "we found something better."

"Solitaire" was one of my first stories. The initial drafts were done on an electric typewriter, the most sophisticated writing tool available to me in the late 1970s. I wasn't satisfied with early drafts and it went in and out of desk drawers for over ten years before I finally finished it. Something about this world and the strange, aloof solitaires kept drawing me back until this, the final version.

"Solitaire" was the cover story for the Fall/Winter 1992 issue of Figment *magazine. It was reprinted in the April 1997 issue of* Cosmic Visions.

* * S O L I T A I R E * *

Seeing the crowd balk, Theresa turned. The massive airlock behind her was opening. She moved closer to it, while the people who had been converging on her retreated to form a rough arc a safe distance away.

Orange light from the round doorway silhouetted a giant, inhuman form. Leonine, graceful in free-fall, a wary Solitaire emerged from the lock to stare at the onlookers, the lights and the single nearby human, who bit her lip and smiled back.

Theresa watched its humanoid hands unclip things from the belt around its middle. It loosed something like a camera as well as a small fleet of fan-driven balls that caromed through the air of the hangar. The watchers broke into uneasy talk. The diplomats fidgeted with their Universal Peace Symbols.

"Get away, it's dangerous," someone shouted at Theresa. The Solitaire glanced at the speaker, then returned to its machines.

"Don't come near me," she warned the watchers. "You'll spook it, and who knows what'll happen then?"

"You don't know what you're doing!"

"Oh no, I'm the only one here who does know." She settled on the wall near the Solitaire. It ignored her until she opened her satchel and began letting out lines on which numerous objects were strung. There was everything from wood to vials of chemicals, computer parts to a section of steel plate—as thorough an inventory of the colony as she could construct, made according to the slim data on Solitaire contact she had gleaned from her books. The lines splayed out around her, hundreds of samples turning and looping.

Now the Solitaire took interest. The crowd muttered in consternation and the security men looked grimly at their hand monitors. "This woman's a criminal," said one. "She's out to ruin our contact with the visitor." They edged forward as the alien caught the end of one of the cords and drew the whole skein towards it. It began going through the objects, hunched over like an old man counting beads. Its ears twitched a little this way and that.

She brought out the can she had rigged to look like a bomb. "Stay back," she hissed. "I mean it." The crowd fell silent momentarily, watching the standoff. Cameramen rushed back and forth.

Leaving the can hanging in midair before her, she took a viewscreen and a portable telephone from the pack. Her hands were shaking. Clutching the pack she looked to the Solitaire.

Long tail out, it held onto the edge of the airlock door with the clawed toes of one foot. The other stabilized the turning tangle of samples as it tore a vial marked Chlorine from the line. It sniffed at it a few times then placed it briefly in the door of one of the circling machines. Most of the other vials which had been on the string were ricocheting around the cavernous docking chamber. It kept this one. Quickly, unsure of its next move, Theresa punched up a hologram of chlorine tanks being siphoned, and held out the viewscreen to the alien. It looked at the viewscreen, looked at her, and took the picture out of her hand. The crowd erupted into astonished chatter. Hurriedly she dialed the number of the colony's chemical plant, and when the representative appeared said quietly, "I'd like to purchase as much chlorine as I can." The rep nodded blandly, checked the credit number she gave him, and asked, "When do you want it?"

"Immediately. At the docks." She gave the exact location. Again he nodded; he was obviously not paying attention to the news today, which was her good luck.

"Trace that call," someone said. She disconnected immediately, and smirked at the mob.

The Solitaire was watching her through crimson eyes. It could have no clear idea of what transaction had just occurred, since it had no language nor as far as she knew any idea of what language was. But now it bobbed over to her and took the phone from her limp fingers. She could smell the alien, a salty odor that resembled nothing she knew. She was tiny beside it; it must weigh at least three hundred kilos and its claws, carnivore's teeth and musculature were heavily developed.

It fell to examining the other items on the line, hulking back towards the lock and only occasionally glancing in her direction. It seemed to be waiting. She did not know if it had ever encountered humans in the flesh before. It had no human servant, but that said nothing since a man or woman in the service of a Solitaire could easily die. It might be looking for such a servant, if she was lucky.

No alien had ever visited this colony before, and the military government did not know how to react. The police, lacking orders, began to bring out their riot weapons.

"Get back," she said. "It won't let you interrupt." It made a fluid move towards the crowd, and the people fell back nervously.

"Why are you doing this?" demanded a lieutenant. "What will it get you?"

"Away. Out of here, and away from you. I know there's a warrant out for my arrest; you've been after me for days. Really you should ask, what do I have to lose?"

The Solitaire still held the phone, and it twitched violently when this abruptly rang. It threw the unit into the air. Theresa caught it.

"Courier," said a bored voice. "I'm at the docks. Where do you want these tanks?"

"Berth fourteen," she whispered. "Go straight up to the lock, and don't mind the crowd."

"Sure."

A few sullen, silent minutes later she spotted the courier's airbike, sailing around the curve of the huge torus which was the docking chamber. No one had noticed him yet; the crowd was entertained by the policemen's threats and cajoling, and her derisive reactions. The police could still very easily ruin things, by simply not letting the driver through. But they were distracted, and had no real idea of what she intended. They expected to pick her up the moment the Solitaire left.

Luckily for her, no one here knew much about Solitaires. And except for a very few academics and misfits such as herself, no one had any desire to.

The courier flew obliviously through the crowd and followed her waving arms down. When he noticed the alien he took off his headphones and stared, but he was close enough for her to reach over and turn off the airbike.

"Thanks," she said, while the police shouted at the courier to grab her.

Behind the airbike bobbed five white tanks.

The alien came over and began shaking them to see how full they were. The courier jack-knifed off his seat and clung to the wall. The lieutenant was shouting orders to his men, who reluctantly moved forward.

With two tanks held against its chest, the Solitaire pushed off in the direction of the airlock. Theresa shoved the third tank it had unhooked. Urgency gave her the strength to move the massive thing and momentum carried her to the door. She could see the alien's powerfully muscled back receding down an amber-lit tube to its strange ship. It didn't look back.

This was the hinge of all her hopes. A grimace of despair on her face, Theresa pulled the white tank into the airlock with her.

"Stop!" The crowd surged forward, pressing around the airlock hatch, shouting, exhorting, cursing her. But unwilling to follow. The lieutenant's bewildered voice rose above them all.

Theresa was panting as if she had run a race as she went past the last spars of the human docking structure and into the odd, honeycomb labyrinth of the Solitaire ship. Enfolded in amber light, she located the alien and moved to set the tank beside the two it had placed in a hexagonal opening in a floor. It adjusted the tanks' position and placed a lid over the top.

It looked back at her. She hung in the midst of the space, awaiting its decision. Faint voices reached her. It twitched its powerful tail once, twice, and began rooting through her possessions, sorting them carefully. Then it reached out a furred arm and grabbed her by the arm. She yelped. The alien turned her around, examining her. It tugged at the dun laborer's uniform she wore. She was terrified, but the seed of determination that had kept her going throughout her years as rebel and thief held her still now.

The Solitaire let her go and went to the airlock. It pulled a switch, and the walls of the access tube collapsed together. The concerned and astonished faces vanished and the whole docking structure folded into a heavy knot on the wall.

It was taking her with it.

A wave of incredulous relief enfolded Theresa. After years, and against all expectation, she had escaped.

*　*　*　*　*

The solitaire left. She stayed by the lock, exhausted. Finally she slept in midair, and, waking to find the alien vanished from the maze, felt reduced to aimlessness and indecision. The ship was very cold so she layered herself with clothing. She remained among the machinery for several more hours, a steady acceleration the only indication they had left port. As curiosity got the better of her fear she began to explore, and soon discovered a white-walled shaft leading towards weak gravity. She climbed down and into a centrifuge, where the Solitaire had gone. Gravity increases to near normal, and she emerged in a pale landscape which at first bewildered her.

Solitaires did not seem to like walls. Theresa was in a chamber of unknown limits, filled with meter-thick pillars that like a forest blocked vision over any distance. The ladder to the axis of the ship was in one of the pillars. A blue-white glow came from the ceiling and glared off a floor of white sand. Artificial breezes sighed around the columns. The effect was chilling.

Pieces of scrap metal and electronics, bottles of pale liquid, and tools lay all around, on or in the sand. Dragging her luggage, Theresa moved to a nearby clearing and set up camp for herself. When all was secure and to her liking, she went exploring again. Water was ample from fountains, and many small rabbit-like creatures inhabited the sands, eating leaves that sprouted from the bottoms of the pillars. The leaves, she knew, would be edible if processed properly by her portable kitchen. After she drank her fill at the fountains and washed, she followed a faint trace of sound to the Solitaire.

The alien was in a large clearing examining some equipment. All around were truncated pillars serving as tables or control surfaces. Holograms suspended over the tables showed a three dimensional map of thousands of stars, penetrated by lines and loops of light. Occasional flicking pictures and noises appeared. Between adjustments of its machinery the Solitaire would look at this display and sometimes poke it with a finger, changing colors or sounds.

She settled herself by a far pillar and watched. It noted her presence but continued its work.

The alien, which she had seen before in pictures, could only be fully appreciated when as now it was moving, acting with purpose. With a minimum of wasted effort, it dismantled and repaired huge metal hulks of machinery; its strength let it do the work of five men, and it had created numerous tools to hold, twist and pull at a distance or independently. It jammed these in or on the machines it was repairing and did things she would have thought needed four or more hands. It did not pause to consider its work, unless it was to measure a gap or fitting. There was no doubt it knew precisely what it was doing, and it even seemed that it redesigned when it repaired. Nothing it used was standardized.

She watched, and mused, and tried to ignore the quiet voices in her head—voices which said *are you sure you know what you've gotten yourself into?*

Later that evening as the ship's lights dimmed she sat in her new camp and brought out the viewscreen with her library on it. She called up the memoirs of Richard Abbafi, the first man to travel with a Solitaire and from whom she had learned the technique of Solitaire contact. Over the years she had reviewed these tapes often, in romantic phases, in the throes of desperate dreams of independence and escape. Her familiarity with them was what allowed her to capitalize on the sudden, unforeseen visit by this alien to her colony. When she heard of the ship's arrival, she knew instantly what was possible, what to do. Small matter that it had only been done once or twice before; it was the release of years of bottled frustration that gave her the impetus, as well as the knowledge that this opportunity might never present itself again. Now she cued the first record, the one recorded immediately after Abbafi's own first sight of a Solitaire's home.

Abbafi's face appeared on the tiny screen. He was white- faced, barely in control of himself as he held his camera. The picture shook slightly. "I think this record might be indispensable to future researchers," he said, "though I hold out little hope of surviving to deliver it to anyone. That's not important, as what I've seen in even the last few hours makes it worth the risk.

"For a century these creatures have been ghost ships, completely uncommunicative, rare, never entering human space except to mine asteroids and, occasionally, steal something when they could get away with it. Since they were visible only as ships, we weren't even sure they were organic entities like ourselves until very recently." He turned the camera away from himself, showing a vista of inverted pyramids more softly lit than her pillars, with black sand for a floor. A pile of equipment—medical unit, food processor and research materials—lay behind Abbafi; it was this that she had used as the model for her own kit. "Twenty years ago, at the beginning of my career, I heard a report that a Solitaire had docked at a human colony, and entered it apparently in a desperate search for oxygen supplies. Its ship had been damaged. I discounted this as a fable until I was shown a set of videos made of the incident. It was the first time we saw one in the flesh. And the fact it came to us—albeit not to talk—made me think perhaps there was a way of meeting it."

He looked around apprehensively. "And I did. It took me two decades, and a lot of failure and frustration . . . but yes."

Abbafi had lured his Solitaire into contact by leaving a kind of trail of refined and valuable materials, with himself at its end. He had demonstrated his value as an agent or go-between in the same way Theresa had, and been adopted as the Solitaire's 'pet.' She had the video of their first encounter; the two beings in deep space, suited figures backdropped on total black and speaking in gifts and stances. She had dreamed herself into that picture many times.

"Already from examining this ship I've confirmed several hypotheses: that the alien is incapable of language, does not possess a society in our sense of it and instead of our massive vocabulary, the thousands of words we have and the millions of subtleties of personal relationships which clutter up our thoughts and unconscious minds, it has an instinct and mind directed to technology. I mean instead of all our thoughts and ideas, words and affectations its head is full of plans for physical objects, new systems and details of the old ones which run its ship. It thinks scientifically. As we bathe in the medium of personality, it is immersed totally in its creations. Both paradigms have the same ultimate end: survival."

He continued speaking, pointing out objects, speculating happily. With his voice a reassuring babble she looked up from the screen, thinking of the alien preoccupied with its repairs. That was what drew her— its aura of total self-reliance, self- containment. It was a whole world unto itself, and for her, an ideal. From now on, it would be her study.

It continued working in its clearing; but oddly, even with it so close, she felt safe, as though alone.

*   *   *   *   *

The Solitaire seemed to be patrolling, roaming a clearly defined territory. Theresa saw a great many strange stars and planets pass by, her nose pressed to the tiny windows in the docking area. For a while she was comfortable and happy.

Once the alien actually landed on a planet. She had never been on a planet before, so she snuck into the landing craft behind him to see it.

The world was a cold stone the size of Mars, with a bleached sky and a permafrost of carbon dioxide on the rocks. The Solitaire, a bulky man-shape in its space suit, looked around from the hatch, then left to jog over a hill. She walked around the outside of the ship, taking her first opportunity to view it from without. Its landing section, the front half of the starship proper, was a squat cone colored blue. There were no markings, but four squat silver engines on short arms splayed out into the scorched soil.

Her attention turned to the planet itself. The Solitaire was a tiny figure balanced on the knife-edge of the horizon. The vision before her was overwhelming—there were no walls, no containing vessels, just flat broken land that fell away to all sides as over a verge. There was no one here, the stones before her had never been seen or touched, might never be seen again. There was nothing to hold the atmosphere in; the giant vault of sky over her filled her with an uneasiness that gradually gave way to panic. She ran into the lander and waited there until the Solitaire returned, carting a net full of colorful rocks.

*   *   *   *   *

Theresa's life aboard the ship had become routine. The Solitaire had ended the ship's artificial winter and it was very hot. He had been shedding all over the ship for weeks and had an uneven coat that he scratched absent-mindedly. The short hair accentuated his alien physique.

She had stretched out on the sand to repair the flavor unit of the food processor. Everything it produced tasted like beef. As she pried at it the Solitaire walked out of the pillar forest and picked her up by one arm. She yelled in surprise and dropped the machine; the Solitaire shook her to keep her quiet and trotted towards the docking tube. She was terrified that he had decided to clean house and was going to eject her through the airlock. But when they reached it she saw it was open with white light at the far end—they were in some human port.

It opened a locker and gave her a small metal bar. Then it shoved her at the airlock. She crabwalked in that direction, and it turned and re-entered the shaft to the centrifuge.

She paused at another locker to take out a bag of the Solitaire's discarded tools and trinkets, which she had placed there months before. With this to trade, she went to the lock.

She hadn't even known they were in human space, much less near a port. She floated out into a crowd. There were people in all possible positions and places hanging in the zero-gravity of the docks. They were all speaking at once.

It was a language she didn't know. All these sudden, pressing people unnerved her even more than the planet had. She restrained an urge to bolt back into the ship.

She had always planned to disembark at the first human colony they came to, her escape from her home complete, with fame to boot. This gabbling mob frightened and repelled her, however, so that even when someone speaking her own language addressed her, she shook her head and merely held out the metal bar.

She replied in monosyllables when addressed, looking around herself suspiciously. She did not, after all, know that this place was any better than the one she had left. The people looked as uniform as people anywhere. Her uncertainty grew: perhaps she could disembark, but *this* was not the right place. In fact, these docks looked downright dismal, dingy and small. No. Better wait. Wait for a place where she could walk in with confidence, head high.

When a runner returned with a crate of metal ingots, Theresa took it and handed out the items from the sack she had brought. She could see concern and curiosity in the eyes of the people, but chose to be suspicious of it. With a cold smile and nod to them all she climbed back into the ship. She felt she should cast some word back to them, but there was nothing to say.

*　*　*　*　*

Over the next two years Theresa came to know her alien and his habits well, and from watching him, learned the intricacies of the ship. Within limits she could anticipate him, and over the space of nine more stops in human space she traded advantageously for both of them. In civilized space she was told that she was famous, and a credit account had been set up for her (by who? she wondered) in case she decided to leave the Solitaire. The objects she traded for the alien's needs were worth fabulous amounts and most of this was being returned to her. She did not understand this, and it increased her suspicion when she entered human port. What did these unknown benefactors want with her?

The Engine of Recall

During the long periods between stars she brooded. She had taken ship with the Solitaire to escape the restrictions on her freedom she had felt at home, she thought, but now she seemed incapable of breaking out of her own exile. It was nothing the Solitaire did. He had no awareness of her as a thinking being, so there was no element of malice in his actions toward her. She was his machine.

She could talk, if only to Abbafi's phosphor image on her small viewscreen. He would ramble on about observations or problems, and she would speak into his short or long silences, about her own experiences, about home, about the people she had left behind. Her loneliness grew.

The Solitaire seemed to be having his own thoughts about companionship. He had begun building an extension onto the ship using materials milled in his workshops—a kind of hive that she recognized from Abbafi's own descriptions of his Solitaire's mating behaviour. He enlisted her as a portable winch and gopher to help him. In exhausted evenings, she reviewed Abbafi's tapes on the subject.

"They're smarter than we are." Abbafi stood in a garden structure recognizably similar to what they were building. He had let his beard grow, and he often looked around himself in a distracted way. He had been with his Solitaire nearly ten years when he taped this. "They raise children the way they do anything—as a construction project. The fact that a male and a female come together to do it seems largely irrelevant. Look at this."

"Have you ever considered," she said to his moving picture, "how becoming a hermit is just a social action? Like snubbing someone at a party? It's an attempt to communicate something, not an attempt to get out of something, out of society. You can't get out of society."

The picture now showed four Solitaires, two adults and two cubs which, like animated balls of fur, played in a maze of toys while the adults watched. The toys all had some educational function, and the cubs took them apart, rebuilt them, and tested their different modes of action.

"They learn the way we do," said Abbafi, "by example and experiment. But they do it more thoroughly. No words get in the way."

She said, "I'm thinking lately—just thinking, you understand—that somewhere along the way I've decided to say something by dropping out of the world. Maybe I'm still protesting. The terrible thing is, I suspect no one is listening."

The two cubs fell to fighting. Snarls and thuds sounded. One of the adults, a beautiful creature with brown and gray fur, stepped in and cuffed them apart. They watched it tensely for a few moments, then stalked away from each other into the strange brown foliage of the garden.

Abbafi turned his camera back on himself. "Six years since this pair met. I know these cubs like my own kids, and the one thing I know is that they'll never learn altruism. They don't help each other—it's an imposition. If you're helping one that's having difficulties with something, it interprets this as an attempt to dominate it, and it reacts violently."

She frowned at the screen. "I really doubt it's possible for a human being to say *nothing*. We're always surrounded by an invisible audience, always playing to the gallery if it's only an invention in our own heads. Do you think maybe even the hermits are playing a role for some imagined watcher, some sympathetic or conspiratorial viewer? Somehow, this idea worries me."

"Their temperaments follow the seasons, like any animal that has no sense of the Self. In rut they're extremely aggressive. The males fight. The females fight the males. A human would do best to stay away during this period." His face showed the tension that being a potential toy—maybe picked up and handled roughly at any moment—brought on.

Theresa's Solitaire walked by her clearing, carrying a long object that, after a moment's study, she recognized as a missile.

* * * * *

She spent the next several days in helpless anticipation. The ship was accelerating at a high rate. In the holo display was a small red cross, coming out to meet them: another Solitaire ship.

A space battle is like a joust—two ships pass one another on their trajectories and endeavor to intersect each other's course with a variety of energies and projectiles. Her Solitaire spent the first two days of the approach firing weapons, sometimes along carefully sighted courses and sometimes randomly. The analogue computers controlling banks of energy beams were programmed and left, and several small interplanetary probes had their guts replaced with nuclear charges. Presumably, the enemy Solitaire (they must have strayed into the territory of another male) was doing the same.

He worked quietly and carefully, belying the nature of the situation. A cloud of missiles must be heading to intercept them at thousands of kilometers per second. If they took a hit they would never even know it.

The final day, as the cross moved close enough for energy beams and interception of missiles, the Solitaire donned his space armor and spread several tonnes of sand in a pall ahead of the ship. Then he began heavy braking and maneuvering. Theresa strapped herself into one of the lockers in the airlock and tried to endure the battering to which he subjected them.

When the two ships passed (never at any time close enough to sight by eye) the myriad projectiles and missiles slammed into sand clouds and disintegrated, missed, or exploded violently off target. Energy beams laced space destroying incoming ordnance and probing beyond for the ships. For the first hour Theresa felt only the sudden accelerations of the ship, hearing only the hiss of the beam generators; later as she calculated that impact time for the clouds was at hand a series of snapping sounds and then a long shudder washed through the ship. A sudden hot flush spread through her—some radically dissipated beam had swept the ship for a fraction of a second. Then nothing but a distant roar and a slight acceleration to the side. The battle was over.

She clambered out of the locker and sailed down the tube to the centrifuge. Some force pulled her towards one wall, but she compensated easily.

In the control area the Solitaire was watching the departure of a small red cross on the display. They had both survived the pass. "Yah," she said to him. "Good for you. What did that accomplish?" He ignored her, as always.

But gravity was playing tricks. Vision—the flat floor and straight pillars—as well as habit told her one direction was down, but her inner ear contradicted her. She fell over without knowing why, banging her nose. Standing up she had to rear back as though facing down a steep slope. Once on her feet she immediately fell on her back. The slope had reversed itself.

Lying there helplessly, she watched the Solitaire crouched before the controls, doing an external scan of the ship. The distant roar gained an identity as one of the cameras showed a large maneuvering engine belching fire unchecked into the void. Somewhere a control system had been destroyed. It was flipping the ship end over end and would tear it apart before the fuel ran out.

The Solitaire tried firing the vernier jet on the opposite side of the ship to balance the effect but nothing happened. He sprang quickly along the shifting floor/wall to the airlock tube. Theresa followed, walking like a drunk on an escalator.

He took up a powerful cutting torch and some vicious-looking tools and entered the airlock. But he had neglected to take any shielding against the radiations of the nuclear engine. His helper machines were splayed against the walls, incapable of movement. Theresa forced open a locker and brought out a bundle of silvered blankets. With these and some stout lines she went out after him.

Crawling along the hull to the vernier engine was a nightmare experience. The ship's surface was a white ceiling dotted with aerials and swiveled machines in pits; the stars were spinning dizzyingly beneath and faster with each moment. Every minute the local sun rose, blazing into her eyes, but it was dim compared to the vernier jet. This faced out and away but from its cone a purely blue-white shaft of light went straight out into the black. Shadows knelt away from it. She followed the silhouette of the Solitaire, clinging to hand-holds. Out had become down, and upside down she came next to him, blankets hanging up from her waist.

He took one. Together they hung it from the cables she'd brought and it afforded some shade. The outside of her suit had started to turn brown with the radiated heat, and it wouldn't do that at less than six thousand degrees. They were still meters from the jet.

They worked without consultation, without the weak intermediary of language. Both anchored an end of one blanket to a handhold, and after watching him looping lines through an eye on one corner of the blanket she did the same to the other. He billowed his shield out before him and she let the line out slowly so that it moved with him. Hanging under the burning hull, he moved hand over hand to the engine, one safety rope attached near her, and she swung the shield like an acrobat's safety net under him. A glance at the reflected light from the hull left afterimages in her eyes. She squinted and tried to watch him.

The moment he reached the vernier he attacked it with his tools, dropping a hatch cover into the night and reaching his whole arm into the guts of the machine. Blue electric light shone there. No time for delicacy; he threw one of his giant wrenches into it and several million volts cascaded along a new course, destroying machinery and cutting in the fail-safe. The engine stopped instantly.

This didn't solve the problem. Down was still out and it competed with the rotational gravity created by the spinning living area. The gyration would be fatal unless he could start the vernier on the other side of the ship and stop the spin. He unhooked himself from the safety line and started laboriously moving around the hull, now in total darkness except when the bright star rose and sailed past. Theresa had to grope much of her way by the glow from the vernier's hot cone.

The alien worked during flashes of sunlight to start the other engine by hand. Luckily the fuel line wasn't cut and start-up power was available. She let out the blankets in anticipation of radiation and tethered his line to a handhold when he forgot to.

The engine blazed into life and he stayed with it for the time it took to stop their rotation. Shutting it down they retreated leaving the blankets and lines. Theresa was shaking with fatigue, her space-suit etched by the heat. But as they stripped in the airlock she found herself laughing and smoothing the rumpled fur on his back. "This is called 'cooperation,'" she said. "You and me, we work well together, don't we?"

He shrugged her aside (which she'd expected) but then turned and sent her a very odd, probing look. Her smile faltered.

*   *   *   *   *

"It's taken us a long time," said the man on the screen, "but we finally know who you are, Ms Lewis. Let me tell you, you've been a mystery now for a couple of years. Famous, and mysterious. An 'elemental' the press calls you, a space spirit. We at the Abbafi Memorial Institute at Titan have had a particular interest in you, but we could never anticipate where you and your friend would turn up next. This message, which is being distributed to all cooperating ports, is our compromise solution."

He had a nice face. Over his shoulder the seal of the Abbafi Institute gleamed on the wall, beside a window that showed Saturn hanging in velvet space. He terrified her.

"We understand," he continued, "you were considered a criminal in your home colony, and the Solitaire provided your means of escape. We had been puzzled as to why you refuse the refuge offered by the various ports you have visited in your journeys. We now understand you might have reason to fear extradition to your former home. We can guarantee that will not happen. In fact, as the sole living human to have spent extensive time with the Solitaires, you are priceless to us. The Institute is willing to offer you anything in our power to grant, if you will—"

"No!" She yanked out the data card. It was the twentieth of thirtieth time she had played its message. It had been slipped into her hands at the last stop, where she had felt calmly in control of herself for the first time in months, and wasn't thinking at all about her future. Then to be handed this letter . . .

She'd been happy, at last. "Why," she had said to this Director Alvarez's image more than once, "did you have to call *now?*" Earlier, she might have welcomed his offer. Now, to keep her fragile peace she had to refuse it.

At the same time, she felt triumphant, vindicated. She *was* somebody. She kept returning to the data card, feeling its physical reality, letting its palpable humanity soothe her.

In periods of brooding she watched the Solitaire watch her. He had taken on a whole new manner after the joust, showing increased wariness around her and even, on occasion, playing serious hide-and-seek with her among the pillars. Today seemed to be one of those days he chose to hide—which was fine with her. He was constantly rooting through her things, though her inventory never changed, and her attempts to make some order out of her clearing were foiled.

He'd been quite despondent after the joust. There were some repairs that he'd left until quite recently, though weeks had passed. He was probably rerouting oxygen lines again today, working listlessly, apparently just to keep busy. He couldn't possibly feel loneliness but must be frustrated at not finding a mate. He had combed thousands of light years of space, and had found only another male. She'd thought at first this might explain his new attitude to her, but as his spirits slowly improved, his paranoia towards her worsened.

There was no way to know what he was thinking. After a while she uncoiled from her position by the reading screen, sighed, and went to retrieve the letter from where she'd thrown it. Routine called; it was time for her morning run around the centrifuge. She followed a route where the sand was thinnest and her feet didn't slide under her. She dodged in between the pillars, hopping over equipment and keeping an eye out for the Solitaire's robots, which were seldom where she expected them to be. As she ran her thoughts turned again to the world she had left.

Would she really be free if she took up the Institute's offer? Even rich and lionized, she would be called on to perform for them—their trained Solitaire observer. Would it really be better than the colony of her birth, where she had chafed at the rule of law so often? She thought of those apathetic millions, could almost feel their presence beyond the hull. No. At least here she had an entire independence and uniqueness.

At least, she had thought so . . . She'd thought they were a team, interdependent, but she'd begun to doubt that lately, what with his strange attitude toward her. She was his slave—or slave to her own fears, which was an idea she shied away from. Each trip into human space she had determined to quit, but each time she finished her assignment she fluttered like a moth back to the airlock. She had reveled in the adventure, and found comfort in the Solitaire's silent presence. Now though it seemed that, far from having her own society with the alien she seemed to have been dancing around the fringes of humanity, in some way spiteful in her isolation.

As she ran by the vicinity of the control area a low buzz snapped her to attention. The holo display was showing a view of the ship with one of the Solitaire's damage symbols superimposed over the axis ring. She paused in her run and went over to look.

There was trouble in the nitrogen tanks. That was where he was working, transferring gas from cylinders damaged in the joust. But things were out of hand and nitrogen was escaping into space. There was no way to pinpoint where the alien was, but by now extensive study had familiarized Theresa with most of the control gestures. In a pinch, she thought she could control the ship itself, if crudely. She called up a pro-file of the damage.

It was presented in a series of pictures and action sequences, flicker-ing by at almost subliminal speed. She frowned. One small tank in the new section of the ship had exploded a bulkhead near it, severing some pipes. The gas flow continued unabated. She couldn't locate the Solitaire.

Running back to her clearing, she donned the deep space armour. Clumsily she trotted to the lift shaft.

A wind whistled past as she entered the airlock. From here a hexago-nal complex of pipes, cables and tanks receded into a distance obscured by white fog. The axis of the ship was choked with cold nitrogen and more was arriving from the corridor to the new section. She moved in, between plastic walls that were stretched taut outward with the pressure. At the far end of the docking corridor a white fountain signified the source of the leak: three pipes near a curving tank had been creased somehow. Theresa followed the breeze past rounded walls and spars, looping cables and power lines snaking about in partial darkness—the place where the Solitaire had been working. Snow had settled on everything.

In the hissing haze near the tank she could make out the pressurized tank that had exploded. It was part of a rack of cylinders that the Solitaire had apparently been moving out of one of the collapsible iris-airlocks. The lock seemed to have failed and sucked the rack into it, blowing one of the tanks. It was stuck in the opening and gas was howling into the vac-uum around it. Sliding sheets of plastic flapped in from all directions, sticking to everything. In time they would seal the leak automatically.

The Solitaire was pinned in the middle of the tangle of metal. He had tried to jettison the tanks manually and the frame had bent a steel bar over his arm. He was struggling desperately.

Nimbly she climbed down to him. She took a metal rod and inserted it under the bar to try and lever it away. The Solitaire turned as best he could and stared up at her.

The malevolence in his eyes stopped her. Shocked, she loosened her grip for a second and the alien hit her hard with his free arm. She sailed back and bounced off the nitrogen tank.

He tried to use the lever himself, but couldn't. But he watched her, red eyes narrowed as he hissed in pain. The cold nitrogen had frozen his fingers and he was covered all over in a white filigree of frost. He would die if she didn't get him loose immediately. But the instant she moved towards him the rod came up threateningly.

"No, no you idiot, I'm trying to help you," she said angrily. He didn't change expression.

She desperately tried to reason out his actions. This aggression had all started after the joust with that other Solitaire, and it was nothing she had done. In fact she had been instrumental in saving both their lives, taking her own initiative at a crucial moment. They had worked together without orders, as a team rather than as leader and follower. If anything she would have expected this to endear her to him.

The Solitaire looked like a tortured lion, bent over the rack. When the vernier went, and she had helped him, she'd thought it must be like pulling the thorn from the lion's paw. He should have started treating her less like a slave, should have seen her as she was, a reasoning being.

But the myth of the lion with the thorn in its paw was a story made up by and for men. It made the lion seem more like a person. Maybe it was precisely because he now saw her as a reasoning being like himself that he was hostile.

He had been treating her like another Solitaire, a clever enemy, as all Solitaires were to one another. There was no cooperation. To help was to impose.

"I stuck my neck out too far, didn't I?" she asked him. "I was never there for you, not the way you always were to me. I wasn't ever your traveling companion, like you were mine. And now I am, you hate me for it. Don't you?"

A healthy Solitaire, given the chance, would enslave a weak one. He expected that of her.

"But I'm not a Solitaire!"

And he's not a man.

He went back to levering at his trap. She looked frantically around for some recourse. The Solitaire was shaking the platform as he struggled, and the damaged cylinders were being rattled badly. If they went off, both of them would be killed and the ship would drift on forever. The rack had to be ejected immediately. By working at it she might be able to finish working the frame free. But this would kill the Solitaire.

"You really had me fooled for a while," she told him. "I thought you knew I was here. I thought you *felt* something different with me, that you had a companion. But I was never even here for you. It's not possible for you to be with someone, you're always alone even with your own children. And me, I'm never—" She laughed at herself. "It's not possible for me to ever be alone, is it? I'm always *with* someone, even if they're light years away."

He watched her over one shoulder, torso heaving in his attempt to breathe. If he were to survive this, he would be too badly crippled to run the ship. Now, he seemed to be waiting for something.

The young Solitaire killed the old, inheriting the ship, the properties and technology, and never noticing the increase in its own solitude. This was the expected thing; it was how they lived.

"I'm talking to myself," she said. His red eyes searched her unblinking for some movement, a signal of her intentions. His gaze met hers for a moment.

She saw nothing in his eyes. There was no one there at all.

Theresa went to the bent rack and pulled at it furiously. The Solitaire renewed his struggle to free himself. She bit her lip and felt the blood flow, but there was no one to appeal to about that, or about the pain in her back from straining or about the futility of it all. She just pulled.

A spar snapped and the fist of pushing air sent the massive frame outward. The Solitaire gave vent to a single scream as he fell into the cold endless void.

She hung there in the howling wind, silent herself, as the white plastic sheets sailed in to seal off the breach and the haze of gas (white like the sky of the planet they—no, she—had visited) cleared slowly from her vision. Through frost she looked down into blackness and stars at the tiny rectangle spinning away, and at the giant form held to it.

At last she pulled herself back into her ship. Exile was over.

"Allegiances" was commissioned for the anthology The Touch *(ibooks, 2000, Steven Altman, editor), a project whose profits go to benefit the war against AIDS. The stories all surround "deprivers," people who have contracted a disease that causes them to remove one of the senses of anyone they touch. We usually think that we only have five senses, but there are others, whose loss can be just as devastating . . .*

Irina stood in line, trying to imitate the look of dejected patience worn by the other women. The sky had decided to be gray today, darkening the squares of shot-out windows in the houses around the square.

"Who is working the table today?" Irina asked the woman in front of her.

"Gersamovic." The woman drew her shawl more tightly around her shoulders. "He is a butcher."

"I know."

"Six times he's made me line up. Something's not right each time."

"They say he lets younger women through."

The other gave Irina a once-over. "Oh, yes," she said. "You're his type. He'll certify your papers. But at a price."

Irina shivered. "Anything to escape this god-forsaken country." She let her eyes rest on the vista of broken rooftops that, when she was a girl, had glowed gold like magic in the evening light. She saw only gray slate and upthrust splinters now.

A commotion had broken out on the other side of the square. Probably another squabble over food.

"I hope somebody kills him soon," said somebody behind Irina.

"Hush," said the first woman. Irina didn't know either of them; the town was overrun with strangers these days. "Don't even think anything like that. Ostovac's men have immunity. Even the UN won't touch them."

"Yeah, I hear he had his own lieutenant shot. An old boyhood chum. Dumped the body in the river, then went swimming."

"Ostovac," said Irina under her breath.

They were nearly at the head of the line. Just a few more minutes, and she would have what she wanted . . . or not.

"*Witch!*"

All heads turned. A man had burst into the empty center of the square. He stood, a gray pillar in the red mud. He held a rifle in his hands.

"I know you're here!" he shouted. "Show yourself, or by God I'll kill all of you."

"That's Terajic," said the woman behind Irina.

Other men, members of Ostovac's private police force, ran over. Two of them began struggling with the man.

"You don't understand! She's here! She'll come for you too if we don't find her now." Terajic broke free, staggered, and raised his rifle. It was pointed at the line of visa applicants.

Irina and the other women hit the dirt. Nobody screamed, the way they might have in the early days of the war. There was a shot, then another. Then only the sound of men cursing.

Irina ventured a peek. Terajic was down, slumped with the unnatural looseness she recognized as death. The other soldiers were clumped around him, babbling to one another, shouting and accusing, ignoring the still crouching women.

Gersamovic stood up from the metal table they'd hauled into the street that morning. "Get him out of here!" he shouted. "You! Tell Ostovac Terajic's dead. Nobody's to blame, I saw the whole thing. Go on! Get on with your business."

He sat down again, puffing out his swarthy cheeks. "Come on! Next!"

The women stood. Irina heard someone behind her weeping. The two she had been talking to wore pragmatic frowns, like herself, as they examined their muddied clothes.

"What was that all about?"

"What do you mean? Isn't it obvious? He snapped."

"But why?"

Irina looked down her nose at them. "Guilt," she said, with satisfaction.

*   *   *   *   *

"Next!"

It was her turn. Irina walked slowly up to Gersamovic, smiling as winsomely as she could. The effort to hold the expression hurt her face.

"I haven't seen you around here before," said Gersamovic. He took a posture characteristic of him, fingers wrapped around the far ends of the desk to emphasize his size as he leaned forward. "Just arrive?"

"Actually, I grew up here." *So I've known the alleys to take to avoid you.* "I've seen *you.*"

"I'll bet you have. So you want to leave, do you?"

Irina looked around pointedly, and shrugged.

Gersamovic laughed. They said he laughed when he shot people. She didn't place much stock in stories, but he was Ostovac's man, and part of the occupying force. Irina didn't need extra incentive to hate him.

"Tell you what," he said. "I'll stamp your little paper there, and you can go see Ostovac tomorrow. But first you see me. Tonight."

She held out her papers, unable to continue smiling. Gersamovic's stamp was necessary for her to get in to see Ostovac for the actual emigration interview. It was joke bureaucracy of course, there to satisfy the letter, and flout the spirit, of the UN peace terms.

Irina turned her hand as Gersamovic reached for the papers, so that his fingers collided with the inside of her wrist. She let her skin slide over his fingertips and dropped the papers in the center of the desk.

He blinked at her, squeezed his eyes shut for a second, then looked down at the papers.

Mechanically, he reached out and slammed the stamp down on the top sheet.

"Thank you." She snatched up the papers and walked quickly in the direction of the crowd that was gathering because of the shooting. She spared a quick glance at Terajic, who was being dragged away by three cursing men. She smiled.

When she reached the crowd she looked back at Gersamovic. He was staring at the face of the woman who had come after Irina. His face held an expression of almost comic bewilderment.

Suddenly he stood up. "Shit!" His chair toppled back, and the woman recoiled with a shriek.

"Stop her! Where is she?"

Two of his men ran up. "Who?"

"The woman! The one who was just here. Where did she go?"

The men exchanged a shrug. They had been watching Terajic's corpse leave the square.

"What's she look like?"

"Like . . . like . . ." Gersamovic's face was turning red.

Irina smiled. She was dressed with absolute conservatism today. She could be any of these women, or they her. Only her face might betray her, to a man who could remember it.

In the moment when she touched him, Gersamovic had lost that ability.

It was terrifying but exhilarating too to stand there while Gersamovic stalked up and down the square, grabbing people and staring at them as if he didn't know what he was seeing. Well, he didn't, in fact, and when his eyes lit upon her there was no recognition in them at all.

"What's she look like?"

"I don't know." Finally he stood there, shaking, tears starting in the corners of his eyes. "I don't know, I don't know, I don't know."

Satisfied that he wasn't going to seize upon an innocent bystander at random, Irina turned and walked away. She let one hand caress the papers in her pocket. She was one step closer.

* * * * *

When the emptiness came over her late that night she was ready for it; this was the third time she had deliberately used her curse, and she was beginning to understand the way of it. She lay in bed, biting her lower lip, blinking away the tears but curiously calm under them.

Yes, there was a pattern to this. First the anger came, and the gloating ambition to take revenge on the invaders who had destroyed her family and her life. She would walk the streets tingling with anticipation, feeling that for once her affliction was her ally. She would hunt her prey single-mindedly, and in the moment of touching them, feel a terrible satisfaction.

Then, in the night, would come the despair. She had destroyed another man's life, and still her son remained dead. No amount of revenge upon those who had killed Mikhail would bring him back.

Irina let herself cry. Her breath steamed in the dark air. It was utterly silent after curfew; she was sure everyone within a block would hear her, but who would notice one more woman crying these days?

The first time, she had wanted to die. She hadn't believed she could deliberately do to these men what she had accidentally done to her own husband and son years ago. Do it—and like it. She was evil, an abomination.

Irina had never told her old friends here the truth about her return to her home town. Her husband had cheated on her, she'd told them, and lied well enough to get custody of Mikhail at the end of it all. They believed her; she was shattered enough for the story to be convincing.

No one asked why she wore long gloves even in the summer, and took no new lovers. People here were used to the strange grief of widows and cast-outs. She moved among them like a ghost, tracing long circles through town that began alone at her front door and ended there the same way, carrying the few spoils she could afford from occasional accounting jobs. She read, she watched the streams of people, and she hid her face from the sight of lovers kissing.

She hardly noticed the war until the day that refugees from her husband's town began streaming down the road. They were all women or girls. The men were dead. The boys were dead. Ostovac had come, and purged the countryside in the name of his own people.

Taking station in a field on the edge of Brcko, Ostovac had made the townspeople parade past him. He separated them by ethnic type. His own people he sent back into the town. Of the others, the women were sent down the road, while the men—including her husband, who could not tell invader from neighbor—were marched to the woods behind the field. Irina heard that the gunshots went on for hours.

Ostovac was indiscriminate. He allowed himself to make mistakes, erring on the side of thoroughness. Mikhail was dead, along with a dozen boys who were probably Serbian, and could have been saved.

Irina had let that knowledge prey on her. In the silent times before dawn, when she couldn't sleep, she would sometimes admit to herself that she felt better blaming Ostovac's men for shooting Mikhail. It lessened her own guilt. The more she focused on that blame, the less she hated herself.

So she had begun to stalk him. And tonight she finally had the pretext she needed to get within touching distance. These hands that had maimed her husband and son, forever separating her from them, could at least be revenged on the one who had killed Stephan and Mikhail.

Or so she told herself, as she lay hugging herself, staring at the ceiling and crying. It had taken weeks for her to recover the anger, and strike again after the first time. Days, after each of the next two. Meanwhile she would wallow in self-loathing and horror. She felt it now, overwhelmingly.

She closed her eyes and gritted her teeth. Gersamovic would talk. They would figure it out. If she was going to go after Ostovac, it would have to be tomorrow. She couldn't wait to feel better about herself, or remind herself of all the reasons why he deserved it. She was going to have to decide if she was going to do it despite her guilt.

Irina didn't sleep that night.

*   *   *   *   *

Most of the houses in the town were of new, cheap construction. Irina had grown up in one of these—cinder block walls, metal roof, some attempt at ornamentation around the windows. The house Ostovac had taken over was old, at least two hundred years. Its roof had been replaced with corrugated iron recently, but the windows were of leaded glass that looked pebbly and uneven, as if those bullets had miraculously missed the original glass all these years. As she approached she could make out a patina of bullet holes in the whitewash, and if she looked closely she recognized hundreds of older dents in the stonework, made by bullets in previous wars. The house had stood through all of it; who knew how many times it had changed sides?

Two of Ostovac's thugs stood guard behind the concrete pylons that ringed the front door. Although hostilities were officially over, they were armed to the teeth; she even spotted a rocket launcher leaning in the shadows near the door.

She held out her papers, looking closely at the face of the man as she said her name. "Irina Ulaj." Had they made the connection between herself and Gersamovic? It wouldn't matter if they figured it out in the next ten minutes; it was just a case of whether she could get in this door.

The guard made a good show of looking over the papers, then shrugged indifferently. "Go in." But he didn't hand the papers back. She eased around him, thankful again for the cold weather that allowed her to cover so much of her skin.

Inside she smelled cigar smoke, cooked sausage and the particular, unidentifiable smell that distinguishes individual houses. It was cold in here, almost as cold as outside. Five men bundled in greatcoats were playing cards in the living room; sunset light through the windows made crosses on the far wall. One looked up, said, "Upstairs, second room," and went back to the game.

Ostovac had made his office in the smallest room, presumably because it was easy to heat. As she entered he sat in a metal-frame chair with his hands behind his head, back near the small fireplace in an obvious attempt to soak up as much heat as possible. He was more than an arm's length from the battered desk strewn with papers; she wondered why he didn't just drag the desk closer to the fire?

There were two other chairs in front of the desk; aside from that the room was empty except for pyramids of paper stacked everywhere. The floor was wood. The wallpaper was a dull green.

Only his eyes moved to follow her as she entered and sat at the desk. He had a broad face and black hair, with the wide moustache that seemed like a military standard these days. He reminded her of Stalin, and she remembered reading how Stalin's mask of calm had become so second nature that even during the war he neither wept nor smiled at misfortune or victory. God forbid any son of hers should grow up this way.

"My name is Irina Ulaj."

"I know." He continued watching her. His voice was a baritone, pleasant even. His continued gaze unnerved her, and deliberately, she stripped off her gloves, allowing herself a glance at the white skin of her fingers as she laid them on her knee. Her weapons were ready.

"They . . . they took my papers at the door."

"You want to leave the country."

"Yes. I want . . . a passport."

"All right." He finally moved, hopping the chair up to the desk where he picked up an envelope. He tossed it across the table; she caught it as it was about to fall off the edge.

He's tense, Irina realized. She cleared her throat. "That's it? That's all there is to it?"

"No." He looked somewhere distant over her shoulder as he said, "You'll have to earn it."

Just like Gersamovic, she thought. But her mouth was dry as she said, "How?"

Ostovac finally looked at her. He allowed himself a small, ironic smile. "By doing what you presumably came here to do anyway."

Her heart began to race. "And that was?"

"Whatever it is you did to Gersamovic yesterday."

Irina's mind went utterly blank. All she was aware of was his eyes, dark and calm, gazing into hers.

"You killed my son," she heard herself say.

Ostovac lost the smile. He sat back. "I've killed many women's sons," he said, not proudly, but matter of fact.

"Other women's sons are not my concern," she said. She had crossed the Rubicon; she was dead now, or worse, so it no longer mattered what she said. She would say what she felt. "I don't want impersonal justice for you, not some anonymous war-crimes trial. No, I want you to know that it is for Mikhail my son that . . ." *I'm going to do this,* she finished in her mind as she silently watched him unbutton his shirt cuff and stretch out his arm.

"How is it done?" he asked mildly. "Is it enough for you to touch my hand?"

A momentary silence hung in the air.

"So now you mock me." He was going to snatch his hand away at the last minute. Ostovac was an adrenalin addict, she realized. Of course, what other man would rise to his sort of position?

"I'm not mocking you. I saw what you did to Gersamovic. We had a doctor look at him. He said it's something called aphasia. He said he'd seen it before in a soldier who had the side of his head shot off.

Gersamovic can't recognize faces anymore, and he has trouble with names—though he did remember yours from the papers. Good thing. He's sedated right now, by the way. It's hit him hard."

"Good." She was surprised at the viciousness in her own voice.

"You know why I became a soldier?"

"I don't care. Did Mikhail know?"

Ostovac sat back. "Ah. Well, that's hit the nail on the head, hasn't it? But let me explain: my parents were killed when I was twelve. It was one of you who shot them. Who? I don't know. Might have been someone you know, a relative, your father even. I didn't know, that's the problem. Every day while I was growing up I saw you people, I wondered, *is that one there remembering how he shot my parents? Is he laughing at me inside?* Somewhere out there was the man, or woman. I couldn't hit them directly. But I had to hit them."

"By killing my son."

Ostovac shrugged. "It can take a lifetime for a man to grow up. It took me my whole life to reach this point—this day, this room and you."

"What do you mean?" She had no idea what he was talking about, and that was more frightening than any certainty about her fate might have been. Irina realized she had a death-grip on the arms of her chair. *Well,* it *will never identify me,* she thought, and almost laughed at the absurdity of the thought.

"You see," Ostovac went on, "you and I are both driven by the same thing: revenge. Even a month ago, I would have said there was no difference between us. I'd have shot you there in that chair without a second thought."

"So? Why don't you?" she managed to say.

His eyes were darting around the room again. "I'm sure you heard about it. Two weeks ago I gave the order to have an old friend shot. It's raised my standing in the eyes of our fighters, because Vlacic was a peace-monger. Well, maybe. At the time that was the way I was thinking.

Afterward . . . I remembered our times together. We drank together—here, actually, down the street. Used to be an inn, but of course it was burned down in the first days of the war. I remember that night . . ." His eyes focused on her again. "Was that revenge? I don't think so."

He laughed, nervously shuffling the papers on the desk. "After that I thought about killing myself. I never had any trouble shooting you people. Christ would have us make no distinction between others, but I do. I do, and I can't stop myself. I look at you and I see a damned Croat. I'm not going to lie to myself, I'll never forgive and forget. So what, then? Shoot myself and go to Hell? I've seen men do that.

"I would have, though, except that something happened. One day Malacek went crazy. He didn't recognize anybody, started shooting wildly. We had to take him down. Two days later, same thing happens to Terajic. But all he did was babble about witches: he meets a mystery woman, and she steals peoples' faces. Until yesterday when he lost it in the market square."

Ostovac fumbled in his khaki shirt, and drew out a cigarette. Absently he offered it to her and she shook her head. He lit it and blew smoke down at his lap.

"At first I was horrified. To be unable to tell the enemy from your own! But as I thought about it, the words 'all are one' kept coming back to me. The more I thought about it, the more it seemed like the answer I had been looking for."

Irina stood up, knocking her chair over. "No! I'll not save you from yourself!"

He had rolled himself back to the fire. Now he absently put one hand down to the warmth while staring at her fixedly over the glowing end of his cigarette.

"I could force you," he said. "All I have to do is grab your hand, that's true isn't it?"

She stood poised, ready to run for the hall. He could shout, and his men would block her way in an instant.

"Well, I asked myself this morning, when does a man begin to atone for himself? You have to draw the line somewhere. Go if you want, and maybe I will shoot myself. Just answer me one thing first."

"What?"

"If you were my mother, what would you want Irina Ulaj to do?"

"Bastard!" She launched herself around the desk. Ostovac didn't flinch as she raised her hand, then she slapped him. He fell off the chair, and her own hand stung with the force of the blow.

He lay on his side, hand to his cheek. Then, he slowly lowered it, and levered himself up on his elbow. His face was utterly serious, and all he did was look at her.

Trembling, Irina reached out, and took his face in her hands.

*　*　*　*　*

It took hours before the feeling that she was having a heart attack subsided. The pain in her chest was intense, but she finally knew it for what it was: grief. So she walked with it, not seeing the faces of the people she passed, or the bullet-scarred facades of the houses. Eventually she found herself sitting in her own parlor, the envelope from Ostovac on the desk before her.

They had just let her go. That seemed the cruelest thing now; she had been told to live with it all. Ostovac's men didn't know what she had done, and she didn't know how long he was going to try to keep it from them. It couldn't work for long. Unless she used the contents of this envelope now, and left the country, they would be coming for her soon.

Maybe that would be best.

As evening fell she rose automatically and lit a lamp. In its light she had a sudden moment of perception, seeing this small room as it had been before the war, during one of the periodic blackouts that plagued the towns during the otherwise peaceful Communist period.

Irina and her mother had sat together in this kitchen with a candle between them, joking to pass the time. Her mother had told Irina how she had baked with her mother before they had electricity; in the evenings they would wrap the cooling bread for tomorrow's market. Her mother associated candle light with such times.

Irina herself would forever associate it with the war.

What would mother want for me?

Tears starting in her eyes, she plunked herself down at the table and tore open the envelope before she let herself think too much about it.

A travel visa fell out.

A second visa fell out.

Irina blinked. Was this a mistake? Ostovac must have given her the wrong papers. She picked up the visas.

One was made out to *Irina Ulaj.*

The other was made out to *Mikhail Ulaj.* It had a sheet of paper clipped to it.

Hands shaking, she spread out the paper by the candle. The first thing she saw was Ostovac's signature on the bottom of the white sheet.

Irina Ulaj, he had written. *When I learned it was you, I checked your background. They told me about your husband and son, so I checked our records.*

Atonement has to start somewhere.

The only other writing on the page was an address.

Apartment 12

782 Byelosj Street

Brcko

Irina began to cry. It felt like she had waited to weep like this for five years.

"Mikhail, Mikhail," she murmured through her tears, and for the first time in years she knew she was not speaking to the dead. "You won't know me."

The Engine of Recall

Mikhail wouldn't recognize her, no matter how much time she spent with him. No matter how she loved him, his eyes would never light up when she entered the room. The last time she had seen him, he had barely known the sound of her voice. By now, even her name might be a fading memory.

Ostovac had stepped willingly into that same shadow world. He no longer wanted to be able to tell people apart. Such blindness was his only hope of salvation.

Funny, that. As her tears dried, she found herself stroking the visas, thinking about Ostovac walking into the night, hands outstretched for the touch of another human—innocently indiscriminate, non-judgmental, pure.

Had she ever held the hand of another and not judged them, by age, race, sex or color? Of course not; and at last she knew that she had walked away from her husband and her son not because she felt guilt at what she had done to them, but because she could not bear the thought that *they* could not judge her.

Because they would not punish her, she had punished herself.

By morning, she was packed and on the road to Brcko.

Like the hidden valleys of Titan or the smouldering kernel of Chernobyl, the cloudscapes of Jupiter have always fascinated me. They are a place as real as the places we know, however inaccessible they may be. Am I alone in dreaming of what it would be like to walk among those clouds?

"The Pools of Air" was my first anthology sale, to Tesseracts3 (Press Porcepic, 1991). The Tesseracts series of annual anthologies has been a tremendously influential contribution to Canadian SF, and I was very excited to be accepted for this edition. As it turned out, this publication opened many doors to me and in a very real sense, launched my career.

✶ ✶ T H E   P O O L S   O F   ✶ ✶
A I R

About to shoot from the unique angle this window presented, Megan Scholes put the camera down instead and wiped at her eyes. *Oh, Hell,* she thought, *what good is this doing?*

She slumped against the window, motionless until she realized she was recording a nice shot of the floor. "Damn."

The window showed appalling wreckage, all that was left of the forward crew compartment of the Wave Rider. According to Moore, the aircraft's weather radar had likely just not believed whatever it had seen coming. Large solid objects were not supposed to exist in Jupiter's atmosphere. The Rider had not tried to avoid it.

Turbulence jarred up through her feet. From the doorway, her Talent on this shoot, Vandna, said, "We seem to have a new problem."

Megan gnawed a fingernail, and stared at her. Still in her exotic Jupiter gear, Vandna stood framed between two hulking machines by the yellow-chevroned door. The turbulence disturbed the oxygenated liquid, called hemolin, which they used for air on the Wave Rider. The ripples made her shimmer in a kind of glycerin haze. *Nice shot,* thought Megan automatically.

"What?" She realized she'd missed something.

"Woolgathering? Moore says something is spraying out of an aft bulkhead. He thinks it's hemolin."

"Oh, shit." Vandna popped out the door, and Megan followed. She was very tired; the buoyancy of this liquid she breathed offset the extra gee-and-a-half Jupiter pulled her body with, but according to Moore that only worked for her outsides. Her joints ached, her stomach felt full and she suffered periods of dizziness.

Vandna moved easily in this strange place, but she'd been to the Wave Riders before. That was why Megan had sought her out to narrate her documentary. Very young, pretty and brainy, Vandna was the perfect figure to place against the terrible hammer-heads of Jupiter's cloudscape.

Vandna clattered lithely down a stairway. "It'll be bad if we lose the stuff," she said. "Not only do we have to fall back on gaseous air, it means we lose the body support. It'll be the wheelchairs for us soon." She sounded tense, but not overly so. Megan envied her.

Vandna led her to a frost-walled passage lined with windows. The frost stood out horizontally in slabs which they had to edge around. Moore stood scraping at a window. He'd uncovered all but this one; the others were starting to frost over already. He pointed with one blunt finger. "Look at that."

Megan took the window next to his and looked out.

They were facing aft, away from the carnage that filled the forward portholes. She could see the sharp horizon of the Wave Rider's wing, and a blur of heat-haze past it, then the full sweep of Jupiter's skyline. A solid-looking wall of brown thunderhead large as a continent bulked up as background to a vista of every other possible kind of cloud. Nearby, whipping past quickly, were deceptively earth-like puffballs, huge and pretty. They receded in the plane of the Wave Rider's flight, grown smaller and fading together, until far away, well under the brown thunderhead, they merged into a white line across the sky. Below them herring-bone shapes of pale blue made a false crisscross landscape.

And above, the sky glowed like a Michelangelo ceiling. Clouds opened on distant heavens and pavilions of air, blue and green and shining gold, with the sun a jewel set in rings of flashing crystal.

Where Moore pointed, a thin stream of white cascaded into the Wave Rider's slipstream, scarves of snow tearing up and vanishing against the skyline.

"We've got to find out where that's coming from," said Moore. He scratched at the glass. "A lower level. I think that's where they keep the hemolin aerators." Glancing at Megan, he scowled. "Why are you still carrying that?" He pointed to the camera. "We have more important things to do now than take pictures."

"Sorry," said Megan nervously. "What do we do? You're the expert."

"I wish. I'm a meteorologist, I'm no engineer." He grimaced. "Sorry. I know where to take a Wave Rider, but damned if I know how they work."

"There's a stair back the way we came," prompted Vandna.

"All right." They followed her. Megan touched Moore's shoulder. "You feel like you should know what to do?"

He closed a hand on hers. "I work with the Wave Riders. I'm crew. You people are passengers. So I'm responsible."

"Get it out of your head. Not," she added ruefully, "that I have any idea what to do either. But who could have seen this coming?"

"I should have. It's my job."

Down the stairs a gallery looked out over silver pipes beaded with tiny bubbles, arrayed in a dim hall. A rushing sound, sharp through the liquid, came from the far end of the place. Vandna had stopped, distressed.

They stood looking for the source of the sound for a minute. Then Moore shrugged and went down the ladder to the floor of the tank room. They watched him thread his way through the metal cylinders until he vanished behind one. A moment later furious swearing drifted back to them—then, surprisingly, Moore's laughter. Megan and Vandna looked at one another, then clattered down after.

He stood over a set of frosted white pipes which emerged from the floor. "I forgot," he laughed, "the basic job of the Wave Rider is to refine helium 3 from the atmosphere, right? These pipes are from the separators; I guess the Wave Rider is just lightening up its load by jettisoning the stuff in the tanks."

"So we're safe?" asked Vandna.

"For now, yes. God," he said, wiping his eyes. "You realize we've been awake almost thirty hours now? We're not even *doing* anything, just running around looking out the windows. It's crazy."

Megan nodded. They needed sleep. But she wasn't reassured by these pipes or his explanation of what was happening. She was terrified; but Vandna seemed calm, and if she could be Megan was determined to as well.

It was only a minor setback. That was all she would allow it to be.

* * * * *

Leaving them asleep in the locker they'd made into a temporary bedroom, Megan slipped next door to review her footage. She told herself she should check the rushes as usual, because to give way to panic the way the other two were, would be unprofessional. But in fact, she couldn't sleep. She needed the reassurance that her images were safe.

Moving by touch in the dark room, she hooked her monitor up to the camera and switched it on. The bright, diffuse light of the screen unveiled jumbled boxes and pipes. She drew her jacket around her—though it gave no warmth in the hemolin—and hunkered down to watch the screen.

The first shot was of the scramjet and she almost fast-fowarded past it. But she had to be sure it was all here. The scramjet was shown in orbit. Vandna's voice-over mumbled faintly; she turned it up.

"—Are the only way down to Jupiter and back. We'll have a long fall, and when we arrive at the flying factory (we call them Wave Riders here) we'll be at the most inhospitable place ever visited by humans. Outside the Wave Rider's hull, there's fatal cold, an atmosphere of chemicals in constant hurricane motion and gravity two-and-a-half times as strong as Earth's—"

She rewound a bit to the going away party at the orbital tanker. She'd recorded it on a whim. She hadn't known either Vandna or Moore, their JoviCorp supervisor, before the shoot. Vandna was a Joviology student who was already notorious for having visited the planet as a child. Moore was a taciturn bear of a man who avoided the press almost fearfully. By the end of the party they felt a bit like a team. They were daring Jupiter together, after all. The adventure would put them in the ranks of a brave few.

The hemolin slipping around her felt strange—disturbing. This was the first time she'd had a problem with it. Megan shrugged angrily and went on.

Shots from the scramjet of their approach to the Rider: it grew from a tiny arrow-head shape to a giant hypersonic vessel, piercing the atmosphere under perpetual lightning and the slewing light of an eight-hour day. The scramjet fell into a zone of calm behind it, and landed smoothly on its back. She remembered the panic of waiting for the *clunk* of touchdown.

The Wave Rider soared on through a night and another swift day. There was nothing to see except cloud, but clouds were heavy here, not the diaphanous creatures of Earth's sky; they collided, and abraded past each other, and tore into sullen shreds of storm and evil color. The Wave Rider threaded through them, measuring out its drops of Helium-3, priceless fuel for the orbiting industries. Alone in the giant automated plane, with Moore as guide, Megan and Vandna did their narrative head-shots and walking tours of a place only maintenance robots and scientists had ever seen. Vandna performed well for the camera. Megan posed her against the backdrop of Jupiter's sky, and shot scene after scene until they were both exhausted.

They were back here, in the aft storage warren, when something hit the Wave Rider. A meteor, was Moore's theory; but Megan had been shooting through a skylight and had seen nothing overhead. Suddenly, there was a terrible lurch and a sound like wailing cats followed by a *bang*. The skylight was obscured by black smoke.

Whatever it was, it scored the nose of the Wave Rider and plowed right through the forward compartment. Emergency doors had thudded down across all the passages that led back to it; but those same passages were their only way of reaching the scramjet.

Megan watched her footage to the end, then rewound and started over. The feeling of uneasiness in her stomach was growing. She reviewed the shots more closely, trying to concentrate. The more she concentrated, the worse she felt.

It was the hemolin. The way it moved over her skin, oily, like a total rainfall, reminded her so much of hunkering down, under a leaden sky . . .

She sat back, feeling for the camera. It was safe. So many times she'd used it as a talisman. She'd hid behind it when she was a war correspondent as though by recording what she saw she could be safe. The camera was her second self, the footage, an immortal half.

But too vividly, the dimness, the feel of the hemolin, and her desperation—they all brought back a memory she had not wanted to keep.

Her hands were shaking as she thumbed the monitor off. The screen faded just as sharper light cut across the floor from the door.

"Megan?" Moore was silhouetted in the doorway. "Are you okay?"

* * * * *

"Listen," she said. "I'm terrified. I can't believe this feeling, like I'm going to explode."

Moore nodded. "Me too."

"How do you handle it?" She drew her knees up and sat with her arms wrapped around them, watching him.

He made a vague gesture. "I've . . . been scared like this before. The situation was different, but the feeling's here again."

"Tell me."

"On Mercury. A warehouse I worked at. There was this giant iron bin full of ball bearings. Millions of the suckers. I was working on the fifth level of a set of metal-floored galleries. The bin was eight levels high. Anyway, there was a quake and the bin ruptured. I hear this sound like the surf, and turn around to see a tide of bright little balls pouring at me. On Mercury the bearings didn't weigh much, but taken together they would have torn me to shreds.

"I had my back to the gallery railing. And somehow—I don't know how—I found myself hopping over it. Could kill myself on the floor below too, cause all the bearings were going to fall on me. So I grabbed the edge of the platform and swung under. There was a strut supporting the floor and I held it with just the tips of my fingers. I hung there and watched this flood of metal go past, right in front of my nose. It took the rail with it—*chunk*. The noise was awful.

"Anyway . . . they had to pry my fingers off the strut later."

"God." She reached out. He took her hand and pressed his face to it.

"The thing is, it was *funny*. It was a big joke in the cafeteria later. A dumb way to die. And in the end, it was really that which scared me, and it scared me much later, only when I'd had a chance to think about it."

She nodded. "I—was just remembering . . . .When I was a child, huddling in the rain in the back of my parents' building, trying to see the pictures in a family album. My mother had thrown it out. It was all pictures of my brother. He'd disappeared during the Bolivian water war. The pictures were all just painful memories for her, but not to me. I wanted him back. By the time I found out and ran out to get it the album was soaked and crushed. I remember pulling the crumpled pictures out in the rain, and just crying and crying over them. Somewhere, I still have them.

"People accused me of thrill-seeking," she said, "said I'd be stupid to come here. I guess I was, you know? I had to, but I don't know why. The idea that something isn't recorded, isn't known . . . it's terrifying. But now I've gotten you and Vandna into trouble."

"It's not so bad," he said. "The Wave Rider—I don't know if flight control is damaged. It could keep flying for years."

"That's not reassuring."

"But they might rescue us."

"They can't land. Our scramjet's still topside, and there's only that one mooring spot. They could never do a mid-air transfer, you know that."

"Maybe we can get to the scramjet."

She drew back. "The access passages go to the forward deck. That's gone."

"I mean from here. Outside."

"*Outside?* You mean walk on top of the waverider? We're hypersonic!"

"Yes, but—"

She stopped his mouth with her hand. "I don't want to be snatched into the sky. I don't want to fall into Jupiter, and drown in air. Better here."

He relaxed against her. "We have to try something."

"I can't think about this. Later. Later."

A slight sound came from the door. Megan looked up. "Vandna? Moore, she's alone." She ran to the door.

Vandna stood apologetic and awkward in the hall. She smiled tearfully at Megan. "I can't sleep."

"I'm so sorry, Vandna. Come in."

* * * * *

A rushing sound woke her. Disoriented, Megan fought the sheets, which bellied and swam oddly. She got them off, and they slid to the floor and crawled along it. Megan screamed and hopped back, hitting Moore and waking him.

"What the hell is it?"

He followed her pointing finger. A slow rattling vibration came through the floor as she put her feet to it; the sheets had stopped moving, pressed against the door of the locker.

Moore went to the door and opened it. He staggered forward and something mirror-like and quivering shot into the room over his head.

Vandna hopped up from the floor. "Air!"

Moore gripped the doorjamb and looked back. "We're losing our hemolin. There really was a leak."

Megan could feel the liquid flowing around her like a strong breeze. "We can breathe that air no problem, can't we?"

"Probably not. I expect the bubbles are full of hydrogen, not oxygen. That's if this stuff is coming from outside, which is likely." He gestured at them to hurry; they practically fell against him as more giant bubbles swept in overhead. "Grab my hands." They daisy-chained into the hall, fighting the current. The sheets slipped past Megan's ankles, flew off and nipped around a corner of the hall.

"Hurry," snapped Moore. "The hemolin could react with the bubbles; it's full of oxygen, right? It'd be like being inside a gasoline bomb."

"We have to try the air chambers," He pulled them down the hall away from the hemolin's drag. "Topside. There's a set of airlocks above which it's nitrogen and oxygen, earthside normal. Those areas are almost never used, 'cause they're in full gravity."

"Let's go then," said Vandna.

"Wait! My camera." Megan, at the back, let go. Moore cursed, ducking bubbles. She let herself slide back to the room, and found the camera just edging its way out the door. She grabbed it protectively. Moore scowled.

"It's important," she said defensively. "It's why we came here."

They mazed through the halls, ducking hydrogen bubbles. Soon the upper quarter of the space was empty of hemolin and they had to walk bent over, fighting the current but afraid to stick their heads up.

At the end of a hall Megan hadn't been in before, was a crimson-chevroned door. The flattened pyramid sign for high gravity was stenciled across it. Moore got the door open just as the lights went out. They tumbled through. Red trouble lamps lit the hall they'd left.

Megan got the camera to her shoulder and recorded the sight as the doors closed.

In darkness, she heard Moore turning some kind of wheel. Light split above them. The level of hemolin dropped with a lurch. "Hold your breath," commanded Moore. "When you get up this ladder pitch over the side and empty your lungs. Like you were trained."

Oh boy. Megan had hoped to cross this bridge in happier circumstances, and had tried to put it out of her mind. The oxygenated hemolin filled her lungs, and if she was going back to air she had to drain them. She remembered when she was first fitted for contact lenses. She'd fought, her body reacting against foreign objects going in her eyes. This, she imagined, would be much worse.

But Vandna went up the ladder into what was presumably now safe air, and flopped over the side at the top of the shaft. Moore waved for her to follow.

"Shit." She went up, and as she left the hemolin felt the brutal drag of full gravity again. Moore put his hands under her and pushed, but she was now dragging weight equal to his own added on hers. She strained halfway up the ladder, dropped the camera, and opened her mouth to gasp—drawing nothing. Crystalline liquid poured down her chin and she fell back into the hard bath.

She couldn't talk, and pushed her head under the stuff, sucking it back into her lungs. The level was dropping, and she had to curl up on the floor. Moore's hands dragged at her, and his voice came distorted and faint from above. He sounded desperate.

I'm going to die, she thought. The hemolin was draining away around her, and Jupiter was reaching up to press her to him. She couldn't have the strength to resist that.

Moore stopped tugging at her. She saw his hand come down through the glistening meniscus and take the camera. He pulled it up, and first one, then his other leg lifted out as he climbed the ladder.

He's leaving me. She rolled on her back, and watched his distorted form move up the ladder. She felt outraged. And why was he was taking the camera?

The scramjet. He must still have that mad idea of going outside to get to it. He hoped to survive, and he was abandoning her in favor of her work.

Enraged, she dragged herself to her knees, and tilted her head back as the hemolin poured from her nose. She would show him she was better than the camera. She clamped her hands onto the ladder and hauled herself to her feet. In lurches, she went up. Then four hands were on her and she jumped, sprawling painfully over the side of a hatch.

She hit her nose on metal flooring, and in frantic retches, let go the stuff in her lungs. Hands put a yellow hose in her mouth. Dimly remembering the lessons they'd given her, she let it slide down her throat. A horrible suffocating sensation overwhelmed her.

* * * * *

She could breathe. For a while she concentrated on that.

Moore sat, a frown creasing his features. Windows in this small chamber let in pale sunlight. He was tightening the straps of a sort of sandal. Black elastic material swathed his calves and thighs. More black material lay flat beside him.

It was the same Jupiter gear Vandna had worn throughout the shoot. The girl stood now, looking down at Megan in concern. She wore arched sandals which bound the ankle and calf and tight knee-length shorts of a material that put pressure at all the right points. She was adjusting a corset and wired bra. A kind of torc rested on her shoulders, from whch graceful curves of white metal curled down her arms to the fingerless gloves which flickered as she tightened her straps. Similar loops outlined her thighs and swept up from the small of her back. The vocoder which allowed her to speak under the hemolin was a gold disc on her throat.

"There's more of these," said Vandna without preamble. Megan felt ashamed of herself. "Better put one on."

Moore pulled black bands up his arms to cover his biceps. "A bit better," he said. "How do you feel, Megan?"

"You honestly think," she said, sitting up awkwardly, "that we can walk to the scramjet?"

"It's not a question of whether we *can* or not," he said in a reasonable tone. "We have to."

She dumbly took the gear Vandna handed her.

"Look," said Moore. "The point is, you can always turn around, but never go back. We're in the same position as the Wave Rider now: no matter what happens, we have to keep going forward. That might kill us, but staying still *will* kill us."

"I know," said Vandna tightly. "I know, all right?" They'd been talking about this already, Megan realized.

"Look, it's not so bad as it sounds," grunted Moore, standing. "A Wave Rider flies belly on. The shockwave is deflected around the edge of the hull. Because of our angle of attack and velocity, objects on the upper hull are actually in near vacuum. That's why things like the scramjet are safe there. Gravity keeps us on the hull itself, so there's not too much likelihood of being swept off."

"But there's all sorts of wreckage all over," said Vandna. "Some of it's cutting into the slipstream."

". . . Which is causing turbulence, sure. The Wave Rider can obviously correct enough to fly. Look, I don't know how strong the slipstream might be out there. It's more the fact that it's going to be a wind of supercold hydrogen that worries me."

"We won't be able to breathe."

"By my estimate," he said sitting down again, "we have about two minutes out there before we're dead. It'll take about thirty seconds to run to the scramjet. The emergency airlock is facing us from this position and all we have to do is hit 911 on the keypad and fall into it."

It came to Megan that they were, no speculating anymore, going to do this. She saw her hands shake as she pulled on her sandals.

"The airlock is through there," said Moore, pointing a thumb to a narrow hallway leading from the locker they were in. "It has windows by it. I suggest we spend some time looking at our route." He rolled to his knees and stood up, and walked an old man's walk down the hall. Vandna followed with an almost normal stride. Megan, deciding to damn dignity and save her energy, crawled.

The route was deceptively clear. The scramjet sat just a few meters away across the stepped gray hull of the Wave Rider. It was beautiful, a long glistening black lozenge without wings or exhaust ports. Its body was its engine. It looked undamaged by flying debris.

Megan stared at the edge of the Wave Rider's hull visible past the scramjet. She was looking for turbulence, flying objects, any indication that anything other than perfect peace reigned out there. The shockwave cut into the sky only meters away, torn cloud shot past in white blurs every few seconds. But that was the background. The foreground, between them and the scramjet, seemed still.

She was standing now. Adrenaline gave her strength. "All right." She slung the camera across her shoulder. "Hold our breath and go? What are we waiting for?"

"I—can't," said Vandna. She drew back from the window.

"We have to," insisted Moore quietly.

"It's just a quick run," said Megan. "A sprint, like we've all done before."

"You don't understand. I've . . . never been outside before. Outside of anywhere. Without a suit. Under a sky . . ."

Megan stared at her. She hadn't expected this. But Vandna had never been to Earth. She'd been born and raised in the O'Neill colonies, and in the caverns of the Jovian moons.

"As long as it's out the window, it's just a picture," said Vandna. "I can deal with it ,cause that's all it is. And this," she touched the metal wall, "is so familiar. But the second we step out there, it's not going to be a picture any more. It'll be . . . Jupiter. And I know too much about that to believe we'll survive."

Megan hugged her. "You can't think about it. You just have to do it."

"You can do it. You've always been doing these things. I watched your shows, I always wanted to be so adventurous. When I came here before, it was just another place. I was too young to know the difference. And it really never hit me where I was. But I thought you knew. You knew when you stood up here that first time, I could see it in your eyes. And I didn't know what that feels like, how you could go on."

Megan remembered foundering in the Hemolin. She'd thought she was afraid before that, but the reality of the situation—that she would die if she didn't get out—only hit her then. Moore knew her better than she'd thought; he had taken her camera to goad her into action. A jealous hatred of her own work, her lifelong obsession, had finally driven her to act for herself.

"I went on," she said, "because I was a fool." She glared at the camera. "I thought: as long as my pictures are safe, we're immortal. It's a madness I've been living for . . . too many years. But I have to throw it away now. And I'm going to."

Vandna wiped her eyes, watching her. "But—your camera. All our work—"

"It's all useless if it drags us down—and it does. It's what I'm most afraid of losing but I'll drop it if I have to. You're going to have to drop your own fear, Vandna. You can do it.

"Watch me, Vandna. I'm going to let it go."

Then Moore had the door open and walked through without a word. The air left in a great gust.

Megan stepped out into Jupiter's sky. Colossal vistas, a firmament of magnificence, greeted her. Moore was running toward the scramjet, beautiful in his determination.

She felt at the very center of time here, her life all around, like these clouds, vistas past present and future. And she could turn and gaze, and turn and gaze, her life not trapped in frames, but like an endless sky.

The camera twirled at the end of its strap, and as she saw Vandna following, she let it go.

And finally we return to Gennady Malianov, who of all my heroes knows best how to live in the blank places outside all maps. "Alexander's Road" appears here for the first time, and caps the thematic thread that has run through all these stories: the idea of the inaccessible place. *We glimpsed it in an empty parking lot in "Hopscotch," found it inside a computer in "Making Ghosts." In "The Dragon of Pripyat" it appeared as the Chernobyl sarcophagus; in "The Engine of Recall," it was in tight orbit around a burster star. So it's fitting that I should close out the volume with a ride in the ultimate in Cold War impossibilities: the obscene (and historically real) invention known only as* Project Pluto . . .

* * A L E X A N D E R ' S * *
R O A D

Gennady Malianov peered over the crest of the ridge. Dusty shrubs dotted the hillside, blurring together into a black tangle at the bottom. Where a dried riverbed cut the scrub like a scar, eight olive green tents stood baking in the sun. A man cradling a machine gun sat near one.

"How do you know about this place?" Gennady asked Baylar, his guide.

The bearded Azerbaijani grinned at him. "During the war we hid anti-aircraft missiles in there. Now, they hide smuggled stuff. Same job, different company, you could say."

Men in blue jeans and parkas began trickling out of a dark opening in the cliff wall to Gennady's left. The mouth of the mine shaft opened where the narrow canyon ended in tawny bedrock; there was no approach to it other than back along the canyon floor.

It looked like the men were packing up to leave. As he watched, Gennady said distractedly, "So you were in the army, then?"

"Yes. Hated it. Happy now," said his guide. "Mostly I'm a brick-layer. Lay bricks all day, come home, watch *The Young and the Restless.*"

Gennady smiled. The famous American soap opera had recently become available, in its entirety, on black-market data chip. "Who's your favorite character?" he asked.

"Victor Newman."

Engines coughed into life below. Gennady and his guide watched as several dilapidated humvees rattled in a circle and away down the riverbed.

"You think they have uranium down there?" Baylar watched the dwindling dust cloud skeptically. "They wouldn't leave it unguarded."

"Sixteen men came, sixteen left. Nobody came out of the tents or mine when they arrived. I think they're confident that this place is well hidden. Else why leave the tents?" He stood up and began the jerky steep-hill walk down to the canyon floor.

"It's like Ali Baba and the forty thieves," he shouted back. "They don't believe anyone's around to hear them say 'Open Sesame.'"

Baylar followed in cascades of dust. "Ali Baba had a brother, you know."

Gennady started to run to keep from falling. "What's your point?"

"The forty thieves killed him!"

Gennady waded through tough bush, trusting that his khakis wouldn't tear. Finally he popped out next to one of the tents. Panting, he walked around and looked through its flap. "Empty." He headed for the mine entrance. "You don't have to come with me, you know."

"But I feel responsible!" The mouth of the mine was a dark square; somebody could be standing a meter inside and Gennady wouldn't see them. He walked in anyway.

"Stolen uranium is everybody's business, isn't it?" added Baylar as he reluctantly followed. Gennady pulled out a flashlight and his battered Geiger counter and waited for him to catch up. Then they strolled into the darkness.

The Geiger clicked once or twice, registering the usual background radium levels. The tunnel ran straight for a hundred meters, then abruptly stopped at a flat granite wall. Dozens of long crates were stacked at its base. Gennady put the flashlight down where it could light the scene, and set to prying open one of the crates. After a nervous glance around, Baylar knelt to help him.

The dusty lid lifted with a creak, and Baylar grabbed the light. They peered inside at long lengths of gray pipe.

"Could be uranium processing tubes?" said Gennady doubtfully.

Baylar shook his head. "Oil well casing. Non-standard, though—way too big for your average well."

Gennady roved the Geiger counter over and under the stack, but there was no radiation here. He cursed. Suddenly Baylar grabbed his shoulder, pointing upwards. "What's that?"

He flicked the flashlight up, catching a star-like glint of light just under one of the tunnel's wooden beams. Gennady frowned. "That, my friend, is a web-cam."

The realization hit them both simultaneously. Without another word, they both turned to run up the tunnel. Before they got within ten meters of the entrance Gennady knew it was futile: he heard engines.

A small crowd of men with guns was waiting for them as he and Baylar stepped blinking into the October sunlight. Gennady grinned weakly as a black-bearded man with tiny, crazy eyes stepped up to him. Holding up his IAEA card, Gennady said, "UN inspector. Sorry to—" The man knocked the card out of his hand.

"I could shoot you both and dump you in the bush," he said. "Unless you've got something to trade for your lives?"

Gennady and Baylar looked at one another. Then Baylar reached carefully into the breast pocket of his jacket and pulled out a data chip the size of a postage stamp. He proffered it to the bearded man.

"Victor Newman," Baylar said.

*   *   *   *   *

"Lucky for you we have a ransom budget," said the IAEA director. "Not like the old days."

Gennady grinned weakly. Director Jafarov sat in partial silhouette, a tall window behind him showing a nice view of Ahmed Javad Street and, down by the harbor, the Maiden's Tower. Having Baku's most famous landmark as a backdrop seemed to be a kind of status thing with the director. But the vista eclipsed Jafarov himself, continually drawing Gennady's gaze away when he should be looking the director in the eye.

"At least," Gennady said jokingly, "they were polite kidnappers." The men who'd caught Baylar and Gennady had given them tea at a truckstop about ten kilometers from the mine while they waited for their boss to show up. "You see, they were not smugglers after all."

The mine was a nicely dry location to store drilling supplies. After an hour or two of banter with the men, who turned out to be oil wildcatters, Gennady watched in bemusement as a shiny new Rolls Royce pulled into the pot-holed, overgrown Azeri caravansary. A huge man with a face as flat as a Kamaz truck got out and walked over. He wore a fine woolen suit with a beige sweater in place of the vest. "Mikhail Faradjev!" he shouted, pumping Gennady's hand vigorously. "I hear you had a run-in with some of my boys!"

Faradjev was using the mine to store drilling equipment because it was dry and relatively secure. "He seemed to think he had a right to hold us for ransom," said Gennady. "Catching trespassers was a business opportunity."

Director Jafarov shrugged. "More or less. As I say, we covered it."

Gennady sat back, relieved. "Then everything is all right?"

"Well . . ." Jafarov turned his chair and gazed out at the Old Town's rugged stone walls, above which the Maiden's Tower rose like the fist of a giant. "The fact is, the ransom fund is for IAEA employees. You're a freelancer."

"So . . ."

Jafarov grinned like a shark. "We'll expect a full refund. You can stop by the accountancy department on your way out."

Gennady tried not to slump in his seat. There went his income from this venture—and maybe a chunk of his savings as well. Faradjev had thought Gennady and Baylar were worth a lot more than Gennady himself did.

"And the job?"

"Ah, well, that's an interesting story." Jafarov flipped through some papers on his desk. "It turns out that the stolen uranium was laced with thorium. Makes it unsuitable for weapons production. So it's not so urgent as we first thought . . ."

Gennady's heart sank even further. He wondered how much a ticket back to Kiev would cost him. Maybe the weekly bus to Grozny—

"But we have a more pressing problem in any case," said the director. "A bigger job and they're pulling in everybody. Money's no object. You're off the uranium hunt and on to this one, along with everybody else."

Gennady perked up. "What's the job?"

"Nukes," said the director. "Two one hundred kiloton hydrogen bombs from the Russian arsenal are missing. We think they're coming this way by ship. It's an international emergency, Malianov. Overtime, danger pay, whatever. Are you in?"

Gennady didn't have to think about it. "I'm in," he said.

＊　＊　＊　＊　＊

Back in the Soviet era, party members had flocked to the beaches at Baku. The best and brightest of the communist world could sip tea in the local cafes and admire the ever-changing hues of the Caspian Sea, while their children played on Shikhov Beach or chased each other up and down the Boulevard.

As Gennady walked the Boulevard now he was acutely aware that he was an outsider. Up the hill they'd built a monument to locals massacred by the Soviets in 1990. He had no intention of visiting it, but it remained in the back of his mind as he walked the streets, like the north pole for some compass of inherited guilt.

NATO had installed their headquarters in an old hotel near the white curve of the Shikhov. The hotel had a nice view of the rusting oil derricks that dotted the harbor. As Gennady checked himself in at the faded beaux-arts lobby, he could hear loud voices arguing in the ballroom upstairs. A bewildering variety of accents were involved, though the language was English. He recognized one of the voices, and hesitated before trudging up the steps to the ballroom.

"When I ask for a cordon, I don't just mean roads! I mean air, water, and God damn it, *under*water!" Jack Caiter was on a roll. Four field operatives cowered under the NATO liaison's wrath, their faces lit by a bank of flat-screen TVs that showed various maps of western Kazakstan. "You mean to tell me your people didn't notice a couple'a big cables hanging off the back of that boat?" Caiter shook his head. "You can't rely on the detectors. You have to use your eyes, damnit."

Gennady skirted the edge of the room in the opposite direction. He'd spotted a Belgian arms inspector he'd worked with before. When Nadine Marceau saw him she smiled and came over to shake Gennady's hand.

"Good work on that Chernobyl thing," Marceau said warmly. "It was brave of you to go straight in there like that."

Gennady flushed. "Uh, I take it they lost the trail?" he said, nodding towards Caiter. Marceau nodded mournfully.

"These were some of the last warheads slated for decommissioning," she said. "They'd been sitting for years in a high-security bunker outside Volgograd. Last week the place was raided. Not a sophisticated job, but security had deteriorated over the years. They got away with two hydrogen bombs."

On the way over here Gennady had been thinking about what might have happened. This sounded all too close to his speculations. He'd seen just how badly nuclear safeguards had slipped over the past few decades. "But if they were in Volgograd, what's the connection with Baku?" Volgograd was east of Kiev, hundreds of kilometers north of Azerbaijan.

"Two of the attackers were killed," said Marceau. "They were both identified as Azeris."

"*This* is your local agent?" Caiter had spotted Gennady. "The Russian ambulance chaser himself?" He stalked over. "I heard your last job was shooting radioactive camels on the Chinese test range. And I heard most of them got away. How does that qualify you to find two active nukes?"

"Active? The nukes were decommissioned," said Gennady. He didn't add that checking a wild camel for radioactivity was no easy task. He held his ground against Caiter but only because he had no choice; having just turned over all his cash to Jafarov's ruthless accountants, he had no financial alternative but to take this job.

"Commissioned, decommissioned, whatever. Those bombs are still capable of wiping out a city," said Caiter. "And they could be anywhere by now. We know the thieves had lined a shipping container with lead. We blocked the roads, but it's beginning to look like they half-flooded the container and then towed it underwater down the Volga. Behind a fishing boat!"

"To Astrakhan," said Gennady with a nod. "And the Caspian Sea."

"They could be halfway to Tehran by now."

"We're searching all ships on the Sea, of course," said Nadine Marceau. She led Gennady to a set of tables where file folders lay spilled open. "But they had a few days' head start on us. If they went by boat . . ."

"They could offload anywhere," nodded Gennady. "Turkmenistan, and straight into Afghanistan. Or Iran. Or they could have put in at Makhachkala, taken them through Grozny and to Black Sea . . ."

Caiter groaned. "This is not what I want to hear. This has all the earmarks of a carefully planned operation. They've covered their tracks in advance, used decoys, planted false leads . . . It's a mess."

Gennady was flipping through the reports on the table. "They're trying very hard to hide the nukes," he mused. "So we won't find them by looking for the nukes."

"What are you talking about?"

"These bombs are twenty years old." Gennady pointed to the IAEA manifest. "When was the last time they were recharged?"

"Re—" Caiter suddenly fell silent.

Gennady nodded. "Hydrogen bombs are plutonium wrapped around a tritium gas core. Tritium has a short half-life. It has to be replaced every few years. These bombs are useless until somebody recharges them."

Caiter's field operatives had stopped to listen; the rest of the room was looking over as well, apparently because Caiter was suddenly so quiet.

Gennady smiled slightly, looking from Marceau to Caiter. "Follow the tritium," he said. "Then you'll find the nukes."

∗　∗　∗　∗　∗

Two trucks loaded with welding supplies had visited Baku in the past week. They made for a promising start. Over the next several days Gennady and the other inspectors fanned out through the city and its sprawling, post-soviet suburbs. Gennady met every welder in town; most just watched in bemusement as he ran his Geiger counter over their acetylene tanks. He felt like a nosy foreigner, another Russian come to interfere with local affairs.

On an unseasonably hot Friday afternoon Gennady stood at the top of the Shikhov, frowning out at the Caspian. The investigation had hit a dead-end. Out in the bay several children were splashing unconcernedly. A couple of divers were spouting as they swam into shore, presumably coming from an inspection of one of the tottering oil derricks. Gennady was debating whether to kick off his shoes and go wading, or just trudge back to his hotel, when someone shouted his name. He looked up to find the oil tycoon, Faradjev, waving at him from a nearby sidewalk café. "Inspector Malianov! Come join me for tea!"

Faradjev had a big grin on his face, but as before there was no malice in it. Gennady felt uncomfortable chatting with people at the best of times, and idle conversation with a man who had held him for ransom just a few days ago seemed unthinkable. But Faradjev was an important local figure. So Gennady sighed, smiled, and went to sit across from him.

"You look tired, inspector," said Faradjev. "You need to become rich, like me, so that you can take the afternoon off whenever you need to."

"I don't have that luxury," he said stiffly. "Especially since you now have all my money."

"*Your* money? It was Jafarov I stole from. I know all about his ransom budget. He told me about it at a soccer game one time."

"Did he tell you the budget's only for IAEA employees? And that I'm not one?"

"Oh." Faradjev looked contrite. "I am sorry. Let me buy you a cup of tea, then." He waved imperiously at the waiter. "Meanwhile, how's your hunt for that stolen uranium going? Not well, by the look of things."

Gennady shrugged in irritation. "It's not a simple job. But at least I'm working."

Faradjev scowled. "I was joking about taking the afternoon off. I'd love to be out there, believe me. But I've just come from shutting down another off-shore rig. It's dry—like every other well in this God-damn country."

The oil rigs leaned in decrepit majesty, most of them little more than giant birdhouses now. Once, Baku had presided over the richest oilfield in the world; the battle of Stalingrad had been fought for these wells. "It's ironic, you know," said Faradjev. "Back in the Soviet days, the oil flowed out of here and the wealth went to Moscow. Then for a while we had it to ourselves, but all the money went to our fight with Armenia. Now that things have finally settled down and we have peace and our own state at last . . . the oil is done."

"But you're still drilling."

Faradjev shrugged. "If you drill, you *always* hit oil. So you suck it up, but it runs dry in a few days or weeks. The problem's with the bedrock, see—there's lots of oil still down there, but it won't flow through the rock.

So unless you want to put a well every ten meters through the whole country, you won't get at it."

"Sorry to hear that."

Faradjev peered at him. "I believe you are. Well. I'm sorry too that you lost your money, Malianov. Maybe I can make it up to you—as a soon-to-be-poor man to an already poor one."

Gennady tried to act nonchalant, thanking the waiter as his tea arrived. "What can you do for me?" he asked.

"I may have a lead on your missing uranium. That is, if you're still interested."

Cup to lips, Gennady hesitated. Nobody was supposed to know about the missing bombs. Officially he was still searching for uranium, unimportant as it had now become. He sipped the tea, then said, "Of course I'm interested."

"There's a man I can introduce you to," said Faradjev. "Name of Humaira Musharraf. He's a rich Pakistani, a pariah in his own country. Makes beer for the market here and Grozny. Maybe you've seen it? Alexander's Road Lager?"

"Humaira? A Muslim making beer?" Gennady shook his head.

"As I say, not well liked at home. The point is, he owns a ceramics factory here in Baku. Makes beer vats. But one of my boys was asked to cast some unusual shapes for him last summer."

"What kind of shapes?"

"Long bricks, six-sided, with holes through them lengthwise." Faradjev held his hands two palm-widths apart. "That wide. Twice as high. Oh, and something like a fan blade, half a meter long."

Gennady sat back heavily. "Very interesting." He didn't know about the blade-thing, but the bricks Faradjev described sounded a lot like fuel-rod casings for a nuclear reactor.

"Now does that make up for losing your money?"

"Partly." Gennady half-smiled. "Giving it back would make up the rest."

Faradjev shook his head. "I stole from Jafarov. He stole from you. But I can ask my man to send you one of the cast-offs of these bricks, if you'd like."

"Sure, thanks." Gennady stood and held out his hand. "And thanks for the tea, Mr. Faradjev. I think I'll pay this Humaira a visit."

As he exited the cafe, Faradjev called after him. "You'll find him at the airport most days!" Gennady waved thanks, but kept walking.

* * * * *

The ultralight wavered like a butterfly, hesitating to land. Gennady held his breath and watched until the fragile green triangle made it to the ground. Then he let go the breath and walked across the tarmac to meet it. Several young men ran out ahead of him to help steer it towards a hangar.

Caiter might fire him just for being here; the missing nukes had priority over the uranium, and there was no evidence the two cases were connected. But with no leads to the bombs, Gennady would make progress where he could, even on a Saturday. Even if interviewing people made his stomach tie up in knots.

Humaira Musharraf was laughing as he untangled himself from the ultralight's straps. "Did you see that?" he shouted. "It bucks like a stallion!" He was a surprisingly young-looking man, with a black moustache and a mop of disarrayed hair.

Noticing Gennady, he ducked out from under the green wing and straightened up. "Not that I've ever ridden a stallion. Who are you?"

He held out his hand. "G-Gennady Malianov. I own a chain of restaurants in Donetsk. We have a mutual friend, Faradjev?"

"Ah, yes, how is he? Donetsk, you say?" Humaira wiped his face with a towel.

"Yes. I wanted to talk to you about Alexander's Road."

"Ah!" Humaira squinted at him. "My successful attempt to undermine the Western powers by encouraging decadence and vice! Glad to hear it's spreading."

Gennady smiled. "I'm told you're a good Muslim."

"I am. But you're not." He looked Gennady up and down. "Russian?"

"Ukrainian-Russian. Is complicated, these days."

"I can sympathize with that." As they entered the hangar, Gennady stopped in astonishment. The lofty space was crammed with unusual aircraft—ultralights, kit-built gliders, even a half-built drone, its sleek sides the iridescent black of new unpainted carbon-fiber. It was mounted on the back of a flatbed truck. Gennady had a momentary thought that it was big enough to carry one of the missing warheads—but nowadays such a missile was easy to shoot down, even from orbit. Only an idiot would try to put a bomb into an aircraft with such a large radar profile.

"Are these all yours?" he asked admiringly.

Humaira nodded. The adrenalin of the landing seemed to be wearing off; a certain placidity was settling over Humaira's features. "I love to fly. Comes from growing up in the Himalayas. And I love to tinker. Nowadays, a man can build his own plane from a kit—even a jet!"

"There's not much a man can't do, if he has the money," said Gennady as he stroked the wing of the drone. "Good and bad, I suppose."

"The superempowered individual? I've heard that theory," said Humaira. "They say it only takes one disgruntled person to wipe out a city. But it takes much more than one to rebuild a nation, don't you think?"

He was referring to Kashmir, of course; Gennady had checked on the way here, and learned that Humaira was from Kargil, high in the mountains. India now had undisputed control over Kashmir, but Pakistan would not forget.

"I'm not sure I can help with that," said Gennady blandly. "But I'm willing to import your beer to Donetsk."

"Of course. But why come to me? I have an orders department."

"My sister lives here. I come here every year, the autumn's gentler in Baku. Anyway, I'm thinking of starting a small brewery of my own and I'm looking for inexpensive casks. I was wondering if I could tour your ceramics operation."

Humaira looked Gennady in the eye for the first time. "What for? Surely you can buy beer casks in Donetsk."

"Actually, no. Not ceramic ones, at any rate."

"Well, then. Go ahead. No need to ask my permission; just show up." Humaira walked over to a table where a laptop sat. "Now, about that order?"

Gennady jumped as his cell phone rang. "Excuse me." He half-turned way and put the phone to his ear. "Hello?"

"Gennady? Nadine Marceau. Get down to Ops right away. We've got a lead on the, uh, items!"

"My sister says I was supposed to take the boys to the beach this morning," Gennady said to Humaira. "Mind if I email you the particulars of the order?"

Humaira shrugged. "If your sister runs your life, I suppose you can do it that way."

"Thanks. You'll have that order!" Gennady trotted out of the hangar, feeling like the worst kind of amateur detective. He was sure Humaira's eyes were boring into his back all the way to the rental car.

*　*　*　*　*

The hotel's parking lot was empty; the concierge pointed Gennady to the new glass and concrete police station down the road, which rusted in a permanently half-built state after the municipal budget dried up. Its visitor's lot was packed with NATO humvees. "Ah," said Gennady. "Of course, thank you."

On the walk over, he'd scanned the streets to see who else was watching. A lot of people, seemingly. It must be no secret by now that the international community had descended on Baku like locusts hunting for a crumb. Luckily for the terrorists Caiter sought, there were several well-shaded cafes near the station, and their patios were packed with silent young men sipping individual cups of tea. Gennady sighed and took the long way around the block, knocking politely at the station's back door.

Inside, Caiter was arguing procedure with the local chief. Nadine, Jafarov and Caiter's flacks had taken over an interview room and piled its table with laptops and file folders.

"We got one," said Nadine tersely. "He's in the holding tank right now, on suicide watch."

"You got one? One bomb, or just one man?"

Nadine grimaced. "Just a man. But we dug a bullet out of him that matches one fired at the raiders in Volgograd. The wound went bad so he finally had to come into the hospital. That's where we got him."

"Not a very dedicated terrorist," commented Gennady dryly. "Should have dug the bullet out with his teeth."

"He's just a boy, Gennady! Bright, an economics student at the University. Had a great future up until last week."

Caiter stalked over. "Won't say a damn thing without his lawyer," he said. "It doesn't matter; he's got residual traces of radioactivity on him consistent with handling a quantity of tritium sometime within the past few days."

"That's good."

Caiter shrugged. "It might be too late anyway."

Gennady felt a chill of sudden fear. "Why?"

Nadine handed him a sheet of epaper. "It's a mail message we decrypted. It was sent between two anonymous remailers; no idea where the destination is, but the origin was somewhere in Baku. But see here," he pointed, "where it talks about an 'act of revenge that will be remembered for thousands of years.'"

"The bombs must be in Azerbaijan," said Caiter. "We have every drone on this side of the continent in the air, boats on the Caspian, as well as satellites and people on the ground from here to Mongolia. The border's locked down."

Gennady scratched at his stubble. "How scared is the boy?"

"Not scared at all, actually. He's laughing at us!"

"Religious nut?"

"Not according to people who know him at the University. If he is, he hid it well. And we've traced his activities; he has an allowance from Dad, likes expensive toys, and he recently made a small investment in some Azeri oil concerns."

"Doesn't fit the profile," said Nadine. "Suicides don't invest. And he's Azeri. The Azeri have no particular cause, political or religious, these days."

"Other than revenge against Armenia," Caiter pointed out.

"Around here, revenge is personal," Gennady said with a shake of the head. "Anyway, the prevailing winds would make a strike just as disastrous here as there." He thought for a moment. "Which oil companies did he invest in?"

"Local bigwig named Faradjev. We looked into him, he's totally apolitical. And going broke, like the rest of the country."

"He might sell the nukes for cash," Gennady said doubtfully. Rogue Faradjev might be, but Gennady couldn't imagine him doing something so callous.

But Nadine was nodding vigorously. "I've checked his activities. He's taking desperate measures—drilling non-standard holes with untested equipment. Hideously expensive stuff."

Gennady remembered Faradjev complaining about how his wells kept going dry. "I don't think he's a terrorist."

"Well, somebody in this town is!" said Caiter. "And apparently, we're out of time. So we're going to have to go to the next stage. Clamp down. The government's agreed to impose a state of emergency, curfew, the whole nine yards." He took the epaper from Gennady's hand. "This is now officially a military matter. Go home. If we need you, we'll call you again."

"But, we know nothing!"

Caiter shrugged. "That's right, you uncovered nothing for us. So now you're just in the way. Go home, Malianov. We don't need you anymore."

* * * * *

Caiter's people were waiting for a convoy of local troops to arrive before enacting the lockdown. While they waited, Nadine offered to walk Gennady back to his hotel. Gennady stalked along the Boulevard, fuming. "Caiter's going about this all wrong!" he complained. "You have to talk to him. Without knowing who has the bombs, or why, how is he going to know where they are or what will be done with them?"

"He thinks some Azeri terrorist group intends to bomb Armenia," said Nadine. "It's plausible—"

"No, it's not! You don't shit in your own sandbox, for one thing. Bombing Armenia would irradiate Azerbaijan. Plus which this kid they have locked up, he doesn't sound like a terrorist, does he?"

"But Gennady, what else could he be?" Gennady shrugged angrily, glaring out at the metallic-blue Caspian.

"I'm sorry it worked out this way. You did your best," Nadine added. "Listen, I'll keep you posted on what we find."

"Yeah." Gennady tramped on his anger for a moment. "Listen, I did get a possible lead on the missing uranium. A local businessman named Humaira. He's a better fit for our terrorists—a Kashmiri Pakistani. If anybody's going to have a grudge, it's his people. Maybe he's behind both thefts."

Nadine nodded seriously. "We'll look into it. Well, Gennady, it was nice working with you again." They shook hands at the hotel steps, and Nadine turned to go.

Gennady looked inside, and hesitated. He had no desire to kick about his hotel room uselessly at this point. Might as well walk down to the beach. He might not get a chance to get out again after curfew was declared.

As he walked, nerves jangling, he glared out at the rotting oil derricks in the harbor. Caiter had sent boats out to search them, thinking one might be a perfect platform for a bomb. They'd found nothing. Evidently Faradjev's men were still doing their inspection, though; another diver was trudging up the beach towards a boat-house with Faradjev's family crest painted on the side.

Gennady stopped in the middle of the street, thunderstruck. A horn blared and he had to leap out of the way as a truck rumbled past. Then he ran back across the street and into the hotel.

"Mr. Malianov, a package arrived for you," called the clerk at the front desk. Gennady stopped, thought about it, started walking again, then stopped and came back to the desk. The clerk had placed a bundle wrapped in brown paper on the polished teak.

Gennady snapped the tape and folded back the paper. There was the hexagonal brick Faradjev had mentioned, plus a long flat sheet of ceramic, almost like a small wing. Both pieces were cracked.

"Thanks," he said to the clerk. He took the package up to his room and dropped it on the bed, fetched his Geiger counter, then jogged back down to the street.

The diver at the boathouse was talking on a cell phone while shrugging out of his equipment. Gennady sidled up to him from behind and glanced in the hut. "Oh, believe me," the diver was saying, "I'm not going to risk being inside at midnight. I'll be standing in the center of a street, or better yet . . ." There was no one in the boathouse, and the diver hadn't noticed Gennady, so he slipped through the doorway.

The hut was small, four by eight meters, crammed with diving equipment and stinking of oil and old wood. Pegs on the wall were festooned with diving gear, and air tanks were lined up under them. Gennady switched on the Geiger counter and knelt in front of the tanks.

Nothing registered on the dial at first—but as he reached the last tank the dial swung and an incriminating clicking filled the shed.

Gennady cursed. This was why Faradjev had been sitting in the café that day; it was why he had called Gennady over.—Not to be polite, but because Gennady had been standing there watching the tritium come ashore, not even knowing it. With a chill he wondered what Faradjev would have done if Gennady had shown any sign that he knew. He might have had a gun on him, or people with weapons nearby.

He pulled out his cell phone and hit a speed-dial number he'd entered last week. "Nadine! Gennady here, I've found the tritium, it's in a boat-house across the street from my hotel."

Even as he said this he realized that it still didn't make sense; who would Faradjev want to bomb? His own people? The Armenians? But fallout from Armenia would land here. Fallout was an indiscriminate weapon, it wasn't as if you could paint it on the ground where ever you wanted . . .

Then he understood. "Nadine? Listen, the bombs are not the problem! It's—" As he spoke he realized the diver outside had stopped speaking.

A shadow flicked down the wood and something hit him on the back of the head.

*　*　*　*　*

A white blur resolved itself into a tiled ceiling. Gennady tried to sit up, and a blast of pain shot through his skull.

"Careful now." Someone steadied him; he looked around, and realized he was sitting on the edge of a hospital gurney. "Your head's going to hurt for a while, but the scans don't show anything serious," said someone dressed like a doctor. "A mild concussion, we've shot you full of anti-inflammatories."

"What happened?" He had fragmentary memories of going back to the hotel, then of running along the beach . . .

"The soldiers brought you in an hour ago," said the doctor. "Also a friend of yours was here—Marceau? She left a note." He handed Gennady a sheet of epaper. Gennady thumbed it and words appeared in the whiteness.

Whoever hit you had run off when got there, Gen. But the tank was still there—almost empty, but it had held tritium, like you said. We're after Faradjev now, but he's driven into the mountains. Our best hope is that he has the nukes with him.

Good work, Gennady. I'm pressing Caiter to give you a citation for this.

—Nadine

Gennady groaned. "Money would be better." He rubbed his head, frowning. There'd been something else . . . something important. He'd been thinking about Faradjev, how the man didn't fit the profile of a terrorist . . .

"Ah!" He fumbled for his cell phone, finding it at last on a side table in the examining room. He staggered to his feet, said, "Thanks for the help," to the doctor in passing and headed for the door. The doctor said something but Gennady ignored him, thumbing the cell phone into life as he went.

"Nadine, listen, I—"

"The caller you are trying to reach has switched off their phone or is outside reception area," said a cool female voice. Gennady cursed.

He'd had the same problem when he was up in the hills with Baylar. No cell phone towers, and satellite reception was spotty.

His mind seemed stuffed with cotton; he couldn't think of what to do next. Flagging down a cab outside the hospital, he directed the driver to take him back to the Boulevard, but he already knew what he would find when he got there. The hotel war room was empty when he reached it. Caiter's whole team was gone, along with the troops, doubtless pursuing Faradjev into the mountains. He phoned Jafarov, but got voicemail.

For a while Gennady stood there, paralyzed by indecision. His head throbbed like a bass drum. Out of ideas, he finally dialed the only other person in Baku he thought he could trust.

"Baylar? Gennady Malianov. Listen, I need your help right away . . ."

*　*　*　*　*

"I don't get it," said Baylar as they drove away from the airport. "What were you expecting to find there?"

"Nothing. Which is exactly what we found," said Gennady. The motion of Baylar's battered SUV along the pot-holed road made him nauseous, and disinclined to talk. "Listen, the Tower told me Humaira filed a flight plan for Xankandi. And his hangar's empty. If you wanted to scratch out a landing strip somewhere around Xankandi, but out of the way, where would you put it?"

"Not too many good places to land in the hills," said Baylar. "And it's a big job to level terrain. Better to use a stretch of road or . . ." He nodded sharply. "Yes! Agdam."

He spun the SUV out onto the paved main highway. A sign said, XANKANDI, 375 KM.

"It's a four hour drive," said Baylar. "But it's the best spot near Xankandi to hide anything. A quarter-million people used to live in Agdam, but it was totally abandoned after the war in 1993. People have been picking the houses to pieces ever since, for building material . . . Totally desolate, nobody lives there now."

"Good, good."

"I still don't get what is this Project Pluto you keep talking about," complained Baylar. But Gennady was on the phone again, trying to reach

Nadine for the sixteenth time. This time, it seemed, he had a signal. He held his breath as the ring tone came on.

"Nadine Marceau."

"It's me, Gennady! Listen, I'm on my way to Xankandi—Agdam, actually. I—"

"Agdam? You're way off track, Gennady. Faradjev's been surrounded just outside Alat. We'll be there in a few minutes—"

"Forget Faradjev!"

"But he's got the nukes. Our satellites have positively identified them by their residuals."

"Nadine, listen carefully. The nukes are not the problem."

"But if he sets them off—"

"He will set them off, and at midnight tonight I think. The diver who hit me was talking on his cell phone with somebody, and mentioned not being inside at midnight. But listen! It's no problem if Faradjev sets off the nukes. The uranium is the problem. I think it was stolen by a man named Humaira Musharraf, he's our terrorist, not Faradjev."

"Gennady, you're not making any sense. How could two nuclear explosions in a heavily inhabited area not be a problem?"

"Put it together, Nadine. Faradjev's only got one obsession: oil. Lately he's been spending extravagantly on non-standard width drills. *Wide* drills. And where's Alat? It's dead center of the biggest, oldest oil deposit in the country—" The signal cut out. Gennady cursed and threw the phone to the floor.

"Oh, I get it," said Baylar mildly. "But what about the uranium?"

Gennady's head felt like it was about to fall off his shoulders. "Just drive," he said, then he leaned out the window to puke.

∗　∗　∗　∗　∗

Agdam had once sprawled across the top of a broad mesa near the border with Armenia. Baylar pointed out side roads and faded signs just visible in the darkness. "Used to be army bases all through here," he said. "Mine fields and trenches, too."

Gennady couldn't hide his alarm. "Mine fields?"

"All gone. Just set off one microwave bomb over them, the whole field goes up, whoosh! The area's safe now. But too depressing for tourism, if you know what I mean."

The road seemed well-maintained, and as they came to the top of the hill Gennady saw many side-roads branching away. Most of them were just uneven ribbons of cracked asphalt, their edges ragged with ingrown grass. There were few trees, but everywhere he could see the facades of buildings—just a front, or a side, with maybe one or two empty windows. Harsh knuckles of masonry rose to two or three stories here and there, as if whole buildings had been uprooted by giants, leaving only these severed stems. Water-filled pits dotted the vista—originally basements, he supposed.

"Welcome to Agdam," said Baylar cheerfully. "Shall we look for a hotel?"

"Airfield, actually. And I think we should do that on foot," Gennady added. He remembered from his experience at Pripyat just how far engine noise could travel in a ruin like this.

"Right." Baylar parked the SUV in the shadow of a corner of missing building. "What are we looking for?"

Gennady shrugged. "Lights. Sounds. Come on." His head was still pounding, but there was nothing to be done about that. He strode off across the grass-covered rubble, Geiger counter in one hand, flashlight in the other. Baylar hurried after him with a rifle slung across his back.

Walking amid ruined, overgrown buildings was not a new experience for Gennady. He had lived for weeks in Pripyat, the abandoned town adjacent to Chernobyl, while hunting for another nuclear terrorist. Pripyat had its own sort of desolate beauty which had tugged at his soul; this place did too, but it showed what Pripyat would become in time. The buildings still stood in Pripyat, the parking lots, boulevards and playgrounds were all intact. Agdam had been shaven clean of structures, leaving only the leaning stubble of occasional walls and buttresses. As darkness enwrapped the dead city Gennady found himself feeling more exposed than he ever had in that other city. There, countless empty windows had stared down on him. Here, there was nothing but grass.

The darkness easily revealed their destination. Gennady had already spotted the lights when Baylar touched his shoulder and pointed. They crept in that direction down a cobblestone street lined with crumbling stone walls.

Somebody had erected tents and a large plastic-roofed pole shed in a broad plaza. Gennady recognized the flatbed truck from the hangar where he'd met Humaira. A bulldozer squatted in the shadows behind the shed. People were walking back and forth in front of a number of spotlights that shone on something lying on the ground. Long shadows raced away from them as they moved.

"What is that?" whispered Baylar. They had both stopped walking.

It took a few seconds for Gennady to work out the shape from a distance; the thing was black, after all. Silhouetted in the dazzle, it looked like two dark porpoise shapes, one mounting the other from behind. Then it snapped into perspective as he remembered photos he'd seen from a war fought almost a hundred years ago.

"V-1!"

"What?"

He shook his head. "Of course it's not, really. Baylar, that's where the stolen uranium went. I was right. Humaira's gone and actually built a Project Pluto device."

"Project—"

"It's a nuclear ramjet!"

Rubble shifted behind them. Gennady spun around in time to be blinded by brilliant light, as a voice shouted, "Don't move!" He heard a faint scuffling sound off to his right—Baylar had dived behind the crumbled wall and was running into the blackness.

Three men emerged from the shadows; all held automatic weapons. "Hands on your head," said one. They turned Gennady and pushed him in the direction of the encampment.

*   *   *   *   *

"So," said Humaira Musharraf. "It's the restaurateur. I assume you were out innocently picking mushrooms?"

Gennady stared past him at the device sitting on the asphalt. "Looking for stolen uranium, actually." His hands weren't tied, but they had frisked him and taken away his cell phone and Geiger counter.

"The uranium's not all in there," said Humaira, following Gennady's gaze. "We left some in Baku." The ramjet was surprisingly tiny—just six meters in length, with a wingspan of twice that. It was spindle-shaped, perfectly black, and mounted on its back was an open-ended cylinder three meters long, a meter in diameter. The whole assembly sat on a wheeled sled that sat on tiny rails, like the ones Gennady had seen used to carry movie cameras. The rails ran an indefinite distance into the darkness.

Humaira walked around Gennady, who had begun to sweat in the cold air. Meanwhile his men were scrambling to put on night-vision goggles, shouting, running back and forth into the darkness, and waving spotlights. Gennady's arrival had thoroughly spooked them; maybe he could use the fact to his advantage.

"How did you find us?" asked Humaira quietly.

Gennady shrugged. "I asked myself: what kind of airplane needs wings that can withstand thousands of degrees of heat?"

He nodded towards the ramjet. Its wings now had ceramic ailerons attached—like the one Faradjev had sent to Gennady at the hotel.

Humaira frowned, and helpfully shone a light at the craft. "You want to see those wings up close?" he asked sarcastically. He gestured to his men to shuffle Gennady towards the drone. Gennady didn't resist, instead peering down the throat of the ramjet where he could see the honeycomb pattern of an exposed reactor core less than a meter away. Humaira watched him, bemused.

"You know what you're looking at, but you're not panicking and running. Most of my men do, the first time. You're not afraid of radiation?"

Gennady shrugged. "It's not very radioactive yet. Is it?"

"Correct. It's a very simple device, really. See that cable trailing out the back? When the sled gets up to speed, that cable will pull the moderator rods out of the reactor—right out the back of the jet. They're disposable. Once it's turned on, it can never be turned off again."

"Of course." Gennady nodded, dejectedly. "Air comes in the front of the jet, goes through the reactor and is super-heated. Roars out back. It's a supersonic ramjet that spews radiation and heat and shockwave behind it and never stops. You can't shoot it down without causing a Chernobyl-scale nuclear disaster. But where's it aimed?"

"Where's it—" Humaira scowled at Gennady. "Kashmir! Kashmir! The bastards have seized it and we'll never get it back now, not with the India and the U.N. enforcing national boundaries from now until forever. They can't be allowed to get away with that."

"But you grew up in Kashmir. Your home—"

"Anybody who didn't leave when India took over is a traitor. Who else would stay?" Humaira patted the back of the ramjet. "This little monster will take off, shoot up to twenty thousand feet and head for Iran. It's going to follow a course that takes it over the most densely populated cities of the region—but high, so it's safe. Unless you try to shoot it down . . ."

"The route, it's over Iran and Afghanistan?"

Humaira nodded. "Following in the footsteps of Alexander himself, until it reaches the Punjab. There it will drop down to an altitude of twenty meters. It'll start to crisscross the country at supersonic velocity, and when it finishes one pass it'll start another. Whatever is not killed by the shockwave will be incinerated by its exhaust and irradiated by the raw radiation spewing out the back. The whole device will be so hot it will shine like a small sun; the nav computers are all in the wing-tips, they'll be coolest. It will sow the nation with fallout so fierce that nothing will survive there for a thousand years. And it will only stop when it explodes and scatters radiation everywhere."

He nodded to himself. "That, my friend, is revenge."

With a gesture, Humaira had two of his men pull Gennady away from the black drone. They led him in the direction of one of the tents.

"Tell me who you're working for," Humaira said as they sat Gennady down on an overturned box. "And who else knows that we're here? If there's been a leak in my organization, I need names."

"I won't tell you," said Gennady defiantly, his quavering voice ruining the effect.

"Oh yes you will," said the man to his left as he grabbed Gennady's hair.

Humaira held up a hand. "In a while. First, get out there and make sure nobody else is around." He turned and started shouting orders, while the one man remaining took up a position behind Gennady.

Humaira carried a couple of laptops out of the largest tent and set them on a table. He switched on a wireless base station and booted them up. Meanwhile his men were attaching stout steel cables to the sled that the drone sat on. These they unreeled along the track that led into the darkness.

Gennady checked his watch. It was 11:43 P.M.—and that sparked an idea. "You're going to set this thing off at midnight?" he asked Humaira. The beer baron checked his own watch, looking surprised.

"That would seem appropriate," he said with a nod.

Gennady tried not to smile.

"I thought you said the thing had its own nav computer," he added conversationally. "Why do you need those?"

"Backup," said Humaira. "Direct flight control—see?" He held up a mouse that was attached to one of the laptops. "Just in case we have to change our plans."

He tapped away at the keyboard for a while, then said, "Well. That's it." Walking to the very edge of the lit area, he shouted, "Is the launcher ready?" into the night. Satisfied by some indistinct reply, Humaira walked back to the table. "Seems to me we need a count-down," he mused. Glancing over at Gennady, he said, "Would you like to do the honors?"

With a grunt, Gennady peered at his watch. He'd spent the past few minutes doing calculations in his head, thinking about distances and the solidity of the rock beneath their feet; and so when the watch said 11:59:10, he was confident in saying, "Two minutes to go."

The men faded away into the darkness. Only Humaira, Gennady and his guard now stood within a stone's-throw of the black drone, which sat silent and apparently dead in the fan of several spotlights. Gennady heard crickets. One of his guards shifted his feet nervously.

Humaira glanced down at the glowing laptop screen, and frowned. "Your watch is slow," he said to Gennady. "Give me a count-down now! From ten."

Gennady shrugged. It had been worth a try. "Ten, nine, eight, seven, six," he said, feeling foolish and angry. Humaira's finger hovered over the laptop's Enter key. *Baylar, if you have a shot, now would be the time to take it.*

"Five, four, three," he said more slowly. Humaira looked over, amused. Resigned, Gennady said, "Two, one, kill us all, then."

Humaira tapped the key. Gennady was watching the drone, so he was startled when a snakelike hissing came from well ahead of it. The cable that led off down the track was whipping up into the air and, suddenly taut, it jerked the drone's sled into motion. Lights sprang up along the length of the track, illuminating the whole two hundred meters of it. The drone wobbled on its supports and Gennady thought it would fall off for a precious second; then the whole assembly began accelerating into the darkness.

Humaira whispered something to himself, transfixed at the vision of what he'd done. And at that moment, the earthquake hit.

Gennady had been expecting it, so he simply toppled backwards off his box when the ground began to shake. His guard shouted and dove for cover as the tents wobbled and a deep rumbling rolled around them. Shouts came from the darkness as Humaira's men dropped whatever they were carrying and ran for it, believing the drone was the cause. Humaira himself stood stock-still, his mouth open.

Hundreds of kilometers away, deep below the crust of the earth in the fused rock plates of the world's largest oil field, Faradjev's first nuke had exploded. In the seconds since then, it had carved out a vast chamber for itself, hundreds of meters across; but that chamber was unimportant. The key to Faradjev's plan was the shockwave that Gennady now felt. As the shock radiated out from the well site—a well with a non-standard size, the hole drilled wide enough to accommodate the first of the stolen bombs—it shattered the hard rock planes that kept the region's trapped oil from flowing. Out and out the shockwave ran, unlocking ten years', or a dozen, or a whole generation's worth of oil wealth for a nation that yesterday had been gasping for its economic life.

Gennady didn't care. He was on his feet and running for the table, but stopped as he saw the drone buck off the track too soon. Humaira yelled a curse—for a second the shaking ground was forgotten as they watched the drone arcing up, pitching to the left. It shuddered once as the umbilical running into its back popped out, taking with it a cluster of black tubes. A red circle appeared at the drone's tail.

The circle turned yellow as the drone slewed sideways and touched the grass. Humaira shouted again as its left wingtip pod sheared off. Then the circle turned white, and Gennady could hear a distant, deep hiss as the drone somehow righted itself and undulated up into the air.

"Stop!" Gennady's guard had gotten to his feet. The shockwave had passed. Gennady put his hands up and watched as Humaira tapped rapidly at the laptop, then grabbed the mouse. A dim light was growing from somewhere behind Gennady—at first rosy like a false dawn, it slowly grew yellower and brighter. At the same time a sound like thunder began echoing between the hills.

Something shot through the sky to his left; high already, it climbed with majestic strength, as if trying to claw its way to heaven. In the seconds before it pierced the clouds, he watched a yellow cross with a brilliant white core throw a false dawn over the ruined, empty city of Agdam.

On cue, the ground began to shake again. Gennady rode it out this time, and to his disappointment, so did the others. "How did you know that was going to happen?" asked Humaira.

Gennady smiled modestly. "I am an agent of God," he said. "He will not allow you to do this."

For just a second, he saw doubt in Humaira's eyes. Then the terrorist laughed. "Too late," he said. "I—" He spun around like a doll and fell on his back as echoes of the distant gunshot banged through the ruins.

Gennady's guard dove for the ground again. Without thinking, Gennady grabbed the laptop and ran for the nearest patch of darkness.

* * * * *

They were combing the ruins for him, but Humaira's confidence had been misplaced; Agdam contained more places to hide than even an army could comfortably root out. Baylar's shots kept Gennady's guards pinned down for the crucial few seconds it took him to escape.

As to the rest of the men, they were still scattered and disorganized, spooked by the earthquakes. After a few minutes of running across open, treacherous ground, Gennady spotted a dark maw opening up at the base of a tall pillar of brickwork. He ran over and wedged himself into it.

Flipping open the laptop, he hunted for the network connection utility. With relief, he saw that he still had a weak signal from the base station on the camp's table. He maximized the window of Humaira's remote flight program.

He had time to see a speckled, night-vision glimpse of clouds and a horizon before he heard shuffling just a few meters away. Closing the laptop lid quickly, he held his breath.

"Gennady! It's me." Baylar loomed out of the darkness.

"In here!" Baylar came to hunker down next to him. "Am I that visible?" asked Gennady worriedly.

Baylar laughed. "Not at all. You ran right by me back there, that's all. But they're hunting for us both. What are you doing?"

"Piloting a doomsday weapon, I hope." Gennady opened the laptop again. There it was, an indicator display and a nose-camera view from the drone. He could see clouds lighting up as the thing shot through them at bewildering speed. Every few seconds he caught glimpses of a flat gray surface far below: the Caspian, already.

"The sat systems must have a lock on this thing by now," he muttered. "But they must also see the radiation. Somewhere somebody's trying to decide what to do about it."

"If they shoot it down now, it'll poison the sea," Baylar pointed out.

"They'll be thinking if it goes down here, it will poison this, if it goes down there, it will poison that," said Gennady. "They don't know where it's aimed. So they'll be frozen in indecision."

If the flight computers were working, the monster would soon turn south and make a beeline for Tehran, high in the air and relatively safe.

From Tehran it would follow Alexander's road into Afghanistan, drop-ping to a dangerous height only when it reached the Punjab. National sovereignty counted in decisions about terminating rogue planes and missiles; this late, and with the damn thing flying so fast, nobody was going to be able to react in time.

Gennady put the mouse on a brick and tentatively gave it a roll. The image on the screen turned. "Hell," he whispered. "Humaira switched on the override.

"Keep watch," he said. "I have to concentrate."

Baylar looked down, saw what he was doing, and swore. "What are you going to do? There's no safe place to ditch the thing."

There wasn't. Gennady thought about his choices: he could run it out into the Indian Ocean, head for Antarctica—but the ocean and the continent were fragile ecosystems. That was no solution. The Himalayas? That sounded better; he could plaster the damn weapon against the side of some out of the way, high plateau. Of course that would outrage the Chinese, and make recovery and cleanup nearly impossible. . . .

"We need to bury it," Baylar said.

"Bury . . ." He had it. "You're not going to like this," he said. "But we have to bring it back here."

"What do you mean—to Agdam?"

"No." Gennady named the place. "Will you be able to spot the land-marks from the air?"

"At night, through a tiny camera, on a laptop screen, while keeping one eye out for murderous terrorists?" Baylar laughed. "No problem."

Gennady reluctantly took up the mouse and began a long slow, banked turn. To his relief the drone responded easily. "I'm going to have to bring her below the cloud deck."

At three times the speed of sound, Humaira's monster punched the clouds out of the way and arrowed for the coast of Azerbaijan. Gennady could see the long, low shoreline, glowing towns and faint strings of highway lights; for a hallucinatory moment he even saw blinking lights on offshore rigs as they whipped past. Then he was lining up on the hills, as Baylar said, "Yes, to the left, no not that far . . ."

Brickwork exploded over Gennady's head. "Hell!" Baylar hunched down, then rose quickly to fire the rifle blindly into the dark.

Gennady barely noticed. He was entirely absorbed by the screen before him—almost able to feel the monster's strength propelling him forward, its savage momentum overcoming weather, wind and gravity.

The drone pressed itself faster and faster against the air. If he stood up, Gennady could probably see the light from it against the sky, even a hundred miles away. Its power and heat were building by the second; he could feel it in his pounding temples.

Baylar fired off another shot and then hunkered down. "There! Those are the hills. The canyon will be on the right, after two others drain onto the flats."

More gunfire shattered the night, and chips of brick and stone flew everywhere. Gennady felt something cut his cheek. He moved the mouse ever so gently. At this velocity, the slightest overcorrection could cause the drone to tear itself apart in midair.

It had been weeks since he and Baylar drove into those hills, looking for stolen uranium. It felt like another life, when all he'd had to worry about was being shot and dumped by the side of the road by Faradjev's boys. Gennady hoped Faradjev was still alive; he'd love to explain to him how he'd had to borrow his secret cave.

Now he let the drone drop until it was skimming above the grass. Everything behind it would be shattered and incinerated; but he couldn't think about that now. Ahead, the canyon ran straight and level.

"Come out of there and we might let you live!" The voice was punctuated by another blast of gunfire, this time right on top of them.

There in the distance was a tiny black square in a gray wall.

"Gennady!"

The square expanded with astonishing speed, then—

Static.

Gennady let out a sigh and sat back. He dropped the mouse and looked up, smiling mildly at the two men who were aiming machine guns at him.

"Gentlemen," he said. "You lose."

He heard a trigger cock. Then light bloomed behind the terrorists. Dust flew up as first one, then two and finally four military helicopters swayed into the air over Agdam.

"*Put down your weapons!*" boomed an amplified voice.

Baylar whistled. "I guess the whole country saw that thing take off from here," he said. "We're safe!"

Gennady closed the laptop. "Yes," he said. "I guess we are."

* * * * *

Faradjev shrugged. "Of course it's a hideous crime," he said. "There'll be a debate about whether I should be executed. Not that anybody died." He stubbed out the cigarette Gennady had brought him.

The cell was small, yellow paint peeling off the bricks. Nonetheless, Faradjev looked quite comfortable as he lounged on the tiny cot. "You'll do quite well out of all this, though, won't you?" he asked.

Gennady shrugged. "Didn't want to be famous. Looks unavoidable now."

"I have a great connection in Hollywood," said the Azeri business-man, leaning forward. "I'll make sure he contacts you. Hell—maybe we can sell our film rights together!"

Gennady had to smile. "You're totally unrepentant, aren't you?"

"The Americans tested this technique forty years ago. Nobody charged them with terrorism for it. There was a whole program—what was it called? The Plowshares program. Peaceful use of nuclear muni-tions. But anything to do with nukes, is—" Faradjev waved his hands, making a blubbering sound. "Scary scary! Nobody would listen to me when I proposed using decommissioned nukes to revitalize our oil deposits. So I had to go my own way."

Gennady looked away pensively. "There's a valley inland that'll be uninhabitable for centuries. Most of the radiation was contained when the thing went down the mineshaft and hit the end. But it only takes a little, you know."

"I'm surprised at you," said Faradjev. "You're not afraid of nuclear stuff. That's why you'll be legendary."

"Oh, but I am afraid," he said, standing. "Terrified. Have always been. That is why I am good at my job. That," he said as he turned to go, "is why I do my job."

Faradjev stood and held out his hands. "No hard feelings then. I'm glad we understand each other."

Gennady looked at the offered hand. He didn't take it. "We don't understand each other," he said. "You knew what Humaira was planning. You even knew when he was going to set the monster loose. It wasn't a coincidence that you scheduled your nukes to go off the same night."

Faradjev bit his lip, and looked away. "They'd have shot it down," he said. "Nobody was going to get hurt."

Gennady shook his head. "Thousands were going to die, and you planned to use their deaths as a diversion. In the hysteria after Humaira's attack on Kashmir, nobody would bother investigating a couple of earthquakes in Azerbaijan."

Now Faradjev simply looked sullen. "For my country," he said.

"For your wallet." Gennady left him standing there.

Outside the police station, the weather was finally turning. Low gray clouds promised a cold rain later tonight. The carousels of Shikhov beach were being locked up for the season, and the last tourists had left. The IAEA, too, had pulled out, except for the containment teams working up in the hills.

Gennady turned up his collar and faced away from the cold wind. He was walking back to his hotel when an SUV pulled up beside him. "I suppose you've had enough of our ancient country," Baylar shouted out the window. "Need a ride to the airport?"

Gennady grinned, and went around to the passenger side. Above the streets the Maiden's Tower presided as it had for centuries. People strolled the Boulevard just as if two nukes hadn't been set off the other day; as if no monster had screamed across the heavens at midnight.

Conquerors came and went, but it seemed Baku shrugged them all off in time.

"Thanks," he said to Baylar through the open passenger window, "but I've decided to stay for a few more days."